DISCARDED

Fire *and* Fog

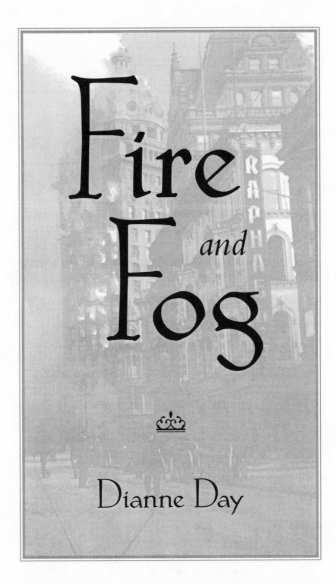

Fire
and
Fog

Dianne Day

Doubleday

New York   London   Toronto   Sydney   Auckland

PUBLISHED BY DOUBLEDAY
a division of Bantam Doubleday Dell Publishing Group, Inc.
1540 Broadway, New York, New York 10036

DOUBLEDAY and the portrayal of an anchor with a dolphin are trademarks of
Doubleday, a division of Bantam Doubleday Dell Publishing Group, Inc.

Permission to reprint photo on previous page granted by
Pat Hathaway Collection of California Views.

Book design by Joseph M. Duraes

Library of Congress Cataloging-in-Publication Data

Day, Dianne.
Fire and fog : a Fremont Jones mystery / Dianne Day. — 1st ed.
p.   cm.
1. Women detectives—California—San Francisco—Fiction.
2. Feminists—California—San Francisco—Fiction.   3. San Francisco
(Calif.)—Fiction.   I. Title.
PS3554.A9595F5   1996
813'.54—dc20   95-44265
CIP

ISBN 0-385-47550-0

July 1996
First Edition
1   3   5   7   9   10   8   6   4   2

❧ For Emily ❧

⁂ Contents ⁂

Fire
and
Fog

❧ 1 ❧

The Bells at Thor's Funeral

I was dreaming that I was Little Nell tied to the railroad track, and a huge locomotive was roaring down on me. Struggling to get free, I woke myself up—but the roar continued. The roar was real, not a dream.

I confess I am rather slow in the mornings. It did not occur to me right away that I should be alarmed. I turned my cheek upon the pillow so that I might see the clock, which read ten minutes past five. The roar continued, building to a crescendo, and in the midst of it church bells began to ring.

How odd, I thought, for I knew it was not Sunday, and five o'clock is too early for a funeral. A great boom sounded beneath the high descant of discordant bells, and I thought: *This must be Thor's funeral, and they are sending the Thunder God off appropriately, with a bang.*

At that moment I was physically jolted wide awake and realized that we were having an earthquake. Later I would learn that my clock was slow, for it was actually twelve minutes past five on Wednesday, April 18, 1906, when the Great Earthquake began.

I was more excited than scared. I had been through one earthquake during the previous year, my first in San Francisco, and had found it an interesting experience. This earthquake, however, was something else. When I tried to get out of bed, thinking that I should like to look out of the window, I could not stand. The whole room was moving!

So I crept to the foot of the bed, as I should also be able to see out the window from there. I live on the third floor of a house on Vallejo Street belonging to Mrs. O'Leary, and I have an excellent view over that part of the city called the Western Addition. I knelt upright, holding onto the foot rail, and looked out. The house bumped and lurched; I tightened my grip. The windowpane cracked and fell out, leaving a jagged frame through which I saw the hills, and all the houses upon them, undulate in shuddering waves. It was a heart-stopping sight, the land heaving like a heavy sea.

Behind me a tall mirror slid from its place on the wall with a thump and a tinkling splatter. I jerked around to find shining shards dashed over the bedclothes and the oval bedside rug. The heavy old oak wardrobe against the adjoining wall swayed, its doors yawned open and spewed my clothes out in a many-hued heap on the floor at the foot of the bed.

Still the shaking went on, and now to the great voice of the quake were added loud creaks and groans from the house. I have sensitive ears; the degree of noise was almost physically painful. A deafening clatter overhead drew my eyes up, and I surmised that the chimney had toppled to the roof, or through it. Cracks charged crazily across the ceiling but it held, raining down plaster dust and flakes of plaster on my head.

Suddenly, eerily, all was still. No noise, no motion. I drew in a deep breath and coughed, for the air was dust-laden. I thought, *It is over.* But I was wrong. I had just loosed my white-knuckled fingers from the foot rail when the quake resumed with even greater force.

"Really, this is too much!" I exclaimed, as I was caught off guard and tossed out of bed. I landed on my bottom on the rug among sharp bits of mirror. I was more startled than hurt, my anatomy being well protected by a thick flannel nightgown. Nevertheless it occurred to me for the first time that I could be injured in the course of this thing. (I admit I am not too clever on the subject of personal safety.)

In that same moment an alarming sort of groan from the wardrobe made me glance in its direction. With wide eyes I watched the huge, heavy piece of furniture tilt out from the wall. For the space of a heartbeat it leaned at an impossible angle, its open doors creaking and dangling, then it toppled and fell heavily onto the foot of the bed. The very place I had been only a moment before!

Whomp! The bed collapsed. I yelped and rolled up into a ball on the rug. It seemed that I lay there shaking and shaken for hours, but it was probably only moments before I realized that the motion, and the noise, had ceased again. I kept my arms wrapped around my head and my knees pulled to my chest, remembering that I'd been fooled once before. But nothing happened. Stillness prevailed.

"Fremont!" a masculine voice yelled from below. "Fremont, are you all right?" It was Michael Archer, who lives on the second floor.

"Yes." I uncurled, and my voice came out in a squeak. Clearing my throat, I tried again, more loudly: "Yes, I'm all right! Don't bother with me. See about Mrs. O'Leary!"

"Will do!" Michael agreed heartily. He sounded quite his normal self, for which I was of course glad, but I did wonder if anything could faze the man.

Still stunned by the good fortune that had saved me from certain death-by-wardrobe, I got slowly to my feet. My balance was unsteady, as if the room still moved. I found my slippers, shook splinters of mirror from them, and put them on. My robe was on the chair, where I always leave it at night—unaccountably, the chair was the only item in the room that remained in its usual place. I put the robe on and belted it with quivering hands. Then I tried to shake some of the dust out of my hair, sneezing a good bit in the process. I was sure I must look a fright with my hair all night-tangled, but I did not much care. Instinct was telling me, "Get out of the house, get out, get out!" and I was quite ready to comply.

I picked my way across the hall and down the two flights of stairs. The front door's lovely panel of etched glass was completely gone. With my hand on the doorknob, I hesitated. Where were Michael and Mrs. O.? All her doors were shut. The front hall looked deceptively normal—that is, until one noted the small chandelier gone splat! in the middle of the floor.

"Michael? Mrs. O.? I'll be outside," I called loudly, and without awaiting a reply, hastened to take myself there.

Up and down Vallejo Street, people were coming out from their houses. All in various kinds of nightdress, we made a most peculiar sight. No one spoke; people turned their heads this way and that, looking bewildered. Instinctively we all wandered into the middle of the street and stood there silently taking in the cracked pavement, the heaved and broken sidewalks, the welter of scattered brick and glass.

Following such an excess of violence, the stillness felt strange, all the more so because of the unusual clarity of the early morning sky. We are not given many clear blue mornings in San Francisco; why today, of all days? One of Mother Nature's little ironies, I presumed. I was not amused.

I shook off negative thoughts in favor of more objective observation. As far up and down the street as I could see, not a single chimney remained upon a single roof, and many blank rectangles yawned where windows formerly gleamed. Yet the houses themselves stood tall and looked solid.

This is really not so bad after all, I thought. Many people thought the same at that early hour. Of course we were wrong, but we had no way then of knowing that the worst was yet to come.

From the corner of my eye I glimpsed Michael Archer, and so turned toward him. He was coming down the front steps with our large landlady on his arm. They made such an incongruous pair that I had to smile: Michael was his slim, elegant, neatly bearded self, in a dressing gown of black and olive-green silk paisley—except that his usually sleek dark hair stood up in spikes at the crown of his head;

Mrs. O'Leary had on a ruffled sleeping cap and a pink chenille robe that did not quite meet in the front, revealing a flowered flannel nightdress with flounces that made her appear even plumper than she was. I pulled my own narrow robe of dark green wool more closely together, feeling very plain by comparison with either of them.

Typically, Mrs. O'Leary had no compunction about breaking the silence in the street. "Wot a horrible shakin' that was! Thought it'd never stop!"

"I quite agree!" I said fervently.

Michael looked around, one hand rubbing the silver streaks in his dark beard, the way he does when he is thinking hard. He said, "Um."

"The damage seems not as great as one might have assumed it would be," I ventured. "At least, the houses appear basically sound. Chimneys can be rebuilt, glass replaced."

"Hah! Not on my front door!" Mrs. O'Leary chimed in. "Cost a pretty penny, them etchin's. It's a shame, that's wot it is. Not to mention all my nice dishes—"

Michael's grave voice cut in. "A quake of such magnitude will have done greater damage in other parts of the city. Here on the hills the houses are solidly built and anchored in rock. But elsewhere it is not the same. Particularly in the poorer sections. We should consider ourselves fortunate."

"Fortunate?" wailed Mrs. O. "You show me fortunate and I'll show you a load of cracked china, not to mention—"

In my turn, I interrupted her lament; it is often necessary to interrupt Mrs. O'Leary if one wants to get a word in edgewise, and she doesn't take offense. I said, "I was most fortunate not to have been crushed under my wardrobe when it fell onto my bed."

Michael raised his eyebrows, and a shadow of concern deepened the blue of his eyes in a most gratifying way.

"Why, Fremont, I'd no idea!" Mrs. O. patted my arm. "Thank the good Lord you wasn't hurt!"

"Indeed," Michael agreed with a nod.

Mrs. O'Leary fussed with her cap, whose ruffles drooped over one eye. "Well, seein' as how we're all in one piece here, I can't tell the use of us standing around in the street. The rumbles is over and there's work to be done. Weeks, that's wot it'll take to set things right, not to mention things that's broke and can't be mended! It's a shame, a pure rotten shame!"

How a shame, or anything else, could be both pure and rotten at the same time I did not know, but I said, "You are right, so, shall we go in?" I took Mrs. O'Leary's arm, which trembled with her indignation, and steered her back toward the house. Other people were also returning to their houses. We left Michael standing there, lost in unfathomable thought.

Two or so hours later, as I was walking down Van Ness Avenue toward Sacramento Street, headed for my office, I saw plumes of black smoke to the southeast. Somewhere on the far side of Market Street a fire burned.

Though the smoke looked ominous I was not particularly worried. San Francisco had an excellent fire department, as I knew from Mrs. O'Leary's frequent extolling of their virtues. Her deceased husband had been a high-ranking police officer, and in truth I sometimes thought I detected a note of jealousy when she told me of the firemen's feats.

I had learned a good deal of San Francisco history from my landlady, including the fact that half a century earlier the city had burned to the ground twice in a single decade and been rebuilt. For this reason the Great Seal of the City featured a phoenix rising from the ashes; also for this reason much emphasis was put on firefighting and prevention, and firemen were generally regarded as heroes.

Traversing on foot the route I generally took by cable car, I continued on my way. The cable cars were not running, and I missed their clacking and clanging. The streets were full of people anxious to see what damage had occurred to their places of business, plus a share of out-and-out gawkers. There was a good deal of bustle, but again—as on Vallejo Street earlier—no one spoke. An aftermath of the shock, I supposed. Hard leather soles slapped pavement, carriage wheels rumbled, horses' hoofs clopped, but even the horses were strangely quiet. I heard not a single whinny.

The newsboy from whom I purchased the *Chronicle* each morning was on his corner even though he had no papers to sell. Enterprisingly, he had made himself a town crier. "Chinatown in shambles!" he yelled. "New dome of City Hall demolished! Fires break out South of the Slot!" He stuck out his hand for pennies in return for these bits of information.

"South of the Slot" meant the area south of Market Street, so called because of the slotlike streetcar track down Market's center. Well, that accounted for the smoke I'd seen earlier. The fate of City Hall's new dome, while a pity, was of no immediate concern to me; but Chinatown was the home of my friend Meiling Li. I stopped and dropped a nickel in the newsboy's hand and asked, "How bad is it really in Chinatown?"

He recognized me and grinned. "It's bad, miss. I seen it m'self down t'other end of Sacramento. All the Chinee buildings done tumbled down, nothin' left but a mess of bricks and boards." He stuck out his hand toward another pedestrian, saying, " 'Scuse me, miss, but I gotta make a livin'."

I thought of the House of Li, so grand and secretive. Gone? Impossible to imagine! I hoped Meiling was all right, and promised myself that I would find out soon. *Michael will know,* I thought, as I continued on my way. Michael always seemed to know everything. Or almost everything; I had managed to keep him in the dark as to my own activities a time or two. Michael's ways were mysterious, and the extent of his knowledge on diverse matters no longer surprised me.

My office was in the next block. Already I could tell that Sacramento Street was in worse shape than Vallejo. I looked away down the street and saw a curl—a mere wisp, really—of smoke rising from somewhere on the other side of Nob Hill. I walked on.

I had been trying not to come down with a case of the What Ifs, but the closer I got to my office, the harder it was to stave off that dread disease. I stopped trying and immediately the awful thought broke out: *What If* my typewriter was damaged in the earthquake, damaged beyond repair?

The typewriter was more than my most prized possession, it was my sole means of livelihood. Even more than that, it was the symbol of my freedom. Without the typewriter there would never have been a Fremont Jones living in San Francisco, I would still be Caroline F. Jones of Beacon Street, Boston. I would probably by now have been forced to marry the loathsome nephew of Augusta, my widower father's new wife. God forbid, I might even have given over to convention and started wearing a corset!

My heart beating much too fast from these unpleasant thoughts, I came to the building that housed my second-floor office. The windows of the bookstore on the street level were broken and cracked, and its insides were a shambles. This did not bode well for the condition of my own office. Ted and Krista Sorenson, who owned both the bookstore and the building, were nowhere in evidence. I couldn't blame them for not wanting to face such a daunting cleanup project. Taking a deep breath for courage, I looked up to the second floor.

My office window with its painted sign—FREMONT JONES TYPE-WRITING SERVICES—was no longer there. I'd been so proud of that sign, and now its fragments were being crunched under the feet of passersby. *Well,* I thought, *there is no point in delaying the inevitable.* I took out my key and unlocked the door to the stairway. The stairs were thick with debris that, after a few steps, caused me to stumble, sneeze, and cough. I stopped for a moment to let the dust settle, and suddenly became aware of a profound unease. Really, it was almost fear—and I am hardly ever afraid. So I asked myself: *What am I afraid of? What is the worst that can happen here?*

Worst would be that I should find everything destroyed, including the typewriter. In which case I supposed I would have to give up and return to Boston. My business had been doing quite well from month to month, but I had not sufficient capital to start all over again. My mother's small legacy was long gone; in the bank I had funds to last perhaps a month, no more. When I came right down to it, I doubted there was enough to purchase a train ticket to Boston. I couldn't even return there without asking my father's help—a thought not to be borne!

A kind of black pit seemed to open up inside of me and threatened to swallow me whole. I couldn't allow it, so I did what I had done since I'd first conceived my plan to come to San Francisco: I reminded myself that my name was Fremont, and that the blood of my ancestor, John C. Frémont, fearless explorer and founding father of the Great State of California, ran in my veins. I truly belonged here, and I could be fearless enough. I charged up the remaining stairs.

Ignoring the mess all around, I unlocked my office door and made straight for the desk in the center of the room, and the typewriter on its special table that stood at right angles to the desk. But the typing table was not there; it had slid all the way across the room and come to a stop by the broken-out window. The typewriter was nowhere in sight. "Oh, no!" I cried, rushing around the desk, stepping over I knew not what, feet sliding on the sheets of paper that littered the floor.

I found the typewriter. It lay on its side where it had fallen, half in and half out of its dust cover. I went down on my knees beside it, removed the dust cover, and tugged the heavy machine upright on the floor. It thunked and made some clattering metallic sounds that to me, in my state of mind, were quite terrible.

Nevertheless, the typewriter looked all right. All its round, silver-rimmed keys were present. I ran my fingers over them, and over the high black carriage, as if the machine were a person and I a doctor searching for broken bones. I opened the cover in the way one does to change the inked ribbon, and conducted the same search on the inside. The slender ribs of the striking mechanism seemed sound. The ribbon was loose; I fixed it. Then I let out my breath in a long sigh. Absently I wiped inky fingertips on my skirt as I arranged myself cross-legged on the floor in front of the typewriter.

I took the piece of paper nearest to hand, ignored whatever was typed on it, and turned it over so the blank side came up when I rolled it in. I closed my eyes. (Somehow hope comes easier when one's eyes are closed.) My fingers found their well-known positions, and I typed: *The quick brown fox jumps over the lazy dog.* Three times. The keys felt firm and made a crisp sound as they struck the paper.

I opened my eyes and read what I had typed. It was letter-perfect, and tears of joy streamed down my face.

At some point in the process of restoring my office to rights, I realized that I was engaged in an impossible task. I didn't know how long I'd been at it, because I'd lost my pendant watch somewhere in the bedroom on Vallejo Street.

I had picked up all the papers from the office floor and reassembled them into their respective documents. A tedious process, to say the least. Nothing was missing, but there were a considerable number of scruffy-looking pages that would have to be retyped before I could hand them back to my customers. The question was, *where* would I be doing the retyping, the handing back? Not here, that was almost a certainty. If my office were any measure, this whole building was a wreck!

Before now, I really had not registered the full extent of the damage. Whole sections of the wall had ripped away, exposing the wooden laths beneath. A huge crack zigged and zagged in one corner from floor to ceiling; most likely this crack went all the way down into the bookstore below me. The more I looked at it, the more I fancied that the crack widened before my very eyes. I glanced up at the ceiling, then quickly away: it looked like an eggshell about to yield to a strong-beaked baby chick.

Still, I reflected, I had not heard any ominous creaks or groans in the building, nothing to herald its potential or imminent collapse. Surely it looked worse than it was?

A gust of wind shot through the glassless window, bearing on it a sharp scent of smoke. I turned my head and looked out, frowning. Was it only my imagination, or was the day getting darker? No matter; I had to decide what to do here. This was all such a bother. The telephones were out, and the electricity, and I assumed some intelligent person would have shut off the gas mains at their source. How was one to proceed in this unprecedented situation? And where were the Sorensons? It was their building, after all.

I decided to explore the other two rooms on my floor. Perhaps if one of them was in better condition than my office, the Sorensons would allow me to move into it until repairs were made. I went out into the hallway.

Here was something I had not seen in my headlong rush into the office: a part of the hall ceiling had caved in, with a stout beam poking down at an angle. I walked under it gingerly. The room next to mine had been vacant since I'd rented my office—in fact I had a long-range plan to expand into that room someday. But when I shoved the door open with some difficulty, I found that, unbeknownst to me, the Sorensons had stored crates of books there.

When had they done that? And why? How could they afford such a large inventory? The back room was the place they used for storage. I knew this because I'd seen similar crates there several months earlier.

I returned to the hall and proceeded to the back room. I did not think I would find anything except more crates, but I might as well be thorough. The door would not open; it was either locked or stuck.

There are few things that pique my interest more than a stubbornly closed door—especially when, at a previous time, that door has been open to me. Whether what is behind the door is my business or not is quite beside the point. (Unless, of course, there are people behind it, in which case I should certainly respect their privacy.) I set my shoulder to the door and pushed with all my might. It did not budge. Reflecting that a woman's shoulder is not the strongest part of her anatomy, I set my hip against the door and again pushed as hard as I could. Still the door did not budge, whereby I concluded that it was indeed locked. How very curious!

I stood back, tapping my foot. There were ways, one heard (or read—I am a great fan of Mr. Sherlock Holmes), to open a door without the key. I wondered if I could do it. . . .

And shortly thereafter discovered that I could. I used a hairpin I had found in the bottom of the capacious bag I carry for a purse. This is not the most fashionable of accessories, indeed Augusta and her ilk have been known to call my preference for it absolutely perverse, but time and again I have been able to find whatever I need among the things that accumulate there. I wielded the hairpin until, with considerable satisfaction, I heard a click and felt the lock disengage. Then I turned the doorknob and entered the room.

The crates were there, as expected, but while the middle room had been in fairly good condition, this one was even more of a disaster than my office. Curious as to the extent of the damage, I edged my way among the crates.

I was not really paying much attention, rather I was thinking that, of the three rooms on this floor, only the middle one could serve me for an office, and perhaps I could persuade the Sorensons . . . I stopped, looking down. I stood stock-still.

How amazing, I thought, *how fascinating!* And most likely, how very, very wrong!

❧ 2 ❧

Fire and Fog

The earthquake had tossed the large wooden crates about as if they weighed no more than egg cartons; what had once been an orderly storage arrangement was now all higgledy-piggledy. One crate in particular had been slammed against the back wall and suffered the additional insult of having a part of that wall fall down on it. Not too surprisingly, it had broken open and spilled out a part of its contents.

The crate contained books, yes. But also something else. Many somethings else. Artifacts, I supposed one would call them. Objects that belonged in a museum, or the most expensive sort of shop. One item in particular drew my attention: a golden knife with a narrow blade that was curved like a scythe—it had a large, dark blue jewel in the hilt. If that was a sapphire, it was certainly the largest one I had ever seen. I bent closer. The curved blade was inscribed with a kind of squiggly writing—I had no idea what the language was. I reached out to touch it but snatched my hand back before making contact. Somehow I did not think touching any of these fascinating things was a good idea.

There were a number of items made of leather, decorated with brightly colored beading. Some of these had fat red or gold tassels hanging from them. Ceremonial pouches of some sort, I presumed; I would have liked to examine one more closely but did not dare. I strained my eyes in the dim light and saw more: brass or bronze or perhaps even gold vases of various sizes, cut in swirling designs, some inlaid and some enameled in more bright colors; several little chests of elaborately carved dark wood, about the size of a sewing box, inlaid with ivory; long strands of beads that looked to be made of semiprecious stones, or they could have been precious, for all I knew of such things; and finally what I guessed were the hilts of a great pair of swords, their blades obscured under a pile of books. There was much more I could not see well enough to identify.

I virtually itched with curiosity and frustration! Keeping my hands to myself with a good deal of effort, I got down on one knee and peered into the crate through the part that was broken. This observation confirmed that the exotic things were contraband: in the part of the crate that was still intact, books were packed around the sides, top, and bottom only, leaving a central space that must have been intended to hide the treasures, for treasures they assuredly were.

What had we here? A smuggling operation? And if so, did the Sorensons know about it? If they knew, would they not have rushed to their building at the first opportunity after the earthquake?

It was a puzzle. . . .

A commotion on the stairs made me start guiltily. Ted and Krista Sorenson, come at last? Or someone else, someone more sinister? Anyone who knew about the contraband was not likely to be pleased at finding me anywhere near it!

I hastened out of the back room, remembering to close the door behind me. Whoever was pounding up the steps, I hoped that I could make it back into my office before I was discovered—but, by the sound of it, I would not.

I was still frantically thinking up excuses when I saw that I would not need them after all. Out from the stair enclosure emerged the familiar figure of Michael Archer.

"Michael!" I exclaimed. "What are you doing here?"

"I've come to help you remove your things." He started for my office door. "Not the furniture, there isn't room for that, but at least we can save your typewriter."

I hurried after him. "My office is in bad condition, but the next room seems all right. I thought I'd ask the Sorensons to move the crates out so that I— Oh! Michael, I found the most extraordinary thing in the back room. Come with me, you should see—"

"Fremont, really, there's no time." Michael was the picture of impatience, already striding toward the typing table to which I'd restored the typewriter.

I fisted my fingers and planted them on my hipbones. I do not like being bossed and was ready to stand my ground. "I think you are overreacting. I've been in the building for quite some time, and it shows no signs of falling down."

He turned to me with a most serious expression on his face. "You've no idea what's happening out there, do you?"

"What do you mean?"

"Come to the window. Now," he said as he joined me there and put his arm lightly about my shoulders, "lean out and look down the street." I did so, Michael leaning with me. His lips near my ear, he asked quietly, "Now do you understand?"

Eastward, toward Chinatown and the Bay beyond, the sky was black with smoke. The smell of it was thick on the air, I could almost taste it on my tongue. Bitter, ashen, horrible, it tasted like death. "They'll stop it," I whispered.

"Not soon enough," said Michael.

All the people who had gone in that direction were now returning, walking rapidly but in an orderly fashion. No one was panicked. I said, "But—"

"But nothing. Come, Fremont, or I swear I'll carry you bodily out of this place and your typewriter be damned!"

"Really, it is not necessary to be rude!"

Michael rolled his eyes but made no rejoinder. He picked up the heavy typewriter with a good deal more ease than I had done when moving it from the floor. "Bring only your most important papers. And hurry!"

I hurried, grabbing from the drawer my files in their folders, and cramming typing ribbons, pencils, pens, etc., down into my purse. I had caught Michael's mood of urgency and emerged rather breathless from the building. Then I blinked in disbelief.

"Where did you get that—that *thing?*"

"This *thing* is a Maxwell, and I've had it for a short time. There is no place to keep an auto at Mrs. O'Leary's, which is why you haven't seen it before. Here, hand up those folders to me and get in."

"Well!" was the only comment I could summon. I'd never ridden in an automobile before; I thought them unattractive and completely unnecessary, given that the world was full of horses needing employment. Still, I am always ready for a new experience, even one I have been somewhat opposed to. I put my foot on the running board, gathered my skirt in one hand—and paused. About half a block away two blond heads stood out above the crowd streaming toward us. The Sorensons, surely, as they were both taller and blonder than most people.

"Come *on,* Fremont!"

"But the Sorensons are coming. They own my building. I must speak to them, Michael."

"Believe me, there is nothing to speak to them about. This whole block will be nothing but cinders and ashes before the day is out."

"You are so certain," I observed as I climbed in reluctantly and settled myself. The area behind the seats was piled high with Michael's possessions, mostly books, and my typewriter rode on top of them.

"Regrettably, yes." The engine of his automobile was already running, making a sound like a giant percolator. He did something with a lever near my knee, and we were off.

"I think you are wrong," I said. "Where is your faith in the fire department?"

"While you went to your office, I scouted around the city, and I learned a few things," said Michael, setting his mouth in a way that I knew all too well.

"Things you do not intend to divulge," I said with some asperity.

"Later."

I had to content myself with that; usually he did not promise even that much.

It was quite remarkable how the Maxwell took the hills all on its own, in a sturdy, chugging fashion. I began to revise my opinion of automobiles. (I am not often wrong, but when I am, I hope I have the good sense to admit it!) The sensation was like riding in an open carriage with the horse at a gallop—but without the horse, which, of course, was what had given rise to the name "horseless carriage"— though the vehicles were seldom called that anymore. Nowadays one said "automobile," or "auto" for short.

I said, "I must admit, I've been unreasonably opposed to this manner of transportation. The ride is not at all unpleasant. Where do you stable your auto? Though I suppose 'stable' is the wrong word."

"Ah, now you are about to learn some of my secrets," said Michael, turning briefly toward me. He smiled, more with his eyes than his lips. Michael has nicely shaped lips, well framed by his beard.

"Is that so?"

"It is. I have space in a garage at the Presidio—one garages an auto, Fremont. I also have a room at the Presidio. This is an emergency, so I doubt anyone will object to my storing your things in the room, along with some of my own."

How very interesting! Glancing over my shoulder as we chugged up Van Ness and past Vallejo Street, I said in a deliberately offhand manner, "The Presidio is a military establishment."

"United States Army."

"Aha!" I pounced on the word in my most Sherlockian fashion. Mrs. O'Leary and I are of the opinion that Michael Archer is some sort of spy. Of course, he will neither confirm nor deny it. He says he is retired, but his "retirement" seems of an intermittent sort; when he is not busy being retired I am sure he is spying. For whom, and on whom, he spies are questions that I have been able only to speculate upon—though he did once admit that he is of Russian descent, so one suspects that Russia figures into it somewhere. I asked baldly, "Are you a military spy, Michael?"

"It's called military intelligence, and the answer to your question is no. I am not in the Army, Fremont."

"Not in the Army? Hmm. Actually, I never thought you were. However, I note you do not deny being in some sort of 'intelligence.' And you must be in government service," I insisted, "otherwise you would not be given space in the Presidio."

"Um-hm."

"And if you were anything other than a spy, you would not be so secretive about it."

"As usual, Holmes, your reasoning is without flaw."

"Thank you, Watson," I said graciously.

"If you ever repeat any of this, especially to a particularly nosy landlady, I will—I will—"

"You'll what?"

"I'll think of something."

"Something unpleasant, no doubt." I smiled. It is so gratifying to have one's suspicions confirmed, and all the more so when those suspicions are of long standing.

The gates of the Presidio were before us. Michael stopped the auto and showed some identification to a uniformed guard. I scanned the area with interest.

"Look behind us," Michael said softly.

I half rose in the seat, turned, and looked. From the heights of the Presidio, the view was astounding. And far, far more terrible than I could ever have imagined. I gulped, and said the obvious. "San Francisco is burning!"

✥

That night Mrs. O'Leary and I climbed to the top of Russian Hill and watched the fires. Michael was not with us. The police had pressed every automobile they could find into service as an ambulance. Hospitals had to be evacuated and people injured in the quake or the fire transported. This effort included the Maxwell, with Michael as its driver.

The hilltop was elbow to elbow with people. When anyone spoke it was in hushed tones.

"It is fascinating, in a horrible way," I said to Mrs. O.

"I see wotcha mean," she replied briefly. She had spent the last of her garrulousness on convincing Michael that she would not leave her house and take shelter in the Presidio. I was glad to stay with her, for I thought she was right, and Michael—for all his good intentions—was being an alarmist. Before being summoned for ambulance duty, he had removed a large number of his books, his papers, and all of his clothes from the house to his room at the Presidio. Because he insisted, I had done the same. We made more trips back and forth than I could count. But Mrs. O'Leary would let Michael take none of her things.

Now she muttered, as she had done at least twenty times before, "The fire won't come up on these hills, they'll see to that." There were more mutterings around us in the same vein.

All humans are fascinated by fire. I suppose it is an atavism, a soul-deep remembrance of ancient times when fire was worshiped for its heat and light and held in awe for its destructive properties. We stood awestruck on our hilltop for hours. The clear weather had held all day and into the night; visibility was good, and we could see for miles. The sky to the south and east blazed orange, brighter than dawn. Below us, in a direct line from Russian Hill to the Bay, North Beach lay dark, untouched. But a mere few blocks to the south the entire business district was dotted with more fires than I could count—and these were but the remains of a general conflagration that had consumed the area during the day. Farther south, a wall of fire raged, seemingly limitless. I dared not think how much of the unfortunate area South of the Slot had burned, and was burning still.

The wind shifted, and a great gasp came in unison from our crowd as a curtain of fiery sparks billowed in our direction. But they did not reach us on top of Russian Hill, they showered down over Chinatown, which was already gone. We all sighed in relief. Mrs. O'Leary crossed herself. I wondered if I should get religion before this was all over.

When I judged it to be well past midnight, I put my hand on Mrs. O'Leary's arm. "We should go home and try to get some rest. We don't know what we'll be called upon to do tomorrow, and certainly we will need our strength."

She merely nodded, and came with me.

Many people sat on their steps, not wanting to go back inside their houses for fear another quake would come and trap them inside. The lurching aftershocks we'd felt from time to time fed that fear. While I shared it to a certain extent, I thought it unreasonable, owing to the comparative mildness of the aftershocks, and I wanted my bed.

I asked my landlady, "Will you come in?"

She shook her head and sat down heavily on her own front steps. I started up them. "Ain'cha afraid, Fremont?" she asked in a querulous voice, quite unlike her normal tone.

"Not very," I replied gently, "but I *am* very tired and I'll sleep better in my bed. At least this time the wardrobe can't fall on me—Michael helped me shift it off the bed, and it's flat on the floor. Good night, Mrs. O'Leary."

I did not know what time it was when I went to bed, for every timepiece in the house was broken. Unhappily, this included the pendant watch my father had given me for my twenty-first birthday. Only two years ago, yet it now seemed another life altogether.

As I curled on my side and lay waiting for sleep to come, I thought I must find a way to get word to Father that I was all right. San Francisco's telegraph lines were down; I wondered about Oakland, across the Bay. Surely from there, or somewhere, the rest of the world would have heard by now about our earthquake and the fires raging.

"Fremont, Fremont, wake up!"

I opened one eye, then closed it again. "Michael, you are becoming a bother."

"On the contrary, you're the one who's a bother, and Mrs. O'Leary is worse!" He shook my shoulder.

I opened both eyes and grumbled, "You shouldn't be in here." Then I awoke more fully. "Michael, what are you doing in my room? What time is it?"

"It's about five o'clock, and I need your help. Are you awake now?"

"Yes." I sat up, holding the blanket modestly up to my chin.

"Then get dressed, please, and join me downstairs in my living room. I've brought some coffee and rolls. I have many things to tell you. We've a rough day ahead."

"It couldn't be rougher than yesterday," I grumped, but the effect was lost on Michael. He'd already gone.

I stumbled to the bathroom, where I discovered there was no water pressure. The toilet would not flush, and the faucet in the sink produced only a thin trickle. This was all so inconvenient! Nevertheless, I managed to make myself look presentable enough in the skirt and blouse I'd held back so that I might have a clean change of clothes.

"Early morning is not my best time of day," I confessed a few minutes later, sniffing at the coffee Michael handed me. It smelled delicious.

"So I observed." He sounded amused.

Suddenly I was ravenous. We ate and drank in silence. By my second cup of coffee, I had begun to think, and to feel. My primary feeling of the moment was deep concern for Michael Archer. His face and clothes were smudged with soot, and there were deep circles under his eyes.

"You look exhausted," I said. "Did you sleep at all?"

He smiled. "No, I didn't. Thank you for your concern."

"It's bad, isn't it?"

"Yes." The smile faded.

"What can I do to help?"

"First, you can persuade Mrs. O'Leary to leave this house and come with us to the Presidio. We'll be safe there."

"She won't go."

"She'll have to. The fire has reached the foot of Nob Hill, Fremont. All the houses on this side of Van Ness are to be evacuated. Soldiers from the Presidio have joined with the police to keep order and to enforce the evacuation. They've already started knocking on doors. It will be far easier for her to come now, before they get here. I have the Maxwell outside and we can take one load of her things if we leave soon, but if she waits until they force her out, she'll have to leave with nothing. I think you'll have more success making her understand than I could."

"And if I don't?"

"Then we'll have to leave her to the authorities. I tried to tell you both yesterday evening: the firemen can't keep up with these fires. Many of the water lines are broken, the underground cisterns are inadequate, and there's no way to pump water from the Bay. Last night I learned that Fire Chief Sullivan was knocked unconscious in the earthquake and is not expected to live. Without him, there was no leadership for quite some time yesterday, which only exacerbated an impossible situation. The firefighting is more organized now, with the deputy chief in command. I know today they plan to begin using dynamite."

"Dynamite!"

"They have to make a firebreak. They'll knock down an area broad enough that the fire can't leap across, and then they'll set back-fires. Thus the fire will consume itself—or so the reasoning goes." He ran his hand over his short, dark hair, a gesture of impatience. "I hope to God they're right!"

My throat went all dry as I remembered the pathetic trickle of water from the bathroom faucet. This situation was so hard to comprehend! Every time one thought one understood it, it got worse. I swallowed with considerable effort and said, "You mean the houses on this side of Van Ness will either burn or be blown up. Including this one."

"Yes. That is so."

"In that case," I stood and said resolutely, "I must do my best with Mrs. O."

Michael also stood, and took a step toward me. "One more thing, Fremont."

"Yes?"

"When we get Mrs. O'Leary settled, I want to teach you to drive the Maxwell."

"Me? I mean, I? Drive? What a notion!"

"You'll find it simple. What's most important is that you have the right temperament for the work. I want you to take over transporting the physically injured and the infirm. I'm needed for other things, and I would rather entrust my auto to you than to a stranger."

"Oh. Well, in that case, I should be glad to learn."

Yes, I thought as I went down to wake Mrs. O'Leary, it would be the best of a bad situation if I could feel I was doing something useful.

Mrs. O'Leary would not leave her house. Nothing I or Michael said could persuade her. I don't think she really listened; she just sat on her couch with the photograph of her dead husband in his police captain's uniform clutched to her breast, saying over and over, "No police is gonna turn me out. Himself and his blessed memory won't let that happen."

At last, with tears in my eyes, I said goodbye, embraced her, and left her there. I came down the front steps dashing moisture from my cheeks with the back of my hand. Michael was waiting in the Maxwell with the motor running. There was an unfamiliar hot harshness to the air; half the sky above was black and roiling, the other half a high, clear blue. With a heavy sigh, I joined Michael and we were off.

After a few minutes I asked, "What will happen to her?"

"A tent city has been set up for the homeless in Golden Gate Park. Someone will take her there, or she'll find her own way." He took his eyes from the road and glanced at me. "Don't worry, Fremont. This crisis is bringing out the best in people, as you'll soon find out for yourself. Besides, Mrs. O'Leary has many friends. She'll be fine."

"The homeless . . ." I mused unhappily. "That's us now. We are the homeless."

"Not precisely." Michael turned left. The auto began to climb toward the heights of the Presidio. We passed a gaggle of refugees, some in horse-drawn carts and some on foot, trundling their possessions. Michael kept to the middle of the street, driving steadily and calmly.

He was good in a crisis, as I had reason to know. I would do well to emulate him. I sat up straighter and inquired, "How do you mean, not precisely? One either has a home or has not, and as of our leaving Vallejo Street just now, we are among the have-nots."

"You will have a roof over your head. I've arranged for you to stay in my room at the Presidio until you can find permanent quarters to your liking."

"Oh? And where will you be?"

He drove through the gates. This time we didn't stop to show identification; the guard recognized him and saluted, then motioned us on. Michael said, "When we complete your driving lessons and I've gone the rounds with you once, I'm leaving San Francisco, Fremont."

"I can't believe you! How can you do that? I know you have the most annoying habit of disappearing from time to time, but *now?*"

"Shush! Kindly control your famous temper, or you will draw attention to us. In a few moments, when we're clear of all the buildings, I'll explain; and I'm quite sure I'll tell you more than I should. Does that satisfy you?" Michael arched one dark eyebrow and looked briefly at me.

By way of reply, I glared at him. I was still worried about Mrs. O'Leary, stirred up in general, and in no mood to be mollified.

He drove to a vast open field that he said was the rifle range, and a good place for me to learn the rudiments of automobile operation. He added, "I can talk here without being overheard," and switched off the motor. The auto gave a little shake and a kind of snort before subsiding, reminding me of the absent horse.

I turned in the seat toward Michael and raised my own eyebrows inquiringly.

"I have no choice. I must go," he said softly, reaching around the steering wheel and taking my hand in the most tender gesture I had yet known from him.

In spite of myself, I felt somewhat mollified; still, I snatched my hand away. Bitterly I said, "Spying again."

"No. Not this time. You recall that I have a boat."

I nodded.

"I'm sailing down the coast to Monterey, taking certain, ah, documents with me for safekeeping in the Presidio there."

"It seems there are Presidios all over the place, though I never in my life heard the word before coming to California."

"The word comes from our state's Spanish heritage," said Michael patiently. He reached for my hand again, and this time I let him keep it. "I don't know how long I will have to stay there. I want you to promise me, Fremont, that you'll be careful. Don't take any unnecessary risks. Don't let your inquisitive nature get you into any kind of trouble."

His eyes were on me with a kind of intensity that made me both glad and uncomfortable. No longer a novice in matters of the heart, I recognized that feeling. I did not know whether to welcome it or not, but a thought surfaced and provided a digression. "That reminds me. Have you heard anything of Meiling and the other members of her household? Did they survive the earthquake?"

He shook his head. "I was kept busy with other things; there was no time to inquire. I'm sorry. But don't change the subject, Fremont. I asked you for a promise."

"I promise that I will take good care of your auto," I said, raising my chin slightly. "I'm sure that is your principal concern. Now, shall we get on with the driving lessons?"

Nightfall. Knowing that I was too exhausted either to eat or to rest, I climbed the Presidio's highest hill. I found a place apart from the others who had come for much the same reason as I. The strait of the Golden Gate lay below me, and directly across rose the hills of Marin, spring-green, untouched by the voracious fire that was destroying my beloved city. I turned my back on all that burning and watched the fog roll in from the open sea. Always fog has the power to mesmerize me; I swayed a little on my feet as I let the fog empty my mind.

It moves like an immense creature of great bulk but no weight, a creature that can miraculously conform its shape to fill any space. A silent creature that brooks no argument but inexorably, insidiously, blots out, covers up . . . everything. As the fog moved I turned with it, entranced, following its progress. The Golden Gate disappeared, and Sausalito, and Tiburon; Angel Island, Alcatraz, Yerba Buena; North Beach, Telegraph Hill, the Wharf and the blessedly still standing Ferry Building. Then the creature grew pale gray tongues that lapped into the valleys between the burning hills.

It poured into the fire-blackened saddle between Nob and Russian Hills, then slowly, slowly crept up and over their peaks to rush down their still burning sides. At the same time I felt moisture in my hair and on my cheeks, and I understood: the fog had crept up my hill too. Soon it would cover the Presidio. I should go down, to that unfamiliar room that was now the only home I had. But I lingered.

How beautiful it was, yet hauntingly, seductively evil: the fire glowing through the fog.

❧ 3 ❧

Ashes, Ashes, All Fall Down

For three days and part of a fourth the fire burned; then Saturday night the rain came and at last we could believe it was over. I scarcely remembered a time when I did not know how to drive an auto, or when my eyes did not hurt from driving through smoke. Or when it was possible to get food without standing in line for it. Or when my soul did not ache even more than my body.

Saturday night after dark, I prowled through the mess tent that had been set up for refugees on the Presidio grounds, looking for a discarded newspaper. Three daily papers, the *Chronicle,* the *Examiner,* and the *Call,* were using presses outside the city; the day after the earthquake they had all collaborated to produce one triune issue that was already a collector's item. I had not seen it or any of the issues they had published separately since. I'd had no time for anything so ordinary—indeed, anything "ordinary" now seemed luxurious to me. I had been driving for the Red Cross and supposed I would continue to do so for an indefinite time, as they were coordinating relief efforts all over the city. Perhaps now that the fires were out we might settle into some sort of routine. At the very least my eyes would return to normal. That was progress, and any progress was welcome.

"Can I help you? Have you lost something?"

I jumped; I had thought myself alone in the huge tent. "No," I said, "thank you."

"I didn't mean to startle you." He was a soldier, and a handsome one at that. Young, with a face like a statue from antiquity.

"That is quite all right. I thought I might find a newspaper to take back to my room, that's all."

"I'll help you look."

"That really is not necessary. I'm sure you have better things to do." I was not in the mood for company, even the company of some-one who looked like a Greek god in U. S. Army uniform.

He grinned, and suddenly became wholly American. "I'm on grounds patrol. I'll just patrol in here for a while."

He really was not much help, as he stayed close enough to be my shadow—except, of course, that the dark did not offer much possibil-ity of shadows. I wished I had brought a lantern. We patrolled up and down the rows of boards that, set upon wooden "horses," made tables for the mess. His nearness would have made me uncomfortable except that I was too tired for even that much feeling.

"Aha," I said, snatching at a whitish rectangle on the seat of a folding chair. "I've found one. Thank you for your company. Good evening." I bustled past him.

"I'll escort you to your room."

I snapped open my umbrella with some impatience. There seemed no way to get rid of him.

"I've seen you around," he said, walking now alongside me. He was getting wet, which did not bother him at all. "Allow me to introduce myself: Albright, James, Private First Class. Everybody calls me Jim."

"How do you do." I deliberately didn't offer my own name, but it did no good.

"May I ask your name?"

"Fremont Jones," I said grudgingly, striding as rapidly as I could manage along the path to the building that housed Michael's room. I could not think of it as *my* room.

"Fremont?"

"Yes."

"Odd name for such a pretty woman."

He was fishing for the explanation I usually gave when questioned, but I wanted only my solitude and so I did not produce it. In the doorway to the building I let down my umbrella, nodded curtly, and said, "Good night, Private Albright."

"If you don't mind my asking, how is it that you're in here"—he gestured to the building—"instead of out there with all the others?"

He meant the refugees, who were camped on the grounds of the Presidio, though in fewer numbers than in Golden Gate Park. "The room belongs to a friend, who arranged it for me." Perhaps, I thought quickly, invoking Michael's name might discourage this too persistent soldier. "His name is Michael Archer. You may know him."

"He's an officer?" The classic face, rain-dappled, creased in thought.

"Not exactly."

"Well, I can't say that I do, but never mind. Good night, Miss Jones." He saluted smartly and turned on his heel.

"Good night," I said, and thought no more of James Albright.

It was a great relief to get out of my clothes and into my favorite old bathrobe, a disreputable-looking thing that had once been viridian but through many washings had faded to the no-color of Spanish moss. I should have thrown it out long ago but could not bring myself to do so; I always sought its familiar softness whenever I was sick or in some other way discomfited. I turned up the wick on the kerosene lantern, wondering how long it would be until the electricity was restored; then plumped up the pillows against the headboard of the bed. With a long sigh of relief, I settled against them and picked up the newspaper. It was the *Call*. I opened it but did not read.

For a few moments I simply savored the delicious comfort of the pillows, the stillness of the night, and my privacy in the room. I listened to the rain pattering softly outside the window, soothing as music. A great feeling of peace stole over me, and I was immensely grateful for it. The newspaper fell from my hand; my eyelids fluttered down. Sometime later I awoke for long enough to extinguish the lamp, and then I slept again, dreamlessly and long.

Thus it was the next morning, Sunday, before I got to the newspaper. I read yesterday's news while waiting in line for breakfast. In sensationally tall letters the headline proclaimed, NUMBERS OF HOMELESS CLIMB! The subhead said "Total Expected to Exceed 250,000!" *Good heavens,* I thought. Even though I had been among them daily, I had not realized the numbers were so great. I read rapidly, finding that not much else was of any surprise to me, as I had been, hour by hour, in the thick of it. All the news was of disaster, or of the politics of disaster. Mayor Schmitz, by all accounts, was performing gloriously— the newspapers had not been so kind to him pre-earthquake. Being so tall and handsomely bearded, he did cut a striking figure in the several photographs here.

I folded the paper and tucked it under my arm as my turn came up for coffee, bread, and butter. I would have killed, nearly, for a piece of fruit. Everyone was all smiles and happy chatter this morning. You would think we were at some enormous outdoor picnic, quite a change from the tense atmosphere of previous days. I did my own share of smiling, though I declined to chat; found a place to sit and resumed reading the paper while I munched passable bread and drank perfectly awful coffee. The best you could say for the latter was that it was hot. Also, I mentally amended, free.

On the back page, set off by a black border, was a listing of the names of people now known to have died in the earthquake. I read it with an eye especially alert for Chinese names. I was quite concerned about Meiling Li, because I'd seen the devastation of Chinatown. I'd looked for Meiling as much as I could while keeping up with the rounds set for me and the Maxwell, but I had not yet found her. The names were listed alphabetically, and I relaxed a bit when I passed the Ls without seeing hers. Then I came to the Ss.

Mr. Theodore Sorenson. Miss Krista Ingrid Sorenson.

What? I blinked, put down my coffee mug, and read the names again. Those could not be *my* Sorensons, for Ted and Krista were husband and wife, therefore Mr. and Mrs., not Mr. and Miss. But could there be two sets of Ted and Krista Sorensons in San Francisco? I thought not. I also thought the newspaper had made another mistake, because I knew the Sorensons had not died in the earthquake. I had seen them on Wednesday morning, coming toward me on Sacramento Street.

I should tell the police, I thought, *they will want to know that they have made a wrong identification.* How I wished that Michael had not rushed me off before I could speak to Ted and Krista. If only I'd spoken to them, I could offer that as proof they were still alive.

Then I remembered something that, in the press of fleeing the fire, I had forgotten: the contraband in the back room. Again, if Michael had not rushed me, I would have had time to tell him about it or, better yet, to take him by the hand and show him. I supposed all the fascinating artifacts were burned up now, like everything else in that part of town.

Quite unreasonably, I felt it was somehow Michael's fault that the Sorensons' names were wrongly on this list of the dead. I knew I felt that way because I was still irritated with him for leaving San Francisco, but that knowledge didn't lessen the irritation one whit. I didn't care that Michael had been sent on a mission, couldn't appreciate that he'd taught me to drive and turned his precious Maxwell over to me. Did I really want to be doing all this driving? No, I didn't. I wanted— *longed for*—some space, just a little space, a closet would do, where I could set up my typewriter and be FREMONT JONES TYPEWRITING

SERVICES again! Most embarrassingly, my eyes spouted tears. I left the mess tent in a hurry.

Later, of course, I was ashamed of myself for that outburst of self-pity. I drove along the now familiar route to the Red Cross station set up just outside Golden Gate Park, thinking about the Sorensons and whether or not I should go to the police. Being somewhat distracted by these thoughts, I did not immediately see the figure that stepped into the path of the auto, and had to apply the brakes sharply.

Did my eyes deceive me? Was this tall person in the traditional Chinese garb of long black coat and narrow trousers who I thought it was? Yes!

Joyously I cried, "Meiling!"

She abandoned her accustomed dignity and ran to the auto. "Fremont, I have been looking everywhere for you."

"And I have been doing likewise, for you. Get in, please. I cannot tell you how glad I am to see you." I did not exaggerate, for I am a great admirer of Meiling Li. Though she is my own age or perhaps a year or two younger, she had been the pillar of her family since her grandfather's unfortunate demise the previous year. And though Chinese society is even more repressive of females than Bostonian society, Meiling manages a considerable degree of independence.

She smiled at me and lowered her head slightly in just a hint of the bow that is her people's form of greeting. "I should not be surprised to discover you at the wheel of an automobile."

"It is Michael Archer's," I said, putting the auto in gear.

"Ah. That does not surprise me either."

"He taught me to drive it and then he left town."

Meiling laughed her silvery laugh. "From what I have heard of Mr. Archer, that too is not surprising."

"Um-hm. I recall that your family has known Michael longer than

I have. Meiling, I hope you won't mind riding along with me, as I'm due at the Red Cross station. We can talk as we go, and after I receive my assignment, I'll drive you wherever you like. Is that acceptable?"

She inclined her head again. "Yes, that is most acceptable."

"I've been in the vicinity of Chinatown several times during the last few days. I know that your splendid house is gone. I'm sorry for your loss, Meiling."

"Thank you."

"Were you able to save anything? Is your mother all right, and your grandmother, and the other members of your household?"

She shook her head; the wind generated by the auto's motion stirred her long black hair and flung strands of it across her face. "No," she said, scraping her hair back, "my mother is dead. She was not killed in the earthquake, but when we went to get her to leave what remained of the house, we could not rouse her. I thought she had only drugged herself insensible, which as you know would be nothing new. But she was dead. Grandmother thinks she drank poison."

"How terrible!"

Meiling lifted her shoulders and let them fall, a grave sort of shrug. "It is not really so terrible. Life has been unbearable for her for many years. I am only surprised that she did not take the poison before. She must have been—what is the correct word, not 'keeping' exactly, but—"

"Hoarding?"

"Yes, hoarding it for some time. The earthquake was her great excuse to use it. Now Mother does not suffer anymore. But Grandmother . . ." Meiling broke off with a most uncharacteristic sigh.

I glanced at her. We were nearing the park, but Meiling clearly needed to talk. I pulled into a side street and cut off the motor, explaining, "I can be a little late. Pray continue."

"Grandmother is so frail. I think she does not have the heart to start over. She will not get up from her pallet. I am sure she has decided to die, and her will is strong. She will die soon. I have had so much to think about, Fremont."

"With the proper medical attention, perhaps your grandmother will change her mind. I've been driving doctors to and from various places for the Red Cross, and nurses; I can see that she gets good help. Where are you staying?"

"We are camped out in a little park in the Sunset District. I appreciate what you are offering, Fremont, but it would be disrespectful of her wishes if we were to bring a doctor to my grandmother. She is a very old and honorable woman. My mother's death was an act of weakness, but it will not be so with my grandmother. I am preparing myself. That is why I was looking for you."

I did not quite understand, so I inclined my head in a gesture of acknowledgment and waited.

"I am the last direct descendant in my branch of the Li family. Since Grandfather died last year, I have been expected to marry, even though it is well known that I do not wish it. I am supposed to take a husband and produce a lot of little Lis, preferably male. Only my grandmother's affection for me has kept her from arranging a marriage. Now she feels that she has failed in her duty and seeks a promise from me, a promise that I cannot bring myself to give."

"Whom does she want you to marry?"

"He is a close relative, in English I think one says a cousin; his name would not mean anything to you. I do not particularly like him, but even if I did, I would not marry him. I am a most dishonorably disobedient woman." Meiling turned and looked me full in the face with her lustrous dark eyes. She did not appear at all regretful. "I am going to make a new life for myself. The earthquake was not so much a disaster for me as an opportunity. No one must know what I am planning, but I need help. Will you help me, Fremont?"

"Meiling, you know that I will."

᷍

We arranged to meet at the end of the day, when I would have more time to hear Meiling's plan and my part in it. She declined my offer of a ride back to her camp, saying that she preferred to walk. Excited by the prospect of helping Meiling, I chugged up to the Red Cross station in quite the highest spirits I had enjoyed for some time.

"You're late, Miss Jones," said Mrs. Bartlett, the nurse who gave me my assignments.

"I'm sorry, but I met up with a friend whom I hadn't seen in so long that I was beginning to think she hadn't survived the quake. I really had to take the time to talk with her."

"Well, I can understand that." Mrs. Bartlett had a face like an old prune, but she was a warm-hearted person.

"What am I to do today?"

"First, you can take Dr. Tyler back where you came from, to the Presidio. Some of the refugees there need attention."

"Can't the Army doctors do that? After all, they're right there on the spot."

"Apparently not, they're short-handed or something. All I know is the request came in, and Dr. Tyler's ready to go. Or at least he was— where do you suppose he got to?" She contorted her long, wrinkled neck to such an extent that I thought, like an owl, she would turn her head clear around backward. "Oh, drat!" she expostulated.

"Never mind, I'll find him." Dr. Tyler was already kind of a favorite of mine; I didn't in the least mind looking for him. Besides, in the process I could continue my search for Mrs. O'Leary. She had to be somewhere among the homeless at Golden Gate Park, but thus far I had not seen her or any of her friends whom I might recognize on sight.

"Wait, Fremont," said Mrs. Bartlett, snatching with her skinny fingers at my sleeve. "Let me give you the rest of your assignment in case I get busy with something while you're off after Dr. Tyler. When you've dropped him at the Presidio, you're to go to the train station."

I nodded. The train station, though south of Market, had, with heroic effort, been saved from the fire. Now a steady stream of supplies arrived there daily. Communities around the state and across the country were being very generous to San Francisco.

Mrs. Bartlett tipped up the little round watch pinned to the flat bodice of her shirtwaist. "Have you the pocket watch I gave you?"

I fished in the pocket of my skirt and produced it.

"Good." She nodded, which set off a wavy motion among all the wrinkles in the vicinity of her chin. "Let us synchronize our watches. I have nine fifty-seven."

I pulled out the fob of my watch and made a two-minute adjustment. Mrs. Bartlett was notoriously precise. "Nine fifty-seven it is."

"There is a train due in from Sacramento at ten-thirty with a load of donations. You are to pick up the blankets and bring them here. Nothing else, just the blankets, as they are urgently needed. Others will be along with wagons for the rest, but loading the wagons will take some time and I want those blankets right away. Understood?"

"Understood." I grinned. I felt I should salute. Mrs. Bartlett would have made a great general if she had been of the opposite sex. She already had a good deal of the lingo, and I was picking it up myself, both from her and from the Army types at the Presidio.

"Carry on," she said, and I did.

"I do wish you would call me Anson," said Dr. Tyler. I had found him with no trouble but could not say the same for Mrs. O'Leary.

"Very well. Thank you, *Anson.*" I glanced over my shoulder and smiled at him. He was a lanky fellow, as soft-spoken as he was clean-shaven, with light brown curly hair that had already receded to the crown of his head, though he did not appear to be much over thirty. His eyes were a darker brown than his hair, liquid as a puppy's and always full of kindness, which was why I instinctively liked him.

"I keep thinking that we should be in church," he said, "though I'm sure the rescue work is more important."

It was a measure of how much I liked Dr. Anson Tyler that I did not acknowledge my own lack of religion. Instead I said, "I expect God will understand."

"I'm sure you're right, Fremont."

Mrs. O'Leary was still on my mind; the church she usually went to was called for two saints—Peter and Paul, I thought it was. At any rate, her church was in the vicinity of North Beach and so must have burned on the third day of the fire. If it had not, I was sure she would manage to get there somehow. "If I am not being too inquisitive," I ventured, "what church do you go to?" There was a small chance he might attend the same one as Mrs. O'Leary.

"I live in the Mission District—fortunately, in the part that did not burn—so I usually go to the Basilica Church at the Mission Dolores. I was brought up Methodist, but since coming to San Francisco I've become interested in the Catholic faith. I expect I will become a convert someday. Perhaps soon. The earthquake has speeded up my thoughts on the matter."

"I can understand that. I visited the Mission Dolores on one occasion last year and had quite an interesting chat with the priest there. I rather preferred the little Mission to the large church."

"Yes. I prefer the intimacy of the Mission myself, but it is no longer large enough for the congregation. We will all be crowded into the Mission for services now, however, because the Basilica sustained a lot of earthquake damage while the old building came through with only minor cracks. I find that fascinating."

"Mm, yes. I wonder why that is?"

"Why is it fascinating?"

"No, on that I agree, but why did the Mission, which after all is over a hundred years old, suffer less damage?"

Anson laughed, a rich, buttery sound; you would not have thought such a spare body could produce so mellow a resonance. "I'm sure there is a scientific explanation, but not from my branch of science. Are you a Catholic, Fremont?"

"No, I was talking to the priest about something else, not religion but an old legend connected with the Mission." I cut my eyes rapidly to Anson and back. "And before you ask, the old priest was rather embarrassed about it"—that was an understatement!—"so I won't repeat the story. I'm sorry, I shouldn't have mentioned it at all."

"Fascinating," Anson murmured. I guessed the word was a favorite of his. As it was of mine.

I sailed through the Presidio gates without even slowing the auto. The Maxwell and I had all but worn a rut in the pavement with our comings and goings, and the guards who stood watch had known me by sight long since.

"Do you know where to go?" I asked.

"All I know is, not to the Army Infirmary. They have set up a tent for the sick somewhere out here."

"Tents! I am fairly sick of tents." I braked to a stop and cut the motor.

"Tush, Fremont." Dr. Anson Tyler turned his kind gaze full on me. "If we did not have the tents, largely thanks to the courtesy of the military, where would we be?"

"I know. I am properly chastised." I sighed, and ran a hand across my hair. The wind had tugged some of it loose from the clasp at the base of my neck. "I think I will probably be living in a tent myself soon enough."

Anson picked up his medical bag and rested it on his knees. "You are homeless too?"

"I thought you knew. I have a room here at the Presidio, actually, arranged by a friend. But I do not much like the atmosphere. I find it rather repressive, or regimented, or something. I can shut the door and have some privacy, but it comes at a price."

"It's none of my business, of course, but if I were you I would think twice about giving up a real roof over my head. No matter where it is. Now I'd best be on my way." He climbed out but stayed with one hand on the door. "Will you be coming back for me?"

"Mrs. Bartlett didn't say. What time do you think you'll be through?"

"Unfortunately, I have no idea. If the telephones were working I could call you, but they're not. I do miss the telephone. In a short time it has become important to my practice."

"You could hardly call me on the telephone in the Maxwell at any rate." I smiled at such a preposterous idea. "I tell you what, Anson. I'll stop by around the lunch hour, about one o'clock, and if you're not ready to leave then, at least you might know how much longer you will be. Don't worry, I won't leave you stranded."

"Thank you, Fremont." Anson had a smile that crinkled his eyes and curved his mouth in an attractive manner. "I look forward to seeing you again."

Leaving the train station with my load of blankets, I had quite a scare. A young woman, in a dress that had once been a delicate shade of pink but was now darkly striped with charcoal, lurched off the sidewalk and fell into the street. I brought the Maxwell's wheels to a stop only inches from her head. A head that, on closer inspection, looked familiar.

I set the handbrake and leapt out. She lay face down on the pavement, and her fair hair was tangled and matted. The dress, which looked as if she had been wearing it for days, was not warm enough for the weather, but she had no coat. She also had no purse. The skin of her hands and arms, though smudged, was pale as milk; her fingernails were dirty and broken.

Did I know her?

I took her wrist gently and felt for a pulse. I'm no nurse and could not find it, which did not necessarily mean she did not have one. Her wrist was as thin as a child's, and so was her body, but the style of her dress, as well as the two-inch heels of her shoes, proclaimed her adulthood. She seemed so familiar, even though I could not see her face.

Crouching beside her, I watched closely until I thought I saw an indication that she was breathing. The Red Cross sign on the front of my auto seemed like a bad joke; they should have given me at least some basic training before sending me out with such a sign. I felt a fraud.

Before moving her, I should check for broken bones. I knew that much. I began with her ankle, and as I felt my way up her calf, she stirred. I snatched my hand back as if from a hot potato. She struggled up on one elbow and turned a bewildered, dirty face to me.

In a flash I recognized her, though I had not seen her for many months. "Alice? Oh, my God, it *is* Alice!"

Godsend?

A lice whimpered, high in her throat. The expression in her eyes was that of a wounded small animal, cautious, craving help, yet fearing the human who offered it. Clearly, she had no command of her wits at the moment and therefore did not know me.

"It is I, Fremont Jones," I said, gently taking her by both hands. "You remember, about a year ago you brought me some poems to type."

Love poems, they had been, of a sweetness and innocence that to my mind more than made up for their amateurish imperfections. Her hands quivered in mine. I continued to talk soothingly as I drew her to her feet. "I recollect that you are a librarian, at the public library, was it not? I used to see you there on occasion, but not for the last few months. I wondered what had become of you. I am so glad to have found you again, even in such circumstances."

"F-Fremont?"

Ah, at last a tiny spark of recognition in those wounded eyes. What an extraordinary color they were, like violets. Beneath all her sooty smudges, Alice was a lovely little creature. I said, "Yes, Fremont," wishing that I could remember her last name, but it evaded me.

She whimpered again and her face crumpled, her shoulders shook. She tried to turn away, but I held her hands fast and spoke in the businesslike manner that, I had learned, was most effective with people in shock. "You're hurt, and I am driving for the Red Cross, so you see, we are well met. I shall drive you back with me to the aid station, where you will be cared for. Here, take my handkerchief." I drew it from my pocket and pressed it upon her. Then, still holding one of Alice's hands, I began to coax her toward the Maxwell. I was very concerned about her; there was a lump the size of an egg where she'd hit her forehead on the pavement, and though the skin was unbroken it was already beginning to turn quite a nasty color.

Alice tried to pull back. She ignored the handkerchief, her tears making dirty tracks down her cheeks. "No, I can't, I can't. I have to keep looking. I've lost him, you see, and I have to find him. I have to!"

"Of course you do. I understand. I'll help you look. Do you hear me, Alice?" I doubted that she could, for all her anguished sobbing. I wondered who *he* was, but for the moment that was of less importance than getting her into the Maxwell. I stepped close, took the handkerchief, and wiped her face myself, carefully avoiding the ugly lump on her forehead. I repeated, "I will help you look for him, Alice."

"You will?" She gazed up at me, violet eyes round and full of doubt. She had a mouth like a rosebud. Her chin trembled.

"I will. I promise." I tucked Alice under my arm, feeling like a big sister, although I'd never had a sister, and moved both of us step by step to the auto. "But first we must get you taken care of, or you'll be no good at all to him when we do find him."

"Oh. Oh, I hadn't thought of that. How clever you are! Thank you, Fremont." She managed a wan smile as I handed her into the passenger seat. I got her settled, took a blanket from the pile on the back seat, and wrapped it around her.

"There, that's better." I cranked the Maxwell, which I had become quite good at, and we were on our way.

Mrs. Bartlett, on the lookout for her blankets, marched up as soon as I braked the Maxwell to a stop. Alice cowered, clutching her own blanket under her chin. She seemed confused by all the hubbub of the aid station.

I shut off the motor and jumped out, waylaying Nurse Bartlett. "I have your blankets," I said, speaking in a low tone, "but first my passenger needs attention. She is an acquaintance of mine, though I don't know much about her. Her name is Alice. She fell into the street right in front of me, near the train station. She hit her head, but that is not, I think, her only problem."

"Oh? Yes, well." Bartlett gave Alice a quick visual once-over, then stomped around to the passenger side and opened the door. "Alice? I'm Nurse Bartlett."

Alice whimpered and cringed, almost disappearing under her covering of charcoal-gray wool.

"Hmmm," said Bartlett.

I stood aside, confident that my job was over. I hadn't yet seen the individual, large or small, male or female, who was beyond this nurse's capabilities. I brought them, she and the other nurses or doctors took care of them; that was the way it always went.

"Fremont," Bartlett said, jerking her head to the left and setting all her wrinkles aquiver, "you carry the blankets over to that table for the volunteers to hand out, while I take care of your friend here."

"Of course." I moved to comply.

"No!" shrieked Alice, dropping her blanket and half rising out of her seat. "Don't leave me, Fremont, please don't leave me!"

"Shush, dear," the nurse cajoled, "she's not going anywhere, she'll be nearby, and folks need those blankets. See here, you already have one, and where would you be without it? I ask you. Why, you'd be freezing. Lost your coat, did you? Poor thing. Wrap up, dear, and come on down out of that contraption. Let me take a look at you."

"No," Alice insisted, "I don't know you. What is this place? Who are all these people?" She was becoming frantic, whipping her head around and twisting her torso from side to side. "Fremont, where are you? You promised you'd help me, you *prooooomiiiised!*" She drew the last word out until it became a wail.

Across the Maxwell I made eye contact with Bartlett and she shrugged, stepping back.

"I'm here," I said hastily, redepositing my armload of blankets in the rear of the car. Alice reached over the seat and laid hold of my arm with a clawing grip. Really, she was rather alarming. I assured her, "It's all right, I'll come with you and stay while Nurse Bartlett examines you. Let go of my arm, Alice."

"You won't leave me?"

"No, I won't leave you." It was not easy to keep a note of exasperation from my voice. "Didn't I just say so?"

"You won't let them hurt me?"

A *tsk, tsk* escaped from Bartlett. I darted a glance her way and saw that she had her arms crossed, as if to hold back her impatience.

I pried Alice's fingers loose, saying, "No one is going to hurt you. We're here to help you, Alice, not to hurt."

Still there was doubt in her eyes. When I came around the auto and assisted her down, I found that she was shaking like the proverbial leaf. With sisterly care I looped the trailing ends of the blanket over her arms and shepherded her into the examination tent. Bartlett followed. When I had Alice seated, I turned to Bartlett and whispered, "I fear she has been severely traumatized."

Bartlett inclined her head in acknowledgment, then, with rather less briskness than usual, she set about examining the unfortunate young woman.

"Tell me your name, dear." As the nurse asked routine questions, with keen eyes and gentle fingers she searched for hidden injuries, working her way from the head down.

"Alice Lasley."

"That's a nasty bruise on your forehead, Miss Alice Lasley."

"Mrs.," said Alice. It was news to me. From our scant acquaintance, which was based primarily on her working at the library I frequented, I had assumed she was not married. Most husbands would not allow their wives to work, as a wife's employment cast doubt in the eyes of the world upon her husband's ability as a breadwinner.

"Whatever," said Bartlett. She held up her index finger in front of Alice's face. "Now, I want you to focus on my finger. Keep your eyes on the finger as I move it from side to side. Hmm. Do you feel at all dizzy?"

"No. Well, yes. A little."

"Any nausea?"

"No. I don't think so." Nervously, Alice darted her violet eyes to me. I nodded reassurance.

"Can you remember what it was that caused you to fall and hit your head?"

"I was just walking, and then, and then—" Alice gulped. An expression of panic took her face. "And then, I don't know, I don't remember! F-Fremont was there, she helped me."

"Um-hm. Well, let's be quiet now while I take your pulse. And while we're doing that, Fremont will get you something to drink. See if there's any fresh apple cider, will you, Fremont? And don't you fret, Alice," said Bartlett, interrupting a whimper, "we're all your friends here."

When I returned with the cider the nurse had completed her examination and sat opposite her blanket-wrapped patient. I had to steady Alice's trembling hand before she could take the drink.

Bartlett looked pointedly from me to a third folding chair, and I sat. Alice took one hesitant sip, and another, then in a long draught half drained the glass.

"When did you last eat, child?"

"I don't know." Alice raised a hand to her forehead as if to help herself recall, but her own touch made her wince with pain. "What day is it?"

"Sunday," I said. "The earthquake was Wednesday."

Alice seemed at a loss. Bartlett and I glanced at each other. I leaned forward. "Alice, the person you were looking for—have you been out on the streets searching for him ever since the quake?"

"Oh!" She dropped the glass, spilling the remaining cider onto ground, which had been grassy when the tent was first set up, but now was packed hard and worn bare. The blanket fell from her shoulders. "Oh, I must find him, I can't stay here!"

"Hush, now. Be still." Bartlett was up in a flash, rewrapping the blanket and seating Alice in the chair. "Chances are the man you're looking for is right here in Golden Gate Park. Most of the refugees are; you couldn't have come to a better place for finding someone. Now, dear, who is it you're trying to find?"

"My h-husband." The word unleashed a fresh flood of tears. I fished out my crumpled handkerchief and handed it over. So, she really did have a husband. And he, no doubt, was the cause of Alice's absence from the public library in recent months. She wouldn't have continued to work after marriage.

"He is almost certain to be here," I said with more confidence than I felt. We did not have a listing of all the people who had taken refuge in the park, nor even of those who'd had medical treatment during the first, worst days. Learning the names of the dead had had top priority; of those we had a list, but Alice was in no condition to see it yet. If her husband's name was on it, I feared for her sanity.

"He wouldn't be *here*. Why are all those people here? Why don't they go home?" asked Alice in a whining tone.

Nurse Bartlett's prune-face had the intense expression I had seen at other times, when she was trying to decide whether or not to call in a doctor. There were too few doctors to go around, and the nurses did not call upon them lightly. So I took it upon myself to answer that astonishing question.

"They have no homes to go to. They lost them in the earthquake, Alice." Perhaps her sanity was already gone.

"The earthquake." Again her hand strayed to her forehead, and again she winced. Slowly, in visible pain, she shook her head. "No, that's not it. I remember that; it made a frightful noise and all the pictures fell down. He, uh, my husband was there then. At home. But he—he went out. And he didn't come back. I kept thinking he would—he always comes back, you know—but he didn't. And so I went to look for him, but I got lost. There was . . . there was a fire, I think. Was there a fire, Fremont?"

"Yes." Understatement of the century. Any century.

"And everything looked different, it was all so confusing, and I hid. Somewhere. Everything was so strange that I couldn't find my way."

"Well, that's all over now," said Bartlett, standing, her mind apparently made up. "First things first. You're a very lucky young lady to have taken such a hard fall with so little damage. I expect your head hurts, and you may develop a slight swelling of the brain, but I doubt it will amount to anything serious. What you need most is to get some food into you, and after that a nice long rest. Fremont, take Alice out to a table and get her some soup and bread. See that she eats it all, but slowly. Meanwhile, I'll find a place for her in one of the tents." She switched her focus from me to Alice. "You'll have to share, which is just as well, because you need to sleep, but someone will have to wake you every now and then to check for signs of brain swelling."

Alice was hungry; at the mention of soup and bread, I was pleased to see, a light came into her eyes. She'd risen eagerly, but now she frowned. "I don't want to be in a tent. Why should I? Why can't I just eat and go home?"

Bartlett raised her sparse eyebrows, which in turn arched the rows of wrinkles on her forehead. "Where is your house?"

"You did say this is Golden Gate Park?"

The nurse and I nodded and replied in chorus, "Yes."

"My house is on Haight, not far from here."

"Ah," I said with a shade of envy, "so it's all right then." The

Haight was one of the few districts that had escaped both the quake and the fires relatively unscathed.

"Of course it is," said Alice a trifle imperiously, gathering her blanket around her like a royal cape and proceeding through the tent flap.

"Not quite," said Nurse Bartlett quietly, to me alone. "Fremont, she'll be better off in her own home, but she shouldn't be alone for at least twenty-four hours. So if that husband of hers isn't there . . ."

Which was how I got stuck with Alice.

"You are a godsend, Fremont Jones," Alice whispered to me as I tucked her into her own bed in her own house on the corner of Haight and Belvedere. Her husband was not there, and for the moment she seemed to have forgotten about him, which was just as well.

"You exaggerate," I said lightly, biting back what I wanted to say, which was *I seriously doubt it.* My acquaintance with God is scanty at best; I presume He is more in the habit of sending His obedient servants. Obedience was never my strong point, with God or otherwise.

Alice's blankets were a deep shade of rose, banded in satin that was cool to my touch as I smoothed them over her shoulders. The word "Godsend" had set up a kind of echo in my head, and I recalled that I'd been told that same thing a year ago, by a young man who came to a most unfortunate end. No wonder I had no liking for the term, however well intended.

Alice let out a luxurious sigh, turned on her side, and folded her small hands under her chin.

I turned away from the bed and eased the watch out of my pocket. Twelve forty-five—Alice's problems had taken the entire balance of my morning. If I hurried, I could reach the Presidio in time to fulfill my promise to Dr. Anson Tyler.

I had previously closed Alice into her bathroom with a jug of the Red Cross's precious water—the indoor running kind that we took for granted was still lacking—and instructions to bathe herself. The meal of bread and soup had quite restored her, from which I concluded that her faintness and confusion had been mostly due to lack of food. I doubted she had much brain swelling, but Bartlett had said one could not be sure for twenty-four hours.

Alice had emerged from the bathroom in pristine condition except for the bruise on her head, which had worked its way up to a brilliant shade of purple. *Her* wardrobe had not so much as shifted from its place against her bedroom wall, and contained some very fancy duds, quite unlike those she used to wear when working as a librarian. Apparently her husband had expensive taste. And was a cad, to boot, for going off and leaving her at a time like this.

As Alice seemed incapable of making any decision at all, I had chosen a silky nightdress trimmed with lace and ribbons and helped her into it, and thence into bed. Where now she snuggled prettily.

"Now that you are settled, I must leave for a while," I said, steeling myself against the protest I knew would come.

It did, but I held firm. "I've made a commitment to pick up a very busy doctor at the Presidio and take him where he next needs to go. The Maxwell and I are, of necessity, kept on the run these days."

"But—"

"*But* I will be back shortly. You'll be fine, Alice. Nurse Bartlett has said that you should sleep. I only have to wake you every two hours to be sure your brain does not swell. I'll return before the two hours are up. Now, I must go."

I turned on my heel and closed my ears. Already I knew that Alice was a whiner, but I would have to try to make allowances. In the doorway I paused long enough to wave and smile. "Sleep, Alice, sleep well."

I closed the door behind me and hurried out of the house, feeling a little guilty. Yes, she whined, but she had been through a lot. And anyone could see that she had a fragile, delicate nature; such women were, I supposed, constitutionally more subject to whining and fainting in the street than tall, obstinate creatures like myself. Also, I reflected as I automatically cranked the Maxwell, they are more likely to get husbands.

Good heavens—where had that thought come from? As if I wanted one. Hah! Even if I had a husband, I wouldn't know what to do with him. Nor he with me, I expected.

A few minutes later I drove through the Presidio grounds rather gaily, glad to be back in my usual routine. Anson was waiting, and he climbed into the auto immediately so that I did not have to cut the motor.

"Fremont, how good of you to come for me."

"Where to?" I asked, backing and turning.

"To the Mission District. I thought I'd take a little time out before going back to the aid station. I want to put my office in order and post a sign saying that I will resume seeing patients there tomorrow. My office occupies the front two rooms of my house; I'll give you specific directions when we're closer."

"So you won't continue working with the Red Cross?" I felt a pang of disappointment.

"I'll give them half my time, at least. The need is not so urgent now."

"I expect you're right about that, thank goodness." Acres and acres of the city looked like a war zone, and smelled like burnt charcoal, but along every street we passed there were people cleaning up and picking through the rubble.

As I drove and turned when he indicated, I told Anson about Alice.

"Nurse Bartlett oversteps her bounds," he said in a censorious tone.

"Whatever do you mean?"

"The duty of a nurse is to keep patients clean and comfortable and, when asked, to give assistance to the doctor. That is all. She should not take it upon herself to diagnose. Nurse Bartlett doesn't keep to her place."

"Oh, Anson, I disagree! I realize I have little experience in these matters, but Mrs. Bartlett is an excellent nurse. She uses her good judgment to make the most of your time, and that of the other doctors."

"Nevertheless, I think I should see your friend Alice for myself. Turn the auto around, Fremont, and take me to her house."

"That's very good of you," said I, not slowing by a whit, "but Alice has an almost pathological fear of strangers. When I left she was going peacefully to sleep, which, believe me, is a considerable improvement over her previous state. I am to wake her every two hours, and I promise that if I see any of the signs of brain swelling that Bartlett told me to look for, I will come for you. Is that satisfactory?"

"Women!" He said it like an oath, but grudgingly he smiled. "Actually, I admit I do appreciate a capable woman. And you are very capable, Fremont. You are the only woman driver I have ever known, and you do it well."

"Driving is not difficult," I said, glad to have peace restored between us, "and I enjoy it."

"Not to lessen your enjoyment, but slow down, please. We must turn left at the corner here." A leaning street sign marked it as Valencia Street. "My house is in the next block."

I had not been in this part of town before and regarded the houses with interest. A few days ago I would have thought them modest, but now anything that was still standing looked as desirable as a palace to me. There was some earthquake damage, more than in Alice's neighborhood of larger homes, but less than in so many places.

"Here we are," Anson said, and I applied the brakes. His gray frame house showed the ubiquitous smoky grime rather less than its once white neighbors. It had black trim, too somber for my taste; I should have painted the trim that shade of dark red we use so often on doors in Boston. But then, it was not my house. It had one and a half stories, a pitched roof, and two steps leading from the sidewalk to a center entrance. In one of the front windows was a two-line sign: ANSON TYLER, M.D. GENERAL MEDICINE.

He invited me in, but I declined. I was ravenously hungry and no doubt would have to stand in a long line for food, and then I had to get back to Alice.

"In that case, perhaps you will come another time?"

"Perhaps," I said and drove off, my cheeks glowing from Anson's obvious interest.

Alice slept so prettily that it seemed a shame to wake her. I wondered what I looked like asleep. Like a harridan, probably, with my long, straight hair tangled around my neck—I hate to braid it before bed, because braids leave such horrid kinks. Alice's hair curled, but it needed a wash. I wondered if she kept a tank outside to catch the rainwater; if so, she was in luck because of the recent rain, and I wouldn't have minded washing my own hair. I thought I would ask her, but she was so groggy when I woke her that I let it go. I had her track my finger with her eyes as Nurse Bartlett had done. She did it well enough, and I told her to go back to sleep.

I went downstairs. It was three o'clock, and I had promised to meet Meiling at four forty-five. I would have to wake Alice again before I left. Perhaps I might rest myself, on the parlor sofa. If I lay down in a real bed there was no telling how long I'd sleep. I seemed to be always tired these days, to one degree or another.

Alice's house was grander than Mrs. O'Leary's, with higher ceilings and more spacious rooms. The rooms were arranged on either side of a central hall, whose staircase had a fine mahogany railing and was carpeted with an oriental runner. There were two parlors at the front, one furnished more formally than the other. The formal one was no doubt for entertaining, the other for family use. I went into the latter and reclined on the sofa, closing my eyes. Such luxury, to be in a real house again! How quiet it was, with not even the ticking of a clock to mar the stillness. *Someone should wind Alice's clocks,* I thought.

I opened my eyes. Someone should pick up all the mess, sweep up the glass from the broken picture frames. I had grown so used to such conditions that I hadn't much noticed earlier when I was getting Alice settled. I closed my eyes again. This was not my house, cleaning it up was not my concern. Not any more than was the color of Anson's trim. Being homeless was making me think too much about houses.

Botheration! Here I was with an opportunity to rest for the first time in days, and I could not do it. I swung my feet to the floor and sat up, rubbing my face with my hands.

What was that? The sound of a door opening? And had it come from the front or the back of the house? In a trice I was up and striding across the room. I had not locked the front door, nor had it been locked when Alice and I arrived—we'd walked right in. I hadn't thought a thing about it at the time, but now that seemed foolish.

"Hello?" I called out. In a moment I would most likely find myself face to face with the unknown husband. The disappearing cad. But there was no one in the hall.

The kitchen, then, the back door. I headed in that direction, though I had not been in the back of the house before. Just as I entered the kitchen, I thought I saw the back door close. It was half window, covered by one of those sheer curtains caught on a rod both above and below; through this curtain a vague shadow fell. In an instant it was gone.

My heart began to beat quite fast as I ran across the kitchen, skirting a table and knocking over a chair in my haste. *An intruder,* I thought, wrenching the back door open; the husband would have stayed.

Whoever it had been, if anyone at all, was gone. The house had a small backyard that, surprisingly, was overgrown with weeds. I charged down the steps, tripped on the hem of my skirt, and almost fell, thus losing precious time. When I reached the corner of the house and could see to the street, there was nothing to be seen except a couple of innocent-looking pedestrians. This chase was a waste of time. Nevertheless, I circled the house and looked among the bushes along its foundation before returning inside.

There had been some looting since the earthquake, but not as much as one might have expected. Anyhow it was careless of Alice, and myself, in the extreme to leave the house unlocked. I must find the keys.

I looked in the butler's pantry: no convenient row of keys on hooks, as we had in the butler's pantry at my father's house. I already knew they were not on the inside of their locks, where Mrs. O'Leary so often left her keys. Where, then? I should have to snoop—a prospect I did not find entirely distasteful.

Regrettably, I did not get to use any of my Holmesian techniques, for the keys were in an obvious place. Near the front door stood an extravagantly ugly Victorian thing, one of those constructions of dull, blackish wood that have been carved in embellishment to the point of torture. This one had an oval mirror in the center, pegs for hanging coats on both sides of the mirror, multiple drawers beneath, and stuck on either side of the drawers, a couple of umbrella receptacles. The keys were in the top right-hand drawer of this monstrosity. Two full sets.

Hmm, I thought, taking one set and by the process of elimination finding the key that locked the front door. Then I went to the back and repeated the process, pocketing the keys when I was through. On my way back to the parlor, I went into every room and made sure the windows were locked: kitchen, pantry, dining room, a small and feminine-looking study opposite it, and finally the two parlors. Everything was locked now, but something was not right. I stood in the family parlor tapping my foot, trying to figure out what it was. Something about keys . . .

Two sets of keys. Had Alice left the house without hers, without a purse, without a coat? I had assumed she lost those items, but here were two complete sets of keys. That was odd. The missing husband: had he also left without his keys? Why would they, either of them, do such a thing?

◁ 5 ▷

The Man Who
Wasn't There

The telegram was from my father, in response to the one I'd sent
him as soon as I was able. I almost did not get it because it was
addressed to Caroline F. Jones c/o Presidio, San Francisco. Considering the contents, I could have done without it: MY DEAR CAROLINE
STOP GLAD YOU ARE SAFE STOP IMPERATIVE YOU QUIT YOUR FOOLISH-
NESS AND COME HOME STOP WILL WIRE MONEY IF NEEDED STOP YOUR
LOVING FATHER.

Stop indeed—stop telling me what to do! Seething, I set the telegram aside while I changed my clothes. Then I charged out of my
room in a huff, straight into the path of Private Albright.

"Whoa, there!" he said, pulling himself up short to avoid colliding
with me.

I frowned; he smiled, standing squarely in my way. I said, "I beg
your pardon, Private Albright, but I am in something of a hurry."

"I can see that, Miss Jones. I'll walk along with you, if you don't
mind, because I was coming to your room anyhow."

"Oh?"

"Yeah, to speak to you. I, er, that is . . . maybe first I should ask:
is anything wrong?"

At least he was perceptive, I granted him that. "Not really. It is only that I unexpectedly have to send a reply to a telegram, on top of all the other things I have to do this morning. There will be a line at the telegraph office—there are lines everywhere for everything these days, which is really quite annoying. It will make me late for the Red Cross and I was late yesterday, so Nurse Bartlett will fuss at me, which I could easily live without." I stalked across the grass, taking the short-est way to the garages; it was foggy and the grass was all wet and so would be the hem of my skirt, but I could not have cared less.

"You have a temper," the private observed.

I glanced at him and caught his infectious grin. In spite of myself, the corners of my mouth twitched. "My friend Michael Archer often says the same. However, my temper spends itself quickly. What did you want to speak to me about, Private Albright?"

"I, er . . ." To my surprise he blushed, but pressed on, "I'm off duty tonight. And I heard the Palace Theatre's open. They have a variety show, you know, singing and dancing and telling jokes and all. Some of the fellows have been and said it was good, so I thought, that is, I was hoping . . . maybe you would like to go with me?"

I halted. "A variety show?"

He nodded. His skin had resumed its usual fairness. He was really an exceptionally good-looking young man. Not that looks mean any-thing, but they do influence one just a tad.

"I think I would enjoy that, especially the jokes provided they are not too risqué."

"Oh, the Palace doesn't do bawdy shows. At least, I don't think they do. Not too bawdy. I wouldn't ask you to see something like that. You're not that kind of woman, anyone can tell."

"I am relieved to hear it," I said dryly. "I'd be delighted to go with you, Private Albright. What time?"

"Jim, please? Seven-thirty?"

"Seven-thirty, *Jim*. Now, I really must be going."

"I'll come to your room for you. See you then, Fremont."

I waved and he saluted, and I reached the garages in considerably better spirits than when I started out.

Jim Albright had been rather a pest over the past couple of days, but on this occasion his intervention into my fit of pique may have been fortuitous, I reflected as I drove away from the Presidio. My father's telegram was burning a hole in my pocket, especially the word "foolishness"—it smacked of Augusta. On his own, Father might apply certain unfavorable adjectives to my various activities, but "foolishness" was not one of them. If Albright—Jim—had not intervened, no doubt I would have sent Father a hotheaded reply. Along the lines of: FATHER STOP NO INTENTION OF RETURNING TO BOSTON STOP MY WORK IS NOT FOOLISHNESS STOP KEEP YOUR MONEY STOP YOU WILL NEED IT FOR AUGUSTA STOP MY NAME IS FREMONT STOP I NO LONGER ANSWER TO CAROLINE.

Yes! A telegram like that would certainly tell him what was what.

It would also hurt him, and I loved my father. I even understood why he'd married Augusta. He was lonely after my mother died, and Augusta was a perfectly proper, presentable, available woman of the right age. Also narrow-minded and not overly bright, which apparently did not bother him as much as it did me. At any rate, I could not send an angry communication. I couldn't hurt Father any more than I already had by leaving, and besides, I might still find it necessary to return to Boston.

I sighed, and pulled the auto over to the side of the street. I had to decide where I was going, to the telegraph office or to the aid station in Golden Gate Park. No doubt some of my ill temper was due to the fact that I'd sat up all night in order to wake Alice every two hours— thank goodness that was over! Except for a mark on her forehead that looked like a relief map of Africa in shades of purple, Alice was fine, certainly better rested than I. I had returned to my room at the Presidio this morning only to change clothes, and had found the telegram pushed under the door with a handwritten inquiry attached: *Is this for you? If not, return to the Adjutant.* The telegram was dated the twenty-first, which was Saturday, and now it was Monday. Father would be anxious for a reply.

I was caught in a quandary. Driving Michael's Maxwell for the Red Cross gave me the illusion of both freedom and employment. Living in Michael's room gave me the illusion of security. I blinked at a sudden ache behind my eyes, or perhaps the ache was in my heart, for the reality was quite different from the illusion. All I really had was some clothes and a typewriter and, when they finally got around to opening the banks again, a little money. Very little. But the tents in Golden Gate Park were free, and for the present there was a good bit of free food about; if I were very careful with my money, I might find some small hole in the wall that would do for a new office. . . .

I drove to the telegraph office and sent my message:

DEAR FATHER STOP DO NOT WORRY AM FINE FOR NOW STOP AM NEEDED HERE STOP WILL WRITE SOON STOP LOVE FREMONT.

The telegram took the last of my pocket money.

Nurse Bartlett started to fuss at me for being late but I interrupted her. "I need your help, if you would be so kind."

"Bless you, dear, after all you've done, of course I will. What's the problem?"

"I'd be grateful if you could find me a tent space."

"I thought you had a place to live?"

"I do, but it isn't really mine. The Maxwell isn't mine, either— but you know that. Both my room and the auto belong to Michael Archer."

"I remember him." Bartlett nodded her wrinkled head. "Drove for us that first awful day and night—seems years ago, doesn't it?— then turned the job over to you. Good worker. What happened to him?"

"He had to go to Monterey, on business."

"Coming back, is he, and wants his room?"

"No, I haven't heard from him. This is rather hard to explain, Mrs. Bartlett. I don't belong at the Presidio, and I'm not comfortable there."

She snorted. "You wouldn't be too comfortable in a tent, either! I know, I'm in one myself."

"I don't mean physical comfort, what I mean is that I want to get my own life going again. Not that I know exactly how I'm going to do that. But—"

"I understand. We all feel that way. Don't you have family you could go to?"

Not wanting to explain about Father and all that, I merely shook my head.

"Well, for heaven's sake! I wouldn't have dreamed—"

"Mrs. Bartlett, I thought if I had a space in a tent here, I would at least feel that I had my own place to live. I'll continue to drive for you as long as you need me, but when I can get my money from the bank I should try to start up my business again."

She put a bony arm around my shoulders and her head close to mine. "You know, we make assumptions about people without realizing it, and I just assumed you were a well-off young woman with more common sense than most, helping us out until you could go back to your life of social activities and little luncheons and nights at the opera and so forth."

I smiled; it was a good description of the kind of life I'd run away from.

"But I see I was wrong." Bartlett gave my shoulder a squeeze and stepped back. "You just leave it to me. Now, for this morning, I've got a list of places said they'd donate some food. I want you to go around and pick it up, and while you're gone I'll see what I can do about a tent for you. People are moving out already, going to relatives or friends across the Bay, or south down the Peninsula, so maybe I can wangle you a tent of your own. Helpful as you've been, you deserve it."

"Thank you!"

"Now let's see, where did I put that list? . . . Ah!"

She found it and handed it to me. I gave her my mock salute and set off.

"Wait, Fremont. I forgot to ask: how is your friend this morning?"

"Alice? She's fine, physically, but when I left her this morning she still seemed a little confused. I said I'd check on her later."

"Um-hmmm." Bartlett bit her bottom lip, as if to prevent herself from saying anything more.

"Alice, you really must take hold of yourself," I said, firmly but I hoped not critically. "You are not ill, but you will make yourself ill if you don't get out of bed and get dressed. It's past lunchtime, and I'll wager you haven't even eaten breakfast. Have you?"

"I don't want to eat." She pouted, blinking those violet eyes.

"You have to. Disasters happen, but life goes on." A regrettable cliché, but true. I was not without compassion, but in the days since the quake I had seen many who were much worse off than Alice, and who handled themselves far better. The young woman who had brought me poems to type had seemed shy and sweet; who would have thought this languishing, petulant female could be the same person?

"My husband was my life," she said, tears welling, "and he is gone."

"Nonsense. Your life is your own, you don't give it away just because you are married."

"He left me, Fremont. He's not coming back. I know that now." She screwed up her face and a couple of tears fell on her cheeks.

"You may be right. Alice, I'm not unsympathetic, but if I am to help you at all, you must at least get out of bed and get dressed. If you don't, I shall just have to leave." I could think of no other way to handle her.

It worked. She got up, and I went to the kitchen while she dressed. Cooking of any kind indoors was forbidden, all over the city, until the fire inspectors could make their way neighborhood by neighborhood to certify that the buildings were safe. Meanwhile, gas lines were turned off at the mains, and so was electricity. Alice had a wood stove, but no one, myself included, would have dreamed of violating this regulation, for every citizen of San Francisco had become deathly afraid of fire.

Still, Alice and I would not starve. The night before, I'd searched through her cupboards and found some apples and a loaf of bread that was still edible. Now I unlocked and opened the back door, thinking that the milkman might have made his rounds; he had, so there was milk. I brought it in, pleased by this bit of normality restored. While I waited for Alice to come down, I picked up broken crockery and swept the kitchen floor.

Wearing a blue dress with rows of delicate smocking across the bodice, Alice wrinkled her nose at the bread and fruit. She went to the stove, saying brightly, "I'll cook bacon and eggs. For you too, if you like, Fremont."

I placed myself between her and the stove and explained the facts of life in post-earthquake San Francisco. As her eyes widened I wondered where, figuratively, she had been for the past five days.

We sat at the table and I picked up an apple, both because I wanted it and to encourage Alice to do the same. Between munches I said, "Something has been puzzling me. Yesterday, while you were sleeping, I noticed that your doors were unlocked, so I looked about for the keys. I found two sets in that piece of furniture near the front door. In fact"—I removed them from my pocket and put them on the table—"I should return these to you. It would be a good idea to keep the house locked, even if you haven't been in the habit of doing so. Anyway, because the two sets of keys were there, I wondered: is it possible both you and your husband left the house without them?"

She shook her head. "I don't remember."

It seemed there was a good deal she didn't remember. If I were to find myself in such a condition, I would drive myself crazy trying to fill in the blanks, but that was apparently not the case with Alice, who sat placidly sucking on a piece of bread she'd softened in a glass of milk.

Frustrated, I tried another tack. "I promised I would help you find your husband. Have you notified the police that he is missing?"

Her head jerked. "No! Do you think I should?"

"Certainly you should." That reminded me: I should go myself to the police and tell them the Sorensons were not dead. I had been so busy I'd forgotten.

"All right," said Alice, "I will, as soon as I feel up to it. But it will do no good. If he were coming back, he would have done so by now." She said this dully, as if all emotion were spent where her husband was concerned.

I forbore to mention that he might well have died in the fire. My naturally suspicious mind suggested he might equally have seen the confusion as an opportunity to remove himself for a variety of reasons. None of them salutary.

"Tell me about him, Alice. I'm out and about the city a good deal. Perhaps I might be able to learn something of his whereabouts."

A dreamy look came over her face. "His name is Ralph. Ralph Lasley. He's tall and noble-looking, with the most handsome profile. Like the actor, John Barrymore. We love each other very much. There's no one for him but me in the whole world." Her face changed, the light in her eyes went out. "But I'm not going to think about him anymore."

I ignored the last. "What business is he in?"

"Business?"

"What sort of work does he do?"

"Oh, he doesn't work. He doesn't have to. He's quite wealthy. We have everything we need right here." The dreamy look was back.

That did not give me much to go on, but I had an idea. I got up from the table. "If you'll excuse me, Alice, I need to use the facilities."

She made no reply. Dreaming on, apparently. I went upstairs and into the bathroom, where I observed an absence of shaving equipment. I opened the medicine chest and found a few patent medicines, a large bottle of aspirin, a box of cotton wool, a pile of hairpins, and one prescription tonic with Alice's name on it. I raised the lid on the dirty clothes hamper and poked about; it contained a couple of towels and a petticoat.

I proceeded to Alice's room, which had a double bed but no connecting door such as husbands and wives often have between their rooms. I already knew that the wardrobe held only her clothing. I opened the drawers of a tall chest and saw silks and sheer cottons and eyelet and ribbons and lace—female garments all.

So I went into the next bedroom, which had the impersonal, neat appearance of most guest rooms. I did a perfunctory search with negative results. Next I tried the room across the hall from Alice's. It had the stale air of being long shut up and was dusty, to boot; I saw little point in searching here, but did it anyhow, to be thorough. The drawers and the wardrobe were unsurprisingly empty.

I should hurry; Alice would wonder what was taking me so long. There was one room remaining. As it was the room farthest from Alice's, I could not imagine that it would be her husband's, but I turned the doorknob. The door swung inward with a loud creak. Oh, dear. I didn't want to be caught snooping.

Ears pricked, I waited on the threshold for a sign that Alice had heard; as I waited my eyes scanned the room. The person who had chosen this furniture had the same overwrought taste as the one who'd picked the monstrosity by the front door. The bed was a massive affair, so high it required a stepstool beside it. A man might appreciate such a bed, but not its covering: an ecru spread of embroidered cutwork with a gathered, ruffled drop. Moreover, a great collection of embroidered and beribboned pillows—round and square as well as the usual shape, plus a neck roll—were piled at the head of the bed. My suspicions grew.

Since I'd heard nothing from downstairs, I tiptoed in. The wall opposite the bed was almost entirely filled by a scrolled, pedimented armoire that would have made Augusta salivate. It had four doors, and I opened them all. It was empty, save for a quantity of clothes hangers. I closed it up. The drawers of a huge chest were so heavy, and I was so concerned about time, that I opened them only far enough to peer in. They were empty, except for the bottom one, which held a crumpled something far back in a corner. First glancing over my shoulder, I reached in and pulled it out, hoping for a man's handkerchief, preferably with initials. But it was a woman's lace-trimmed nightcap. It had been worn, and smelled faintly of lavender, with an undertone of something more unpleasant, as if the wearer had been sick.

I cannot possibly say why I did such a thing, but rather than return the nightcap to the drawer, I shoved it deep in the pocket of my skirt. Then I quickly closed the drawer and left the room.

Alice was as I had left her, seated at the kitchen table. She had finished the bread and was slowly eating an apple. She brightened as I joined her, looking more like the old Alice I remembered.

"Fremont, I have the most wonderful idea!"

I smiled. "What?"

"You said that your house and your office both burned in the fire, yes?"

I nodded.

"Well, here am I in this big house all alone. Why don't you live with me?"

"Oh, I don't think—"

"Wait, hear me out. I've been thinking about this while you were upstairs. I admired you so much, you know, when you had your business and used to come into the library. I was too shy to say so, but sometimes I used to hope we might become friends. I know we're very different—you're so independent and I'm not. I've never needed to be, but now I do, and I could learn from your example. I don't suppose you'd want to just live here. You wouldn't want to feel like a guest."

"Alice—"

"I've thought of that. I've thought of everything! Fremont, you could have the family parlor and the dining room behind it. We could get someone to help us change the furniture around. You could make the parlor into an office, I'll even buy a desk if there isn't a suitable one here already, and the dining room could be your bedroom. We'll switch the dining-room furniture with one of the bedrooms upstairs. It'll be like having your own apartment. Of course it would be only temporary, you wouldn't stay forever, I know that. Oh, do say you will!"

An office! It was tempting. I said, "Maybe . . ."

"You could pay rent, if that would make you feel better about it. Not much, just a little. You could get a sign and put it in the front window: FREMONT JONES TYPEWRITING SERVICES! Oh, I can just see it!"

I could see it too, and I could not resist. "Provided you do let me pay rent. And with the understanding that, if the arrangement should become, ah, uncomfortable for either of us, we agree to break it off . . ."

"Of course!" Alice seemed to have become a new person. She stood up and extended her hand in a businesslike fashion. "We will have a verbal agreement."

I stood too, and took her hand. A small hand, cold fingers, but her grip was strong. We shook on it. "Very well. I agree."

"I knew you would, I knew it!" she crowed. She scooped up the keys I'd put on the table and pressed them into my hand. "Here, Fremont. These are your keys now."

⚜

I convinced myself it would work. Besides, there was a mystery here of some sort, and I was more likely to solve it if I were on the spot.

But I could think no more of Alice now, or of our arrangement. I had stayed rather too long at her house and was obligated to ferry nurses from one makeshift hospital to another—a time-consuming business that required several trips. After that, I picked up Anson at Valencia Street and took him to the Red Cross station in Golden Gate Park. Bless him, he did not complain about my being so late. Along the way I told him I had found a place to live and also to have an office, and he in turn asked many questions about my typewriting service. He seemed quite interested in my answers. "I approve of a woman who works," he said. While I hadn't been looking for his approval, the remark pleased me.

Nurse Bartlett had been busy all day and was apologetic when I approached her. She said, "I'm afraid I haven't done anything yet about that tent for you."

"That is just as well." I told her about Alice's offer, and that I had decided to accept.

Bartlett, ever practical, frowned and was frank. "Hmmm. I wonder if you will be happy with the arrangement, Fremont. There's something odd about that girl. I suspect she's not quite right in the head."

I knew the nurse did not refer to Alice's bruised forehead. "I think I know what you mean, but we've agreed to break off the arrangement if either of us becomes uncomfortable with it. I'm not sure what is wrong with Alice, but she is helping me by giving me a place for an office, so if in return I am able to help her in some way, I am perfectly willing to do it."

Bartlett cocked her head to one side appraisingly. "I expect you can take care of yourself. You don't need advice from me. Does this mean I'm going to lose you, then?"

"Not right away." We continued to talk details, deciding that I would have the mornings to myself and drive for the Red Cross in the afternoons until my business was up to speed. Then Bartlett's duties reclaimed her, and I took out my pocket watch.

It was almost five o'clock. I mentally ticked off all the things I had to do in the next two hours, before meeting Meiling. This was the night we were to begin putting her audacious plan into effect. She had told me all about it yesterday; we would have started last night but for my obligation to wake Alice every two hours. I hurried to the Maxwell, wondering if Meiling's clothes would fit me. We had to wear black, and as I am not overfond of dark clothing—it makes me look like one of Mr. Bram Stoker's vampires—I had nothing suitable of my own. Meanwhile, I had to—

Oh, no!

I realized that I had made an unforgivable mistake.

Strange Times
and Stranger Actions

How in the world could I have done such a thing? I felt guilty, and I do despise guilt—it is such a wastefully debilitating state of mind. Still, I had earned it, by promising to spend the evening with both Meiling and Jim Albright.

"Oh, bother!" I said fiercely. I gripped the steering wheel at the top and drooped over it, head on hands. I had made a number of little mistakes lately, mostly by forgetting things and having to retrace my steps or my route. Or I might find myself in a particular place with no recollection of why I was there, and would have to wait anxiously until it came to me. As my memory is ordinarily quite good, such episodes were distressing. I had, in addition, become remarkably clumsy, tripping over things, dropping things, barking my shins, bumping elbows, breaking fingernails, and so forth. Regrettable as such things were, they had heretofore caused no inconvenience to anyone but me. This mistake I could not undo without serious inconvenience to one party or the other.

I raised my head, took a deep breath, and set the auto in gear. No use crying over spilt milk, and all that. I darted a glance over my shoulder and pulled out into the street. There was no question that the private would have to be the one I let down. Meiling had first claim on both my time and my affection.

I drove rather too fast back to the Presidio. Perhaps if I found Jim Albright promptly he would have time to invite someone else to accompany him to the variety show. I stopped at the gate and asked the soldier on duty how to locate Private Albright.

"He's assigned to D Company, miss, but he's not in the barracks or on base. He went out a while earlier, and he hasn't come back. Leastways, I haven't seen him."

"Oh, dear." I certainly didn't want to brave the male bastion of the barracks to leave a note, nor did asking this soldier at the gate to deliver a personal message seem quite the thing to do. So I said, "Very well. I shall have to try again later." I reversed and headed for police headquarters. I had postponed this business of the Sorensons for too long. Surely I could take care of it, pick up some supper for myself and Alice—as I had told her I would—and still have time to run back to the Presidio before meeting Meiling at seven.

"I should like to report an error in your records," I said to the policeman at the desk. His uniform made me think of Mrs. O'Leary as I'd last seen her, clutching the portrait of "Himself," her late husband, in his police captain's regalia. I felt, for a moment, a sense of loss so strong that it stole my breath; I'd all but given up hope of ever seeing Mrs. O. again.

"What sort of error?" The policeman reared back and looked at me through rimless glasses that magnified his pale blue eyes. He was young and kinetic. A nervous type.

I explained, "A few days ago I read in the paper a list of names of people thought to have died in the earthquake. Two people were listed in error. I am virtually certain of it, and I felt it was my duty to make a report."

"I see." He poked at the inside of his cheek with his tongue, frowning. "What's your name?"

"Sorenson," I said, and then realized yet another mistake. "No, I misunderstood you. Sorenson is *their* name, the name of the people who aren't dead. My name is Fremont Jones. I'm a driver for the Red Cross."

As I had hoped, the latter statement gave me some much-needed credibility. "Have a seat," he said, jumping up from the desk. "What part of the city are we talking about? Where would these Sorensons have been located?"

"I don't know where they live, but they had a place of business on Sacramento Street, east of Van Ness. That's where I saw them."

"Wait here, I'll see what I can do." He took off into the crowded room behind him.

I perched restlessly on the edge of a hard chair, looking around. The police, like most people, were housed in temporary quarters. The room was noisy, its atmosphere oppressive. Electric lighting would have improved the gloominess but not the smell, a fuggy combination of sweaty wool and old wet ashes.

I had never been in a police station before, temporary or otherwise. Being somewhat interested in crime and detection, I felt favorably disposed toward those who did these things for a living. However, I wondered why there were so many policemen in the room, some sitting at desks piled high with papers, some leaning against the walls and conversing loudly, with every now and then a burst of raucous laughter. Shouldn't they be out on the streets?

The policeman with the rimless glasses returned. "Sergeant Franks will see you, Miss Jones. Second row, third desk." He pointed, and I made my way down the row until I stood before the desk indicated.

"Sergeant Franks?" I expected the sergeant to rise in greeting, but he did not. Instead, he merely tipped his chair onto its back legs and stared up at me. He was a fleshy man, gray-haired, with a neck so short and thick it almost did not exist. He had undone two brass buttons at the top of his dark blue uniform, and the rest of them strained across his broad chest.

"You're Jones? What was that first name again?"

"Fremont. I'll get right to the point because I haven't much time. There has been a mistake about Theodore and Krista Sorenson, who were listed as having died in the earthquake. Two mistakes, actually. To begin with, they were man and wife and so their names should have been recorded as Mr. and Mrs., not Mr. and Miss. However, that is unimportant, because they should not have been on the list at all. They did not die in the quake. I am rather surprised that no one else has brought this to your attention, since I read it in the papers on, um . . . I'm sorry, I can't seem to remember what day it was."

"Never mind, I know when we gave it out." He narrowed eyes that were already too close together. "What makes you so certain these people aren't dead?"

"I saw them, *after* the earthquake. You see, I had been at my office, it's—I mean it *was*—on Sacramento Street over a bookstore owned by the Sorensons. They were my landlords, they own the whole building. As I was leaving, I saw the Sorensons coming up the street. I'm sure it was they, because they are both unusually tall and blond. I wanted to stay and speak to them, but—"

"You're sure you saw them on Wednesday?"

"Of course I am, the day of the earthquake; I could scarcely mis-remember that!"

"What time was it?"

"I'm not sure. My watch was damaged—well, at that point I didn't know it was damaged, I just couldn't find it because everything in my room was topsy-turvy—" I broke off, aware how awkward I sounded. I wished he had invited me to sit; I felt exposed, standing in a sea of desks. In addition, I was the only female in the room, which ordinarily would not have bothered me but did on this occasion.

"Miss Jones. It is Miss, not Mrs.?"

"Yes." I squared my shoulders and lifted my chin.

"You're the one's made the mistake. Go on about your business. You're wasting my time." He turned his head away and took up a sheaf of papers, stacking them, lining up their edges in a fussy, officious manner.

"I beg your pardon," I said evenly. "I know what I saw."

He glared at me, his face reddening, and flung the papers down. They scattered across the desk. I stood resolute, lifting my chin higher. An expression of disgust came over his face. Apparently he had decided I would not go away, for he asked, "Sacramento Street?"

I inclined my head in assent, not trusting myself to open my mouth at the moment. I was angry; there had been no call for him to be so rude. Plus there was viciousness in the way he'd flung those papers. I quite got the message that he would have liked to throw *something* in my face.

"All right," he snarled, "you want the nasty details, I'll give them to you. It just so happens, *Miss* Jones, I was the officer on duty on Sacramento Street that day. My job was to be sure all the people got out of the path of the fire. I remember that bookstore very well, and the rooms upstairs. Those people were there, all right, and they were dead as doornails. A big blond pair with their heads bashed in where the wall fell on them. Now are you satisfied?"

I wasn't, but I was a little shaken. "Wh-where were they? What room were they in?"

"I don't recall. I was kinda in a hurry," he sneered.

"How do you know they were Ted and Krista Sorenson? You must have removed the bodies—who identified them?"

"You know what you are, lady?" Now he stood up, curled his fingers into fists, and leaned over the desktop with his weight on his knuckles. His whole demeanor was threatening. "You're a busybody, that's what. You're so smart, you tell me how the hell anybody had time to get bodies out of a building with the fire roaring lickety-split up the street!"

I backed a step away, shaking my head. I was intimidated, I admit it.

"We identified them. I don't remember how. I could look it up, but I won't. Like I said a good while ago, you're wasting my time. Now get out of here. *And don't come back!*"

A silence had fallen over the room. I felt all eyes on me as I turned and walked up the aisle with as much dignity as I could muster. My knees trembled and my hands were like ice. I wished to high heaven I had not come, and I left no longer so favorably disposed toward the police.

I was astonished to consult my pocket watch and find that so much unpleasantness had taken only half an hour. My confidence in my powers of observation—no, more than that, in *myself*—was shaken. I sat for a while in the Maxwell, exceedingly discouraged.

I ticked off days on my fingers—I was reduced to that, counting on my fingers like a child—Wednesday, Thursday, Friday, Saturday, Sunday, and now Monday. Six days since the quake, three of them all fire. A small time, but it seemed like a century. Everything had changed, including myself. What had happened to me? Where was the old Fremont who went barging through life, admittedly in a willful and eccentric fashion, but confidently? Now I could not even keep my thoughts straight!

Keep moving, I told myself. I had forgotten to crank the motor and so, of course, the auto would not start. "Dolt!" I exclaimed, climbing out to do it. A man in a bowler hat passing by on the sidewalk turned and looked at me. "I did not mean you," I said hastily, "I was talking to myself." He lifted his hat politely but did not smile. Perhaps he thought me an idiot. Perhaps I thought so too.

Keep moving: those two words had become the litany of my life, this new life that I was living without the faintest notion of how to do it properly, like a person who learns to swim by being thrown into the water to do it or drown. I climbed back into the auto, set it in gear, and kept moving.

To distract myself, since the word had come into my head, I thought about swimming as I drove. I hadn't had to learn that the hard way: I'd taken swimming lessons at Sutro's Baths during the winter. I had always wanted to learn to swim, but the skill was not deemed necessary for proper young women in Boston. (I believe a ridiculous low opinion of bathing costumes had something to do with that.) Sutro's plunges were heated sea water, a pleasant contrast to the nippy winter air. I had quickly caught the knack of swimming. At first, it is truly amazing to find that one does not sink. Soon I was kicking and moving my arms with the best of them. What a splendid feeling, to glide through the water like a fish!

Of course Sutro's, being constructed principally of glass, was ruined now. Well, they would fix it eventually. I would swim there again. Probably. Maybe not. Gloom threatened to reclaim me.

I turned onto Fell Street and headed toward the Haight. I am not normally a Gloomy Gus. Somehow, surely, there would be some good to come, for all of us, out of so much loss. I had lost Mrs. O'Leary, at least temporarily, and I felt Michael's absence keenly, but I was making new friends. Dr. Anson Tyler, for one; Alice Lasley, for another. Then there was Meiling, who saw this disaster as an opportunity, and I was privileged to help her take advantage of it. Aha! Yes, I had known that if I thought long enough I was bound to find some good. With a lighter heart I drew to a stop at the corner of Haight and Ashbury streets.

I sniffed the air and smiled. Something smelled delicious; I realized I was hungry. I felt in my pocket for the money Alice had given me to buy our meal and retrieved a lidded pot from the back seat. All over the city, outdoor kitchens had sprung up. I had not patronized this particular one before, but I expected to do so again because it was handy to Alice's house. I joined a line of rather subdued people, all of whom looked tired. A mother nursed her infant right there in public, and no one batted an eye.

The cooking fire was confined in an enclosure built of brick from the rubble, covered over with a sheet of metal that became the cooking surface. Large iron pots bubbled away, releasing their fragrance into the air. A door on sawhorses formed a serving counter, presided over by a large, florid, friendly-looking man. Hanging down in front of the counter was a hand-lettered sign: MICKEY'S KITCHEN.

"Are you Mickey?" I asked, as I handed him my pot to fill.

"That I am, pretty lady, that I am. Mickey Morelock, at your service, late of Mickey's Pub and Restaurant, which is no more, alas." He did not seem to lament its demise; he grinned and so did I, for he was so clearly Irish that he reminded me of my former landlady. "And would your pleasure tonight be the beef stew or the fish chowder?"

"A choice!" I crowed with delight. "That's the first time I've had a choice of what to eat in so long that I don't know what to say."

Mickey leaned toward me across the makeshift counter with his ladle aloft. He whispered and gave an exaggerated wink. "I'd have the stew if I was you."

"Thanks for the tip," I said softly, and more loudly, "The stew if you please, Mr. Morelock."

"Just Mickey, pretty lady." He ladled a generous helping into my pot and finished with a theatrical flourish. Then he reached into a box behind him and brought out a parcel wrapped in newspaper. "A bit of bread for free, to show you Mickey's heart's in the right place. There ya go!"

I paid, and happily lugged my purchase away. Alice and I would feast tonight.

"I must go," I said three quarters of an hour later. I felt full as a tick.

"But you just got here!" Alice exclaimed.

"I am working on a special project," I said, having anticipated her objections, "and will have to be out in the early evenings for the next couple of weeks. I trust it's still convenient for me to bring my belongings over tomorrow morning? Did you speak to your maid about moving the furniture?"

Alice chewed on her lower lip and ducked her head. "Well, there's a problem."

My heart sank. "You've changed your mind."

"Oh, no! Never! It's just the maid hasn't come, so I couldn't ask her to get someone to do it. To move the furniture, I mean. I'm feeling so forlorn, Fremont. Everyone has deserted me, even the maid! I had to clean up this whole house today all by myself."

"You did a good job of it," I said sincerely. I got up from the table and carried my dishes to the sink. "I expect I can find a couple of men at the Tent City who would be glad of a few hours' work, but they will want to be paid on the spot. As you know, I have no money at present."

Alice beamed. "I was sure you'd know what to do."

To have Alice pay for everything bothered me more than I liked to admit. "I intend to keep a record of all I owe you, Alice, and I'll repay you as soon as the banks open. The papers said they are waiting until the metal vaults are cool; otherwise, when they open them and oxygen gets in, the money and anything else made of paper will catch fire. I can't imagine the cooling process will take many more days."

"Think nothing of it, Fremont. I have lots of money in the house. But I'm so lonely! Can't you stay now, and sleep here tonight? I can lend you a nightgown, and—"

"No, I cannot, but this is the last night you will have to sleep alone here. Now I really must go. I'll be here, with helpers, about nine o'clock tomorrow."

Alice pouted prettily and followed me to the door, where she stood on tiptoe and touched her cheek to mine—a gesture of sisterly affection that made me slightly uncomfortable. Perhaps if I'd ever had a sister, or even a brother . . . I did not finish the thought. There is no sense speculating about something of which one has no experience whatever.

I did not like to do it, but under pressure of time I had no choice except to leave a note for Jim Albright.

> *I am most dreadfully sorry* [I wrote], *but I cannot go to the variety show with you tonight after all. I had made a previous commitment that I forgot when I accepted your invitation. Please accept my most sincere apology.*

I signed my name and placed the note in an envelope on which I printed his name in big block letters. Locking the door of my room behind me, I balanced the envelope on top of the doorknob and tucked one end into the space between the door and its frame. It seemed secure enough, and certainly he could not fail to notice his own name writ large.

I felt a bit cowardly as I hurried off, but did not let that dampen my enthusiasm for my adventure with Meiling. I was to pick her up two streets over from her family's encampment in the Sunset District. She did not want them to see us together because, if anyone found out what she was doing and that I was helping her, I could be in danger. Or so she said, and I believed her; I well remembered another time when Meiling's company had proved dangerous to me.

The fog had come in while Alice and I ate supper, so I drove cautiously through a whitish haze. *Meiling will be pleased by the fog,* I thought; *it will hide our activities.*

Meiling's was a plan after my own heart, but far more of a risk than anything I had ever undertaken. When I left home, I risked only my father's affection and an eventual inheritance, whereas in pursuit of her own independence Meiling was risking her very life. If American society is repressive of females (and it is!), Chinese society is worse by far. The more highly born a woman is in that society, the more cruelly she is repressed. The upper classes bind the feet of women in childhood to produce a disfigurement they call "lily-foot," which is much prized but has the effect of crippling the woman. How convenient for her lord and master! No matter what he does, the poor woman cannot run away.

Meiling's wise grandfather, Li Wong, had not allowed her feet to be bound. He had also, perhaps intuiting his untimely death, given Meiling a secret gift to serve as her own personal insurance: a pouch of pearls. Pearls that were now buried under layers of rubble and ash.

Because of the pearls, Meiling had been working out her plan even before the earthquake. She wanted to leave Chinatown and become what she called "a real American." She wanted a college education that would prepare her for a profession, and she knew of a university that had accepted women students from its beginning only a few years ago. It is called Stanford, after the deceased son of one of California's four railroad barons, and is located halfway between San Francisco and San Jose. Meiling had already petitioned for acceptance to Stanford as a special student, though she had not yet received a reply. The sale of her secret cache of pearls would provide the necessary funds. Provided, of course, that Meiling and I could find them.

However, there was an even more significant problem: most Chinese women are not allowed to leave Chinatown. Not ever. Indeed, they are seldom permitted to leave their houses. The authority of Chinese males over females is such that a woman can be kept a prisoner, shackled, under lock and key, for the smallest offense—real or imagined. For an offense of such magnitude as Meiling planned, death might well be the penalty. I shivered to think of it.

On the appointed corner, a tall, dark shadow stepped out of a swirl of mist: Meiling. "Keep going," she said, swinging onto the running board, and I complied. She tossed a black bundle onto the seat, opened the door with one hand, and slid gracefully in.

"You are very athletic," I remarked.

"Ha!" she said; she might have smiled, but I could not tell—she had wrapped a black scarf about her head and face so that only her eyes showed. The effect was rather sinister. I liked it.

I looked at the bundle. "Are those the clothes I am to wear?"

"Yes. They are mine; I think they will fit you well enough."

"And shall I also have a scarf to hide my face?"

"Of course! That may be the most important part of the disguise. Fremont," she said in a somber tone, "I have been thinking that perhaps I should not have asked you to help."

"Nonsense. I am honored. You must say no more about it."

I drove in the direction of Chinatown. It was a surreal trip, with ragged ruins looming through the fog on all sides, like charcoal drawings for some gothic horror story. Familiar landmarks were no more; street signs lay twisted and melted, half buried in piles of ash. I was soon hopelessly lost and said, "I hope you know where we are, because I do not."

"The fog is a good omen," said Meiling, "but perhaps you would drive more slowly, Fremont?"

The burned stench was all around us, so thick it made me gag. Our adventure would not be the lark I had painted in my imagination. I coughed. The Maxwell crept along, and I knew that the sound of its motor would carry through the fog and silence. My hands gripped the steering wheel hard enough to hurt; I leaned forward, peering intently into a moving veil of grayish white.

"I know where we are now," said Meiling softly. She directed me to turn left and then right, and then to stop the auto. There was no choice but to stop, as the street ahead was blocked by rubble.

Meiling got out, and so did I. She had chosen a cul-de-sac surrounded by partially standing walls that formed a ragged hiding place for the Maxwell. She thrust the black bundle into my hands. "Change clothes quickly. I will stand guard."

Undress in the open? How extraordinary! But strange times call forth strange actions, and so, without a word and only a slight qualm, I stripped to my camisole and donned a black tunic that buttoned down the front. It felt like thick silk, far too fine to wear for digging in the ashes.

Meiling glanced over her shoulder and whispered, "Hurry!"

My fingers fumbled with the buttons; I skipped a few. Then I took off my skirt and petticoat, and for the first time in my life stepped into trousers. I had long admired Meiling's trousers and secretly desired a pair of my own, though I hadn't the slightest idea where I would wear them. In spite of the tense occasion, I felt a thrill as the silk glided along my nether limbs. As Meiling had surmised, they were a perfect fit. I bundled my clothes into the back seat out of sight and took the black scarf in hand. "Show me how to do this," I requested.

A lifting at the corners of her already tilted eyes suggested a smile as Meiling deftly wound the scarf about my head, covering nose and chin and handing me the ends to tie at the back of my neck. "There," she said, "you look dangerous, like a Ninja."

"What is a Ninja?"

"They are a Japanese cult, much feared by their own people and by mine, for good reason. Come, Fremont. The remains of the Li compound are not far from here. I hid shovels there earlier, and screens to sift the ash."

We set off, creeping like dangerous Ninjas through the fog and gathering darkness. I marveled at how easy it was to move without the encumbrance of long skirts; I thought that if only I had slippers like hers, instead of high-button shoes, I might go along with almost as much grace as Meiling. I was quite enjoying myself.

But my enjoyment did not last long. I became aware of a prickly sensation at the back of my head, down my neck, and between my shoulder blades. "Meiling," I whispered, "I think we are being watched!"

⁊ 7 ⁊

Resurgam: Like the Phoenix I Will Rise

Meiling stopped in her tracks, like a deer, arching her neck and tilting her head slightly in an attitude of concentration.

Chinatown being in a relatively low-lying area, the fog was thick here. "I'm sorry," I whispered, "I've alarmed us both for nothing. If anyone is out there, he can't possibly see us through this fog."

Meiling held her index finger up to her masked lips in the universal sign for silence. I listened with her, intently. After a few moments she said, also in a whisper, "I don't hear anything. Do you?"

I shook my head. "No." We went on. I do not know how she did it—perhaps she numbered Chinese homing pigeons among her honorable ancestors—but Meiling led us unerringly to the place where she had concealed shovels and screens in a frame, such as are used by gold miners for sifting. We worked through the long twilight until darkness closed in, and we got very dirty. We dug up many things, including (most horrible!) a skull and bones that Meiling identified as dog. Not a family pet, she said; nevertheless it was awful. We did not find a single pearl that night, nor on many nights thereafter. And though I did not say so again, I continued to feel that we were being watched.

On Tuesday morning, after my first night of digging with Meiling, I loaded the Maxwell with my few possessions. They seemed to multiply in direct proportion to my eagerness to be done with moving them. As I marched back and forth with my arms full, I kept expecting Private Albright to appear, but he did not. I admit I was relieved; I assumed he must be out of countenance with me for breaking our appointment. Assembling the final load, I inadvertently closed Michael's dresser drawer on my fingers. "Damn!" I swore, yanking my hand out. It smarted terribly, and I was sure there would be some swelling and bruising, to boot. *Keep moving. . . .*

At last I was done. I cranked the Maxwell and got it started, but then I sat there, beset by the notion that I had forgotten something. I couldn't for the life of me think what it might be. Not the typewriter, which occupied the passenger seat. I had my clothes, and the few books I owned. Not nearly so many books as Michael—I had been living in the midst of a veritable library for days.

"Michael!" I exclaimed. I had forgotten to leave word for him as to my whereabouts. I was sorely tempted not to bother. After all, he had not written me a single line from Monterey.

Well, I mused as I reluctantly cut the motor, *it is true that he has been gone only a week.* It was just that this particular week might as well have lasted forever—that was how it felt. Certainly I should excuse him, but I did not want to. He could have written. There were boats and trains steaming up from points south every single day. If he had cared to, he could have gotten a letter to me overnight; what is more, if he had done so, I could have written to him in answer. (Independent I may be, but I hope not forward where men are concerned!)

So went my thoughts, but I slid out of the Maxwell and strode back into the building. Feeling self-righteous as the Queen (Victoria, may she rest in peace), I wrote with stiff, smarting fingers:

Dear Michael: I have arranged a more suitable accommodation, with
Alice Lasley, who lives on Haight Street at the corner of Belvedere. If
your auto is not in the garage here, it is because I am still using it for the
Red Cross. I will return it as soon as they no longer need me. Yours most
sincerely, Fremont Jones.

I left the sheet of paper in the middle of the bed, where he could
hardly fail to find it. I locked the door again and pocketed the key,
reflecting that I was sure to see him at least once more—he would
want his key back. Someday. Would he not? I had a perverse feeling
that I was about to cry.

"Keep moving," I muttered, blinking hard. I did, and I did not
cry.

As I drove away from the Presidio, my foot lightened on the gas
pedal and the Maxwell coughed in protest. What was this, could I be
reluctant to leave? Considering that on the whole I disliked the regi-
mentation of the place, and certainly had never felt I belonged, such
reluctance was difficult to understand. *Perhaps,* I thought, *it is only that*
I will miss the splendid vista. . . .

I did not really think that was the reason, but it was the only one
that came to mind. I pulled the auto over and said a silent farewell to
the sweeping view from the Presidio's heights. The sun had burned
last night's fog down to a thin layer of white that shimmered like
diamond dust upon the surface of the Bay. Boats of different sizes and
configurations sailed blithely through the magical sheen. Farther west,
the strait of the Golden Gate and the Pacific Ocean were as dark and
rich a blue as sapphires.

The Atlantic was never this beautiful, I thought. Oh, dear God, how I
loved San Francisco! Often I had felt my heart would break from the
sheer joy of being here. Yes, even now—I turned my head and forced
myself to look down upon the acres and acres of devastation.

"San Francisco will rise again," I said, "and, by God, so will I!"

❧

I had been at Alice's for about a week when it became evident that someone had taken a dislike to one or both of us. This unknown person was expressing his (or her) dislike by leaving nasty little gifts on the front steps overnight. Invariably I was the one to find them. I cannot begin my day—at least not in a decent humor—without the lift of caffeine, so first thing each morning I walked to Mickey's Kitchen for a pot of coffee.

The first loathsome present was a dead pigeon. I had picked it up and carried it around to the trash bin before it occurred to me that this bird had not died a natural death. Its throat had been cut almost all the way through. Later in the morning, it took me quite a bit of time and elbow grease to scrub pigeon blood off the steps. The next day's offering was a piece of rotten meat, crawling with maggots, that I was only just barely able to dispose of without vomiting. The third gift was a strangled cat, its poor head twisted all the way around backward. This time I left it there and went on to Mickey's, thinking along the way.

Thus far I had said nothing to Alice. She aroused a protective instinct in me; I suspected she did it deliberately but I could not be certain of that. At any rate, I was not averse to assuming some responsibility in return for her hospitality. I am by nature a person who takes charge, whereas Alice appeared to be the opposite. Her state of mind still seemed fragile—indeed, I had begun to wonder if it had not always been fragile—so perhaps I should continue to keep mum about the things on the steps. On the other hand, Alice's situation was far from straightforward. She had lied about her husband, of that I was certain, even though I had not attempted to ascertain the exact nature of the lie. Not yet.

"Where is Mickey this morning?" I asked the hefty woman who filled my coffeepot. She was dressed in black and had a sort of Mickeyish look about her, as if she might be a relation.

"I dunno. Off somewhere," she grumbled, "up to his tricks, like as not."

I would have liked to ask about Mickey's tricks, but owing to her obvious ill humor I asked for a few rolls instead. I paid with Alice's money and headed back, resuming consideration of the problem.

If a man had ever lived in the house on Haight Street, he was long gone. I had not lived with my father for most of my life for nothing; I knew the signs of a man's occupation, and they are more extensive than clothes in the closet and a razor, etc., in the bathroom. For one thing, most men smoke some form of tobacco, and the smell of the smoke gets into the draperies and furniture. There was none of that at Alice's. There were no humidors, no ashtrays, either sitting about or stored in cabinets—I had looked. No large, comfortable chair with a reading lamp nearby. No big desk full of cubbyholes and drawers; no stacks of newspapers that could not be thrown out because he was going to get around to reading certain articles in their entirety one of these days. Likewise no periodicals of a masculine nature. The small study, which was the logical place for a man's sanctum, had furnishings of female scale. The same was true throughout the house.

As I climbed the steps, the dead cat regarded me with glazed, reproachful eyes. Again I left it there. I still had not decided what to do. I held the bag of rolls in my teeth while I unlocked the front door and went in, locking it again behind me. I went straight back to the kitchen.

Alice was not down yet; I had not thought she would be. Her habit was to stay late in bed, and to take a good deal of time with her toilette. I put two rolls on a plate for her—she did not drink coffee—and placed it on the table. I opened the back door and brought in the milk. Then I made a tray for myself and took it into the family parlor, which was now my office. I closed the door as if I were working. Since losing my own flat and office, I had developed a mania for privacy.

The coffee was better than lukewarm, but not by much, as it

always cooled during the walk back. I confess I prefer my coffee scalding hot. Of course in these times one should be grateful to have coffee at all, but I would be glad when the inspectors got around to Haight Street and we could have a fire in the kitchen stove. Another of my idiosyncrasies is that I prefer my coffee in a mug; I had found one solitary brown pottery mug among Alice's dainty cups and saucers. I suspected it belonged to the maid but had claimed it for my own, at least until such time as the maid once more put in an appearance. I sipped and slowly munched on a roll, thinking.

The maid was another puzzle. For the past week, Alice had gone out soon after coming down in the morning. She said she wanted to find out what had happened to her maid; if the woman were in need of assistance, Alice declared an intention to help. When I offered to drive her, she refused. I might have insisted, but told myself it would do Alice good to get out of the house. That was my excuse, but the truth was rather that I appreciated having the place to myself for a while.

Also, there was the question of that lacy nightcap I'd found. Alice did not wear a nightcap. I knew this because not a night had yet gone by when she did not cry out in her sleep; my first couple of nights in the house I had gone rushing up to her room to see what was the matter. I no longer did that—there was nothing I could do about Alice's nightmares—but at least I had learned that the nightcap was not likely hers. So whose was it? Had it been overlooked by a visitor departing in haste? Somehow I did not think so.

If the maid comes back, I thought, *I can perhaps get some answers from her.* I hesitated to question the neighbors, for the obvious reason that I was new here and did not want to get a reputation for being what that awful policeman had called me, a busybody. Perhaps I might approach Alice's former coworkers at the library. . . . But the library had burned—something I truly hated to think about—so where would I find them?

"Oh, fudge!" I said, an expression I had recently acquired. It felt somehow like a swear word without actually being one, which I found most satisfying.

Alice was an enigma within a conundrum. If not for the vile things being left on the steps, I might have decided, for once, to ignore it all. Without information from somewhere, one could not possibly know whether Alice had invented her husband out of whole cloth, or whether there had actually been such a person here briefly, though not long enough to make an impression on the property. The latter explanation seemed the most likely. But, in that case, this large house would have to have belonged to Alice before the marriage, and why would a shy woman who owned such a house force herself out into the world to work as a librarian?

My ruminations were interrupted by a knock and Alice's voice. "I don't mean to disturb you, Fremont, but I thought you might like to know that I'm going out."

I leapt up and snatched open the door. "Good morning," I said. "There is something I must show you before you leave, though you are likely to see it in any case."

"Oh?" Alice wrinkled her brow in pretty confusion. She had done her pale hair up in a pouf, and wore a rose-colored dress with a small bustle and a high lace collar centered by a cameo. She had a lacy white wool shawl about her shoulders and carried white gloves. A reticule on a thin gold chain completed her ensemble.

I by contrast was wearing a flared blue skirt (I do despise bustles, they are such a bother when one tries to sit), a brown leather belt, and a white shirtwaist with no ornamentation other than a few pleats. My own brown hair (which has a reddish glint if one tries hard enough to see it) I had pulled straight back into a clip at the nape of my neck, in my usual style. No wonder I felt plain around Alice.

"What I want to show you is on the front steps," I said.

"Oh." Alice turned to the door and grasped the doorknob, which did not budge. She glanced over her shoulder at me, pouting. "You've locked it again. I always forget."

I took keys from my pocket, unlocked the door, and held it for Alice, following close behind her.

"Eeuw," she said, pausing on the second step, "a dead cat! Well, it isn't mine, Fremont, if that's what you were thinking. Get rid of it. It's nothing to do with me." She held her skirts daintily aside.

I moved quickly around and onto the step below her. As I am so much taller, this put our heads on a level, and I looked her straight in the eye. "This is not just a dead cat."

"Whatever can you mean by that?"

"It is a threat, and it is not the first," I said flatly, watching her reaction.

"A th-thr-threat?" Alice's already pale skin blanched, and she cowered, shrinking, swaying on her feet.

Interesting reaction! I took her by the elbow. "Come inside. We should talk about this."

I escorted Alice into the formal parlor, where I knew there was a collection of decanters on a butler's trolley. "Sit down," I said, mentally adding: *And don't you dare faint while my back is turned!*

By the silver sign hanging on its crystal neck I identified the brandy and poured some into a rather dusty goblet. "Drink this." I wrapped Alice's fingers around the glass. "You need it. You must keep your wits."

She downed the brandy swiftly, without coughing as I would have. I hate the way the stuff tastes and burns going down, but I do like how I feel afterward.

"Now, then." I leaned forward in the chair I had taken opposite her. "Tell me. Who do you think would do this?"

"I don't know, I'm sure. It must be that . . . that the cat just . . . just happened to die there."

"No. The cat was strangled, Alice. Someone killed it and put it there deliberately." I told her about the bird and the maggoty meat, and once again she paled, putting her hand to her heart. Her eyes closed and she slumped sideways.

I have often thought that women faint when it is convenient for them; or else they do it because their corsets are too tight. I find the habit tedious in the extreme. I sighed, picked up the goblet she had dropped while crumpling, and filled it with another inch of brandy. Alice opened her eyes when I shoved it under her nose. She seized the glass and again drained it right down.

"Do you suppose," I asked, "that this harassment is somehow related to your missing husband?"

"I don't know. I must go to my room. I don't feel at all well." She wobbled on the edge of her chair.

I gritted my teeth, once more pulling out the only trump card in my pack when it came to dealing with Alice: "I don't know that I can stay here unless we deal with this."

"Fre-e-e-mont!" she wailed.

Oh, fudge, now I'd done it. "Shush, don't take on so! Talk to me, Alice. If you will only tell me the truth, I can help you. But if you continue to deny that anything is wrong, there is nothing I can do."

"The truth?" She blinked her violet eyes innocently, as if she had no acquaintance with the term.

"The truth about your husband, and why the maid has not returned, and why you have nightmares."

"Those things have nothing to do with that cat. They can't have!"

"Tell me the truth, and we will decide together whether they do or do not."

With her little chin trembling, Alice got to her feet. "The truth is my husband left me for no reason, and so did the maid. I didn't do anything, it's not my fault. And I don't have nightmares, you made that up. I think you are being quite cruel to me, Fremont, to persecute me in this way." She walked unsteadily to the parlor door.

"I'm sorry. I don't mean to persecute you."

"I shall try to forget it. I am much too upset to go out today. I'll be in my room." In the doorway she turned. Bright spots of color burned high on her pale cheeks. "Maybe the cat, and the other things, have been left here because of *you,* Fremont. Have you thought about that?"

She did not wait for an answer. It was my turn to blink. No, I had not. Because I had so many unanswered questions about Alice, I had made an assumption that suddenly seemed unfair. I felt like a monster. I went out and removed the cat, and from then on I questioned Alice no more.

The fourth gift, which arrived the next morning, was the chopped-off head and feet of a chicken. That evening as I worked alongside Meiling, I told her the whole complicated story.

She straightened up and stood leaning on her shovel. "This woman is taking advantage of you, Fremont."

"More likely it's the other way around. After all," I said, keeping my eyes on the ashes I was sifting, "I am living in her house. Not to mention that, until the banks opened this morning, Alice was paying for the very food I ate."

"You, too, are paying, but not in coin." Meiling went back to shoveling.

"Your point is taken." I discarded some unrecognizable bits and scooped up more ashes. I had begun to despair of ever finding Meiling's pearls.

"You will have noticed that all the things left on your steps were in a lifeless state," said Meiling.

"Quite."

"It is a form of curse."

I shuddered, and quickly looked around. This evening, like the one previous, was clear. People in oriental garb had been working in other parts of the ruins when we arrived, but nowhere near. We appeared to be quite alone, and at the moment I did not have that being-watched feeling. I had more than half decided it was in my imagination, anyway. "I suppose I may have made an enemy or two,"

I confessed, "but not recently. You don't think these threats—this curse—are because I am helping you, do you, Meiling?"

"No, I do not think so. The primary person in my family who might concern himself with my activities, or yours in helping me, is the cousin I am expected to marry. These days he keeps himself, how do you say, stuck to—"

"Glued to?"

"Glued to my grandmother's bedside, waiting for her to die. He reproaches me that I do not do the same, but for many months now I have been often out conducting the family business, as I was taught by my grandfather. For all anyone knows, including the cousin, I continue to do the same."

"Then why are we digging in secret? Why do we mask our faces?"

"Because, this way, we could be anyone. We are not Meiling and her friend looking for something."

"Speaking of looking . . ." A huge grin spread over my face beneath the black scarf. "I do believe I've found it!"

I returned to the house on Haight Street in a state of elation. The object I'd found was round and hard and as big as the tip of my little finger. I'd dropped it into Meiling's palm for her to do the honor of wiping off the black dust. It was indeed one of the pearls, and we soon found the rest, eighty altogether, none of them burned. Meiling said pearls are like teeth, they can survive most anything short of being ground to bits.

I allowed that I knew little about pearls, aside from the unbelievable fact that they are made by irritated oysters, at which Meiling laughed. "These should bring a good price," she said. That, I certainly believed. I had seldom seen such large pearls; their size could only increase their value.

We had worked on past nightfall, using starlight and our sense of touch to guide us. It was not difficult, merely time-consuming; once the first pearl had been found, the others lay nearby. When we returned to the Maxwell, Meiling counted out ten pearls, which she attempted to give to me, but I refused to take them.

"Let me keep the outfit, especially the trousers," I said; "that is payment enough for helping a dear friend."

Meiling had inclined her head in her grave way of acknowledgment. She kept a silence that I did not break—I supposed she was thinking about fulfillment of her plan—until I dropped her off on the other side of Golden Gate Park. A quarter moon was just rising. By its pale light Meiling made me a promise: "I will see you again, Fremont, before I leave San Francisco."

Now the thought of Meiling's leaving put a damper on my elation. If only I could have rushed up the stairs and burst in upon Alice, showering her with the good news of how Meiling and I, against great odds, had found her treasure! Of course I could not do such a thing. I had to keep Meiling's secret, and in any event Alice and I were not close.

I undressed, wondering when I would ever wear the trousers again. Certainly not until they were washed; they were quite filthy, as was the tunic, but even in that state the fine silk was luxurious to the touch. My aubergine cape, which I had been wearing to cover my dangerous Ninja outfit in the auto, was also in need of cleaning.

I slipped into my robe and went up to bathe, making rather more noise on the stairs than necessary. If Alice were awake, perhaps she would come out of her room and we could have a conversation. I was all keyed up; in such a state it is difficult to be alone. But Alice's door remained closed.

A hot bath would have relaxed me, but there was no hot water. A cold splashing got me clean, and that was all it got me excepting goose bumps. I prepared for bed but knew I would not sleep; I decided to read for a while by the light of the kerosene lamp in my bedroom, once the dining room. My book was a collection of tales by Nathaniel Hawthorne. I chose one called "Rappacini's Daughter," which I had not read for several years and recalled as engrossing. It did indeed hold my interest, but because it was all about poisons, it did nothing to calm my nerves.

The tall-case clock in the parlor began to toll, startling me nearly out of my skin. I counted its strokes: twelve. Midnight. The final chime reverberated, sharpening the edge of silence. Beyond my circle of lamplight lay a dark void. I closed the book and put it aside. Leaving the lamp beside my bed, I walked into the darkness.

❧ 8 ❧

From Death Springs New Life, and Vice Versa

Behind me I closed the pocket door between my bedroom and the office and waited in blackness until my eyes adjusted. Slowly then, I went to the wide bay window overlooking the street. Here I would hang my sign, whenever the overworked sign painter produced it; I had already removed the lace curtains in order to give the room a more businesslike appearance. Therefore I had an unobstructed view—such as I could see of it. I stood off to one side, staring. Little by little, the street scene revealed itself in subtle dark shadings. An animal, probably a cat, streaked by, its motion making it easy to separate from the black background. That gave me an idea. . . .

Using the thin line of light at the bottom of the door to guide me, I went back to the bedroom and rummaged among my things until I found my trusty weapon. It is a walking stick that conceals a long thin blade, something like a sword. Last year I'd had need of a weapon, but lately I'd used the walking stick only for its overt purpose, at which it functions admirably on San Francisco's hills. I fingered the secret mechanism and drew out the blade in a practiced motion that I was pleased not to have forgotten. I took up my set of keys in my other hand, taking care not to jingle them, and blew out the lamp.

The total darkness that immediately enveloped me was a bit unnerving, but I soon got used to it. The edges of the bay window were just barely discernible. I headed for it, then turned to my left and felt my way to the front door, which I unlocked and opened stealthily. I did not go out, only looked to be sure that the steps were clear. They were. Good. The nasty gift-giver had not yet made his visit. I intended to keep vigil and, when he appeared, I would be ready for him.

I closed the door without locking it; I wanted to be able to spring forth upon the enemy like a fury, brandishing my blade with a blood-curdling yell. Pausing to unlock the door would rather ruin the effect. I inched my way back to the bay window and waited, straining my eyes and ears.

The grandfather clock made an informative companion, melodiously marking each quarter hour and tolling a count of the hours. Until two o'clock I stood, then my legs gave out and I sat in a straight chair. My eyes played tricks on me. I thought I saw moving shadows more than once, but when I blinked and cleared my vision, they disappeared. I kept hearing things that made me jump, until I ascertained they were only the sounds all houses make in the night. Once Alice cried out in one of her nightmares, but she ceased, and all was still.

Morning came, and with it a heavy mist, not quite a fog. I awoke with a start. I had fallen asleep sitting up in the chair; my trusty blade had slipped to the floor beside me. Fudge!

I leapt up, my body protesting with a wrench of pain, ran to the front door, and flung it open. Damn it all to perdition, the wretched perpetrator had been here again, and I had slept through it!

"Oh, dear God," I said as I spied what he had left. I turned my head away, grasping the doorframe for support. When I had regained a modicum of composure, I forced myself to approach the dead dog.

It was the kind of small terrier that women keep as pampered pets, which made its death all the more gruesome. It had long, silky, silver hair that was now matted with blood. Its perky little face was perky no more; that lolling pink tongue would lick its mistress's hand never again.

"At this rate," I muttered angrily, "we will have a horse on the steps next!"

I wrapped the little dog in a kitchen towel and put him in the trash, feeling as if I were the criminal. Probably I should have buried him, but I had no more heart, nor energy, nor anything. I went back into the house, washed my hands, got into bed, and slept far into the morning.

"That Dr. Tyler's sweet on you," Nurse Bartlett remarked as I worked alongside her in the afternoon. We were sorting clothes that had been donated for the homeless. This particular batch had come by train from Sacramento.

"Nonsense," I said, feeling my cheeks color. "We are barely friends. I've scarcely seen him since I reduced my Red Cross hours to part time."

"That's because I've been needing him in the mornings, and he's been seeing patients at his own office, wherever that is, in the afternoons when you're here."

"He has a consulting room in his house in the Mission District, on Valencia Street."

"Been there, have you?"

"Not inside," I said firmly, in response to her suggestive tone, "I only drove him home one day."

"Hah!"

I changed the subject. "Have you been able to find out anything about Mrs. Maureen O'Leary, my former landlady?"

"Bless you, child, you aren't still worrying about her, are you?"

"I am. I've tried not to, but—"

"The only thing I can tell you, Fremont, is that if she was ever here in Golden Gate Park, she's not here now because we've got the names. You mustn't worry. We know she's not among the dead or the injured. I expect she's gone to relatives outside the city."

I folded a very nice pair of trousers and added them to the pile of men's clothing. "She does have a sister, but I don't remember where. I'm sure she told me once, but I just can't remember. Nor can I think of the name of the church she always attended—if I could, I could ask the priest. You know, Mrs. Bartlett, my mind doesn't seem to work as well as it ought. I keep forgetting things. My body doesn't work as well as it ought, either; I cannot count the times I've bumped my elbow, or tripped, usually over nothing. I never used to be this way, and it's very disconcerting. I don't know what's wrong with me."

The nurse gave me an appraising look. "From the circles under your eyes, I'd say you haven't been sleeping well."

I sighed, rolling socks into a ball. "That's true."

"How's your appetite?"

"All right. I don't really mind having to buy food from the outdoor kitchens, since I am only a passable cook. Alice ate like a bird at first, but I must say she has quite picked up in that department. She will get chubby if she keeps up as she has been. We get most of our food from Mickey Morelock, and it is on the heavy side."

Bartlett gave me the once-over again. "Not much chance of you getting chubby, is there?"

I grinned at her, rather enjoying her close attention. "I doubt it. I am by nature on the thin side. I have sometimes thought it would be pleasant to have curves."

Bartlett snorted. "You've got curves enough to suit Dr. Tyler, anyway."

I swatted at her playfully with a sweater. "Stop that! You are only teasing me."

"No, I'm not, but I'll get back to Dr. Tyler in a minute. First, tell me how that typewriting business of yours is coming along."

"Not well at all. When I leave here this afternoon I'm going to try to—forgive the expression—light a fire under the sign painter. If I could get a sign up, that would help, but I'm not sure how much. Haight Street is residential, not exactly on the beaten path of those who could use my services. I expect I shall have to advertise." I sighed heavily. "And I do hate to spend money on advertising. I don't have much, and what I do have has to last."

"Hmmm," said Bartlett. She stopped her work and stared at me in a way that made me stop also. "Fremont, I know what's wrong with you."

"You do?" I was incredulous.

"Unless you've got some symptoms you haven't told me about—"

"I don't," I said hastily.

"Well then, it's like what they call in the military battle fatigue. I saw it in the ones who came back from the Spanish-American War. It happens when you've been through something really traumatic, like a war . . . or an earthquake followed by a fire that destroys half your town."

I laughed halfheartedly. "In other words, it's not an illness. Well, that's good news, I must say."

"No, Fremont, it is a kind of illness. In a way it's the worst kind because we don't really know how to treat it. The best cure is to be with people who care about you, with whom you feel safe. And then you need to get plenty of rest, plenty of good food, and set yourself a regular routine that's not too demanding."

My eyes filmed with tears. "The people who, um, who care about me and with whom I feel safe are gone. Mrs. O'Leary was one of them. I suppose that's why I keep thinking about her."

"And the others?" asked Nurse Bartlett softly.

"The other was, um, had to go away. . . ." My voice trailed off as I thought about Michael, how much I missed him and how I had always felt safe with him, even back when I'd scarcely known him, even when there had seemed to be reasons not to trust him. . . . I cleared my throat, blinked, and went on. "Of course, there's my friend Meiling, she's still in San Francisco, but I don't get to see her very often." And she would soon be gone, too, but I could not talk about that. Not even to Bartlett.

"I guess I don't need to ask about that Alice."

"Alice is something of a mystery," I said with a forced smile. "In that way, she does keep me entertained. If I understand you, Mrs. Bartlett, you are saying that my lapses of memory and so on are the result of this, whatever you call it, this disaster syndrome."

"Um-hm." She nodded, and set her wrinkles rippling. "What I prescribe for you, Fremont, is to take life easier. I can help you with that, though I hate to do it to myself."

I looked at her questioningly.

"We can manage without you now. As of today, I relieve you of your duties as a Red Cross volunteer, Fremont Jones. Your time is now your own. Just promise me one thing."

"What?"

"That you'll take it easy. Don't be running all over the city wearing yourself out. I've seen how you push yourself. By all means start your business, just do it slowly."

I leaned over and gave Nurse Bartlett a hug. "I will, I promise. If you're sure you don't need me."

"I'll miss your company, but I don't need you. And one other thing."

I raised my eyebrows.

"It's about Dr. Tyler. He's a nice young man and he's fond of you. He asks after you every single day. It wouldn't hurt for you to see more of him. How do you feel about that?"

"I have no objection, but I think you may exaggerate. I believe he knows where I am living, so he would have only to pay a social call. Which he has not done."

"He will," said Bartlett, tucking her chin into a cowl of wrinkles, "you mark my words, Fremont, he will."

❦

With no more need of the Maxwell, I thought I might as well return it without delay. In a way I would miss the auto, which seemed to have taken on a personality, as if we were old friends who had been through a lot together; but in another way I would gladly be quit of it, for it reminded me constantly of Michael Archer. I did not like to think about him because my thoughts on that subject were confusing.

I headed out of Golden Gate Park toward the Presidio, but then, on an impulse, turned to the right. The Maxwell and I descended hills like giant stairsteps, going downtown. We passed an impressive amount of work in progress. In some areas whole blocks had been cleared, and scaffolding rose high into the air. I must say it did give one hope, like seeing the way new green growth pokes up through the blackened earth after a forest fire. Hopefully I chugged along, having taken it into my head to pay a visit to the remains of my building on Sacramento Street.

I had to count the blocks after crossing Van Ness, because the old landmarks were no more. Having been through the devastated area so often with Meiling, I no longer became disoriented, and soon found the place I sought. It was deserted; neither clearing nor construction had yet taken place here. A wave of sadness swamped my hopeful mood and drowned it dead. I stopped the Maxwell and got out.

With no preconceived notion of what I might find, I began a random search. In the ruins of the Li compound Meiling and I had worked methodically, one square foot at a time, but I wasn't prepared to do anything like that tonight. Not unless I found something really interesting, in which case I should return under cover of darkness with a shovel. I wasn't even sure what I was looking for. . . .

Ghoulish as it might sound, I suppose I was looking for the Sorensons' bones. I believed they were dead—Sergeant Franks had been most convincing—I just did not believe they had died in the earthquake. If he had found them, as he said he did, before the fire, then what other choice was there but to believe someone had killed them? Especially considering the contraband in the back room . . .

I coughed, took a handkerchief out of my pocket, and held it over my nose and mouth. I had dislodged a blackened lump that in turn set off a cascade of noxious rubble. There are few things that smell worse than old burnt stuff; sometimes I smelled it in my dreams. Bad dreams.

As I had already ruined the hem of my skirt anyway, I knelt down to make a closer examination. Books. Blackened pages, thinner than their original paper, crumbled and dissolved in the air. I moved deeper into the ruins, stirring the rubble carefully with my foot.

No bones; at least, not so far. I had been at this for some time when that all too familiar prickly feeling of being watched came over me. I turned around far more casually than I felt, but I saw no one in the entire block. Nor was there anything left standing that was substantial enough to hide a watcher. My imagination, again.

I did not notice that the fog had come in until it swirled around me. I welcomed its damp freshness, and its concealment, but it cut the light and made my search more difficult. I wasn't finding anything anyway, and that puzzled me. What had become of all that treasure? So much of it had been metal, which might melt into lumps, but the lumps should still be here. They weren't.

"Aha!" I cried, rather too loudly, and pounced. In my grubby fingers I held a hard, round object much larger than any of Meiling's pearls. I rubbed it clean on my skirt and transferred it to my other hand, where it filled the palm. It was the dark blue jewel, perhaps a sapphire, that had graced the hilt of the strange knife. In my mind's eye I could see the squiggly writing on that knife's wickedly curved blade. I thrust the jewel into my pocket, squatted down, and began to dig with both hands, oblivious to how filthy I was getting. There must be some metal here, there must! The curved blade, melted, its squiggles gone; those two huge swords—I had only seen their hilts, but I was certain they were swords; all those brass or gold or whatever vases . . .

I kept at it for a long time but found nothing else. Not a scrap of metal, not the Sorensons' bones. I sighed, swiping hair that had come loose from its clasp out of my face with the back of one hand. Time to give up. The blue jewel would have to be treasure enough for me. Too bad I couldn't keep it, but it was not rightfully mine.

As I picked my way back to the auto, I wondered what in the world to do with the gem. *Michael would know,* I thought before I could stop myself. Since he had intruded into my thoughts anyway, I allowed myself to wish he were here. More than ever I was convinced that the Sorensons had met with foul play, but I could not see how I would get to the bottom of it. No doubt the real Sherlock Holmes could still be Holmes without his Watson, but I could not.

I cranked the Maxwell and got in, surveying my filthy self with some dismay. I could not go to the Presidio like this, not even under cover of fog. I would have to return the auto tomorrow.

"Fremont! Good heavens, what happened to you? Where have you been? It's so late. I've been worried sick!"

"Hello, Alice." She had apparently been pacing the hall, waiting for me, and was now wringing her hands. Alice was good at things like that; I doubt I have ever wrung my hands in my entire life.

"Oh dear, oh dear," she said, "I knew something awful had happened to you, I just knew it!"

I took the watch from my pocket, feeling as I did so the heavy weight of the blue jewel there. "It is only a few minutes past seven, not so late."

"Well, you didn't say you'd be late and you usually get home much earlier than this. Just look at you! Aren't you going to tell me what happened?"

"Nothing happened. I went back to Sacramento Street, where my old office used to be. I was looking for something, which is how I got so grubby. I did not find it." I pushed past her into my office. "If you'll excuse me—"

"Oh. You could at least have told me."

"I went there on an impulse, Alice, it wasn't something I'd planned."

Alice's concern, which had not been for me in any case, became indignation. "That was most inconsiderate of you, Fremont. You know how I hate to be in this house alone."

"I'm sorry." I was saying that a lot these days. My patience, which I was sure I owed her, had grown exceedingly thin. I turned my back on Alice and began to unbutton my blouse. I could not close the door because she was standing in it; perhaps if I began to undress she might take the hint.

"Someone gets in here, I am sure of it," she said nervously. "I hear them moving around, but when I look, there is no one."

So now Alice was adding paranoia to her little bag of tricks. I didn't for a minute believe her. It was only another ploy to gain my sympathy. I continued to undo buttons, then removed my belt, my back still to her.

"Really," Alice pleaded, "I do hear someone, Fremont. Really, I do!"

I suppressed a sigh and turned around. "If you keep the doors and windows locked there is nothing to worry about. No one can get in. In any event, intruders do not operate in the light of day. I can't always be here, Alice. I have my own life to conduct."

"I know." For a moment she looked contrite. Then she tipped her head to one side and had one of her lightning-fast changes of facial expression. From soft to hard, from contrite to accusing. "Where's our supper? Didn't you bring it?"

Now I did sigh; I couldn't help it. "I confess I forgot. Anyway, I could hardly stop at Mickey's looking like this."

Alice sniffed, her turned-up nose in the air. "I suppose you couldn't. You do look quite disgraceful, I must say. But what are we to do about supper? I'm hungry."

I flung my blouse off rather viciously. "Couldn't you go and get it, Alice, just this one time, while I bathe?"

"Oh, no, I couldn't. I couldn't go there all by myself. Especially not at night. It's not safe. A lady doesn't go out alone at night."

There were a thousand things I could have replied to that, but I said none of them. Instead I jerked open my desk drawer and removed a fistful of dollar bills. "Tonight, I will pay and you will go. It's only a couple of blocks in your own neighborhood. Trust me, you'll be fine. There's a little fog, but it's not too bad up here."

"I hate him," Alice wailed, "that Mickey Morelock gives me the creeping heebie-jeebies!"

I shrugged, standing in my camisole, and began to unbutton my skirt. "Suit yourself. I'm perfectly happy with bread and cheese."

Finally Alice got the message: no go, no food. She took the money and stomped out the door. Of course she returned safely, with far more food than I would ever have bought. I thought this a victory of sorts, but Alice did not act like one victorious. Instead, her paranoia grew and grew.

Only it was not paranoia: one week later, Alice was dead.

⊰ 9 ⊱

Sweet Little Alice Blue Gone

During that week before I found Alice's body, everything seemed to be taking a turn for the better—both in my own life and in post-earthquake San Francisco. The electricity had been restored and was being turned on neighborhood by neighborhood as fire inspections were completed. Streetcars ran, and so did the few cable cars that had anywhere left to run to. Telephone service was reinstated, and I ordered one for my office because Alice did not have a phone in the house. The fire inspectors had not yet reached the Haight but were expected any day. My sign was finished, and I hung it proudly in the window: FREMONT JONES TYPEWRITING SERVICES.

I still had not heard from either Michael or Mrs. O'Leary, but I no longer expected to. They were no doubt getting on with their lives, as I was with mine. I returned the Maxwell to Michael's garage space in the Presidio, on the way encountering Private Albright, who was surprisingly civil. I went to a moving picture show with Anson, who did not like it at all, whereas I found it quite exciting; we had a lively discussion afterward. A few of my old clients heard about my office on Haight Street by word of mouth, and they told others, so that a slow but steady trickle of business began to find its way to my door.

After the dog, no more nasty gifts were left on our front steps, which, I suppose, is one reason I had let down my guard. In addition, whatever time I had to devote to mysteries I spent puzzling over the Sorensons and the vanished contraband. I could not very well force Alice to confide in me, or so my reasoning went; and as our two natures seemed always at cross-points, I found it easiest to placate her without really listening.

Then, on a fine, fateful night at the beginning of June, I returned to Haight Street from a dinner engagement with Anson. It was not late, for Anson does not like to keep late hours. He accompanied me up the steps and at the top kissed me chastely on the cheek.

I was pleased; he behaved toward me like a suitor, a novelty I quite enjoyed even though nothing was likely to come of it. I did not ask him in, but stood on the step and waved him out of sight. The night air had a softness that felt like a caress. I stretched my arms out and drew in a deep, delicious breath. I had not, I realized, felt so content for a long time.

At last I turned, unlocked the door, and went in. My jaw clenched involuntarily; I knew Alice would be waiting to bombard me with questions and probably a few accusations for good measure. But the house was silent and dark. So I was not to be accosted tonight, so much the better. My jaw relaxed.

"Alice, I'm home," I sang out, then fled into my rooms and shut the door. I lit the oil lamps in both office and bedroom and began to undress.

I had worn one of my better outfits this evening, a dress of dark green taffeta that is most becoming to my eyes. I also like the way it rustles when I move. I began the tedious process of undoing a multitude of tiny buttons down the back, but in the middle of my shoulder blades I paused. I thought I heard something. I listened. Alice coming down the stairs? No, it had been more of a click, a one-time-only sound. Like a door closing. Hastily I redid the top two buttons—I should look into this.

Alice had continued to insist that someone was getting into the house when I was away, so much so that I'd done a thorough investigation a few nights ago. I'd found nothing, no sign of forced entry, no objects out of their usual place. After my investigation, she changed her tune and began to complain of a feeling of being watched. With exaggerated patience I had explained to her that I'd often felt the same thing of late, both in and out of the house, but had concluded that it was only my imagination. As no doubt, I'd said, was the case with her.

I struck a match and lit the candle that I carry at night when going upstairs to the bathroom. Probably Alice herself had gone into the bathroom and closed the door. But no, it had sounded closer than that. In the unlikely event that there really was an intruder, I should be armed; I grabbed my walking stick and rustled out of my rooms.

I knew I had locked the front door, but I checked it anyway: yes, locked—I went on to the back of the house. The back door from the kitchen was also closed and locked. There were no other outside doors, so I went upstairs, rustling all the way, and feeling a breeze where my dress gaped in the back.

I called out, "Alice?" No reply. I tapped on the closed door of the bathroom; still no reply. I tried the knob, found it unlocked, and opened it. The bathroom was empty.

The doors to all the bedrooms were closed. I went first to Alice's, repeating the knocking and the calling and again getting no reply. Odd! I opened the door, holding the candle on high.

Alice was not in her room; for the first time I felt a tingling of alarm. Rapidly I checked the other bedrooms, then returned to hers, where I put the candle down and riffled through the clothes in her wardrobe. Perhaps she'd gone out—I should be able to determine this by the absence of one of her wraps. But Alice had so many clothes that I couldn't tell if anything was missing.

Besides, I thought as I grabbed up the candle and hurtled down the stairs, she was extremely unlikely to go out at night. Her paranoia had made her a veritable recluse. . . .

The last place I looked was the small study. I pushed the door inward, my candle casting eerie shadows before me. I gasped: the room had been torn apart! In the midst of the wreckage lay Alice in her blue dress, the one with the sweet smocking, and around her neck was a broad band of scarlet. Blood-smell tainted the air. I threw down my walking stick with a clatter and ran to her. Whoever had done this was gone now—that sound I'd heard must have been their leaving. There was always a chance that she was still alive. . . .

She was warm, her arm limp as I took her wrist and felt for a pulse. I couldn't find one. Oh, dear God, there was so much blood! The scarlet about her neck was a blood-soaked rag; more blood had pooled behind her head and spread down beneath her upper body. Blood was in her hair. The taste and smell of it stuck in the back of my throat and I gagged, but I did not turn away from Alice now as I had so often turned away from her before. Poor, pathetic Alice.

In order to see better I lit the kerosene lamp, which remained on the desk, though its Tiffany-style shade had been smashed. Alice's violet eyes were open, staring at nothing. Her mouth was also open, giving her too white face a startled look. She did not appear to be breathing. I placed my hand flat on her chest; it did not move. Alice was dead.

"Oh, God, oh, Alice, oh, God!" I cried. Then I ran into the kitchen and vomited into the sink the excellent dinner Anson had bought me.

I tore out of the house and through the streets, yelling for a taxicab. I don't know how long I ran before finding one; when at last I did it was not an auto but the old horse-drawn kind.

"Take me to the police station," I gasped, "and if you see a policeman along the way, stop. This is an emergency!"

The cabby said, "Right-o," and clucked up his horse. I performed contortions in the carriage, getting my buttons buttoned. I'd left the house without a wrap, without a purse, without keys, without anything. I had also, probably, left the door unlocked—but it no longer seemed to matter.

We did not pass any policemen—they seem never to be about when one needs them—and the trip to the police station took an unbearably long time. I was used to the Maxwell's speed. How I wished I'd kept it! How I wished my telephone had been installed so that I could have called them!

I told myself it did not matter, Alice was dead now, but still it was I rather than the horse who was champing at the bit when at last we reached the police station. I jumped out of the cab, only then realizing that I had no money to pay. "I am so sorry," I babbled, "but something truly awful has happened, so I wasn't thinking about anything except that I must get the police."

"That's all right, miss," the cabby said, "never mind."

"No, it's not all right. Please, if you will come tomorrow to the house on the east corner of Haight and Belvedere, I'll pay you then. Please?"

"If you say so. Good night, miss, and good luck," he said, and I called out my thanks over my shoulder, already running into the station.

The policeman at the desk was not nearly so polite. He growled, "I thought I told you not to come in here again."

Just my luck; it was Sergeant Franks. I took a deep breath, determined that he would not intimidate me this time. "My housemate has been murdered," I said.

He leaned back and looked me up and down contemptuously. "Is that a fact?"

"Yes, it is." I went right up to the desk and stared him in the eyes. "I know, Sergeant, that you have taken an unreasonable dislike to me, but I beg you to put it aside. My housemate, Alice Lasley, is this very minute lying on the floor of her house on the corner of Haight and Belvedere with her throat cut. We must go immediately. It did not happen long ago, because her body was warm when I touched her to be sure that she was dead."

"These things just happen to you, that right, Miss Jones?"

"You accused me before of wasting police time; I won't waste any more of it by responding to that remark. I insist the police return with me to Haight Street to begin the investigation."

A more senior policeman than Franks, to judge by his bearing and silver hair, came up to the desk and asked, "What's this all about?"

"Murder," I said.

"Probably nothing," said Franks, but he lumbered to his feet and buttoned the top buttons of his jacket. "I'll take care of it, Lieutenant, I know this lady."

"Very well," said the lieutenant, "and take Stephenson with you."

Stephenson, whose rank was not mentioned, was dark-haired, thin, and wiry. He looked to be about my own age and never spoke. His job was to drive the police wagon, whose horses might as well have been mules for all the speed they mustered. I sat behind the two policemen, going wild with impatience. As I did not have my pocket watch with me I did not know the time, but it felt late. The streets were for the most part deserted, though as well illuminated as they had ever been, pre-earthquake. There was not a trace of fog, and it was still warm for the time of year. If any softness remained in the air, I could no longer feel it. I strove for composure, which I outwardly achieved, but my nerves were screaming beneath the skin.

Lamplight glowed through the bay window of Alice's house on Haight, giving it a falsely welcoming appearance. I had left my lamps burning, and the front door not only unlocked but standing partway open. "I did not lock up because I was in such a hurry," I explained, entering ahead of the two policemen. I ducked into my office and grabbed the burning lamp from my desk, holding it on high. The hallway was black as pitch. "If you will follow me, Alice is in the study toward the rear of this hall. The room has been ransacked. By the killer."

"Yeah, sure," said Franks.

The study door was shut. Surely I'd left it open? I opened it now. I had also left a lamp burning in here, but now the room was completely dark. I held my lamp out before me; my hand shook, making the light flicker across the room.

"No!" I exploded. "This is impossible!" Franks shouldered past me through the doorway. Alice's body was gone. The room had been put back to rights. I could not believe my eyes. I advanced a few paces and set the lamp down before I dropped it.

Sergeant Franks shoved his hands in his pockets, whistling through his teeth, then pivoted on his heel and glared at me. "Murdered housemate, is it? Well, why is it I don't see no body? Room ransacked by the killer, is it? And everything neat as a pin. Miss Jones, I have a mind to arrest you for making a false report."

"I swear she's dead, Alice is dead!" I rushed past the sergeant, into the middle of the room. "She was right here, right in this very spot . . . Wait a minute. The rug. The rug is gone! They must have taken it when they took her body. There must have been more than one of them, don't you think? One person alone couldn't have handled both the body and a rug the size of the one that was in this room, and also have had time to clean everything up."

Stephenson spoke for the first time. "There was a rug in here until recently, Sarge. Look, you can see where the wood floor is lighter in the middle than it is around the edges."

"That don't mean a thing," Franks sneered. "I know this lady, she's a few bricks short of a load. Hell, she's worse'n that. She's one of them kind that likes to draw attention to herself, ain't that right, Miss Jones?"

"It certainly is not." I cast my eyes about desperately, seeking anything that could persuade Sergeant Franks I was telling him the truth.

He was relentless in his dislike and disbelief of me. His voice took on a smarmy tone. "Well now, I don't see how I can help you. First you come to the station and tell me that somebody's not dead who I know for a fact *is* dead, and then you come—in spite of my telling you to stay away—and tell me that somebody's dead who *isn't* dead." Franks turned to his colleague, his huge hands open in mock appeal. "I ask you, Stephenson, is that any way for a nice woman to treat a public servant?"

To his credit, Stephenson did not answer. He hung his head and studied his shoes.

"I am telling you for the last time," I said through clenched teeth, "Alice Lasley was murdered in this room tonight. I believe—though I cannot say for certain, you will need the coroner for that—that her throat was cut, because there was a bloody rag around her neck. The killer or killers must have returned when I left the house to go to the police station. They took her body away, and the rug because it was covered with Alice's blood. They cleaned up the room, their obvious intent being to make it appear that no crime had been committed. If you don't believe me, look through the house. You will *not* find Alice here. You *will* find all her clothes, all her things. This is her house, not mine; I only rent two rooms from her."

"I'll go look," said Stephenson.

"No, you won't, you stay put," Franks commanded. Then he addressed himself to me. "You said you touched her to be sure she was dead. Right?"

"Yes, I did."

"Then how come there's no blood on you?"

I looked down at myself, until this moment not having thought of whether or not I'd gotten Alice's blood on me. He was right, there was none. My mind worked frantically. "I touched her wrist, to see if there was a pulse, and her chest to see if she was breathing. The blood wasn't in those places, it was at her neck and all down behind her."

"Humph! You got an answer for everything, don't you? Well, get this, lady: *no body, no murder.* You understand?"

I nodded. The words reverberated in my head, as if struck from a gong: NO BODY, NO MURDER!

"I could arrest you for falsely reporting a crime, but I won't. You should be grateful for that."

"I am grateful. However, I would like to report a missing person: Alice Lasley."

"You just don't know when to quit, do you?"

I remained silent. Stephenson fidgeted near the doorway.

Franks leaned toward me. His last meal had been full of garlic and his breath was foul. "The police ain't taking no more missing person reports right now. Things're in such a mess nobody can tell who's missing and who just decided to get out of town, so we don't bother with them no more. You can understand that, can't you?"

I nodded once more.

"All right. Just to show you what a nice guy I am, Miss Jones, I'll make you a little deal. You find the body of this Alice Lasley, then you can come back to the police station and maybe we'll believe she was murdered. Otherwise, you stay away. Come on, Stephenson, we're leaving."

I followed them to the front door. I was numb all over, body, brain, nerves, heart. At the door Franks turned back, and I retreated a step, thinking, *What now?*

"I guess it's only fair to tell you, if you did happen to find Alice Lasley's body, you would be at the very top of my list of suspects. Good night, Miss Jones."

I closed the door after them without a word. Then I leaned back against it and slowly slid to the floor.

⚜

The next morning I sat gritty-eyed at my desk, making a list.

> #1. Go through the study and the rest of the house to see if anything is missing. They were looking for something. What? Might be a motive.
>
> #2. Try to determine how the killers gained entry.
>
> #3. Construct a list of suspects.
>
> #4. Should I stay in this house?

I tapped the end of my pen on the desk, thinking about #4; probably I should have made it #1. Obviously, with Alice dead, I had no right to be here. On the other hand, I could not prove that she was dead without her body. Nor did I feel entirely right about leaving the house empty. I wondered to whom it belonged now. She had never mentioned any relatives, other than the supposed husband, nor had she seemed to have any friends. Now that I thought about it, I found it highly unusual that no one had called at the house to see Alice in all my time here.

I tossed the pen aside and poured more coffee, which was tepid by now. Owing to my sleepless night, I'd been first in line at Mickey's Kitchen this morning. Mickey himself was serving, which I was glad of, because I did not particularly like his surly mother, or whoever that woman was. I suppose I must have looked a fright, because he'd cocked his head to one side and asked, "Everything all right with you this morning, pretty lady?" I'd felt the most absurd impulse to blurt out the whole story to him, but of course I did no such thing. I even had the presence of mind to purchase the usual number of rolls. For the time being it seemed prudent to go on as if Alice were still in the house.

Yes, I decided, that is what I must do for the present: I must act as if nothing unusual has happened until I could figure out what *did* happen. Why was Alice killed? Who killed her? Was it the same person who left the dead animals on the porch? Would this person who killed Alice now come back and kill me? Why, why, why? And, as if all that weren't enough, what if I got the answers to these questions— assuming I remained alive to do so—what was I to do with them? Unless I found Alice's body I couldn't go to the police. They wouldn't care, they wouldn't do anything.

"It would serve that Sergeant Franks right," I muttered, "if I did get killed and he was the one to find my body. That would show him!" Or perhaps he would only say it was the ultimate way of calling attention to myself. Knowing him, that seemed highly likely.

Such a train of thought wasn't getting me anywhere, nor had I any desire to be a victim of any kind. In fact, the very idea made me so livid that it galvanized me into action.

There was something I had not done, nor had I put it on my list: I had not looked for Alice's body on these premises. The house had closets and cupboards and chests, all big enough to hide the body of a small person. I presumed it also had an attic and a basement, though I had never seen either. Wasn't there also some sort of shed in the backyard?

I looked in the closets and so on, which produced no results. Then I went outside. The shed proved to be a gardening shed, with tools lying about and old clay pots both broken and whole, and a shelf with a collection of bottles containing such things as fertilizer and rat poison. The only thing unusual about the shed was that I had never seen a gardener here, just as I had never seen a maid. I did find that strange, not to mention inconvenient; the yard was becoming quite overgrown with patchy grass and weeds and the occasional scraggly flower.

I went back into the house again, somewhat invigorated from my brief sojourn in the fresh air. The attic was reached by one of those trap doors that one pulls down to reveal a set of folding stairs. From the difficulty I had in opening it, and the loud, protesting creaks it made, I thought it unlikely that anyone had been up to the attic recently. Still, I went up. The fusty odor was overpowering, and dust was thick to the point of fuzziness on the floor. I had a sneezing fit. There was no need to go farther; if anyone had walked across the attic floor last night, they would have left footprints in that dust, but there were none.

The basement took some time to find. Its entrance was back outside, a small door hidden in the foundation plantings near the far corner of the house. Inside it was damp and dark; I felt for a light cord overhead, getting a handful of creepy cobwebs before I remembered the electricity was still off. So I left the door open wide to let in the daylight, but even then I could not see very well. It was not so much a true basement as a glorified crawl space, with a ceiling so low I had to stoop. There were pipes from the plumbing overhead but that was all, no vast furnace such as we had in the basement of my father's house in Boston. No coal bin; Alice's cookstove and fireplaces were all wood-burning. The floor was soft dirt.

I held my skirts up around my knees, as there were likely to be all manner of horrid critters down here: bugs, spiders, and slimy things, all of which are perversely attracted to long skirts. I did not like this place. There was a nasty feel to it, and a smell reminiscent of dead rat.

Oh dear. The odor was foul but faint, almost certainly from some sort of animal—but I supposed a dead anything had to be investigated at this point. I went back into the house for a candle and returned to the basement for a closer look. If her murderers had buried Alice down here, it would have to be in a hastily dug grave.

Hunched over, I examined every foot of the dirt floor. No question, it had not been dug up. Nor did I find a dead rat, or any dead animal—that was a little odd, but I did not dwell on it. These cramped, unpleasant quarters were getting to me; with a mixture of relief and disappointment I hunched my way out of there.

No sooner had I gone back into the house than I heard a sharp rap on the front door. I opened it to a man in a fireman's uniform, with his hat tucked under his arm. "Fire inspection," he said. I could have kissed him.

"The owner, Mrs. Lasley, is not at home," said I, a considerable understatement, "but I am her friend and temporary tenant."

"All I gotta do is make sure the place is safe for when they turn the electricity back on in this block. The lady of the house doesn't have to be here, long as you let me in."

"By all means, please do come in." He did, and after some prowling around he pronounced the premises in acceptable condition. I could have kissed him twice, especially when he told me that I could use the wood stove in the kitchen right away and that electrical service would be connected before the end of the day.

Light, blessed light! When twilight fell I turned the lights on all over the house, except in Alice's room, where it didn't seem right somehow. Then I turned them off again in all but my own quarters and the downstairs hall.

I am not particularly good with wood-burning cookstoves, having had a gas ring at Mrs. O'Leary's and a cook who dealt with the stove in Boston, but I was determined to make my own coffee in the morning, so I tackled the thing. I had quite a merry time of it, especially when one piece of wood proved to have bugs that flew out irately around the kitchen. I opened the back door and shooed at them until they all got the idea and flew away. While I was doing that, the fire in the stove settled down to burn steadily without my help. I was glad I'd taken the time earlier to go to the market. I cooked my own meal for the first time in ages, and it was as good as any feast. For a little while, I even forgot about Alice.

When I finished my meal I checked on the stove, remembering something about banking the fire. I did not really know how to do that, but I could figure it out. However, the fire was still burning too merrily; I should have to come back to it later. I admit the sight of the flames, even in their small, enclosed space, made me uneasy. I wondered if for all the rest of my life I'd be afraid of fire.

I continued to sit in the kitchen, where it was warm and cozy. There was a great deal to be done, but I found it hard to move. I'd had a full day following the fireman's departure, with no time to work at the things on my list. The cabby who'd taken me to the police station showed up to be paid. Customers kept me busy typing until midafternoon, and then I'd gone out to do the shopping. On foot, it had been much more of a chore than if I'd had the Maxwell. It was really very irritating how I kept missing that automobile.

Down the hall, the clock struck eight. The house sounded hollow. I got heavily to my feet and walked through the rooms, checking to be sure all the doors and windows were locked, though I doubted it mattered. They'd been locked yesterday too, yet the murderers had got in. Perhaps it was not unreasonable to think they would not come here two nights in a row. Perhaps, even, they had done all they intended to do here and would never return. Dared I hope? Probably not. I sighed.

I was so tired, near exhaustion. I knew my brain would not work well enough for me to do the kind of thorough search needed in order to find out how they'd got into the house. I also knew it would be foolish to take no precautions at all. Dragging myself from room to room, I scattered crockery and pots and pans on the floor in front of all the downstairs windows. If marauders climbed through, they'd make a racket that would either frighten them away or at least alert me so that I could protect myself. I tried to push and pull the Monstrosity in front of the front door to block it, but I couldn't budge the thing and had to settle for the heaviest parlor chair instead. I shoved the kitchen table up against the back door, and while I was in the kitchen, I checked the stove again. The fire inside was glowing nicely. I raked some ashes up over it and hoped I'd banked it properly.

Then I trudged up the stairs to the bathroom. Alice's door stood open, like a reproach. I felt a tidal wave of guilt engulf me as I closed that door upon her empty room. All my life I have thought guilt a waste of time and energy, but I could not escape it now. I *was* guilty. I had contributed to Alice's death, if only by ignoring her when I should have paid attention. I could have pressed her harder to tell me the truth about the husband, the maid, the nightmares. About her exaggerated reaction to the dead animals left on the steps.

There was always the possibility, which Alice herself had raised, that the threats had been aimed at me, not at her; that last night's intruders had been after something of mine, not hers, and poor Alice had only got in the way. For the life of me, though, I could not think of anything I'd done; since the conclusion of certain rather harrowing events last year, I'd led a blameless life. Then too, there was the fact that my rooms had not been touched, only the study. And poor, pathetic Alice.

"I'm so sorry, Alice," I whispered, leaning my head against her door, "so sorry." Too many times I'd said those words when she was living. Now that she was dead they made a poor apology indeed.

There was hot water, another miracle. I had a bath, which I enjoyed, though it did not wash away my guilt. I went all rosy back to my room, intent on going early to bed. I was so tired that I knew I would sleep, and I intended to get a fresh start on all my problems in the morning.

I turned out the light in my office and paused to look out the bay window. The street, bathed by its now working streetlights, was still and quiet. Peaceful—I hoped it would stay that way.

I left my doors open in case I had to move quickly during the night. I would keep my trusty weapon on the bed next to me as I slept; with luck I would not need it. I reached around the side of the bureau, where I kept the walking stick, but it was not there. What? My heart skipped a beat; then I recalled that I had left it in the study when I ran out to get the police.

The walking stick was not in the study, either. I searched for it frantically but did not find it anywhere. The conclusion was unavoidable: the murderers must have recognized my walking stick for what it was, a weapon, and had taken it with them, just as they took Alice.

So I was left without means to defend myself.

⊰ 10 ⊱

Time and Tide Wait for No Man—or Woman

Necessity being the mother of invention, I slept with the largest of the kitchen knives; and I was so tired that I slept rather well. The next morning, as I was finishing breakfast, the doorbell rang and startled me out of my wits. I had never heard it before and had presumed it broken, but apparently it worked on a now restored electrical connection.

None of my customers would arrive so early. I was tempted not to answer it, even though I had already unblocked both the doors, but curiosity overcame me. I opened the front door and there stood Meiling.

"Meiling, what a delightful surprise!"

She bowed her dark, silken head. "Fremont. I am sorry to intrude upon you at this hour, but once again I seek your help."

"Don't be silly, you are never an intrusion. Do come in." I took her hand and drew her inside. "Will you join me in the kitchen? I have coffee made, or if you like I can put on hot water for tea. The fire inspector was here yesterday, so we can cook again, and we also have electricity. It's quite wonderful." Too late I realized there was no more "we."

"I would like to try your coffee," Meiling said with a small smile. "I am most interested to adopt all American customs. In a way, that is why I'm here."

"Coffee it shall be then." I filled my mug and got a cup for Meiling, and we sat sipping companionably at the kitchen table.

Meiling made a face. "This coffee is an acquired taste."

I laughed. "If you would prefer to acquire it another day, I really don't mind making you a cup of tea."

"No, thank you." She glanced out into the hallway. "The person with whom you share this house, perhaps *she* will think I intrude?"

I laughed again, though this time it was forced. "No, she will not think that. Nor will she interrupt us, you may rely on it, Meiling. Pray tell me whatever is on your mind."

"My honorable grandmother went to be with the ancestors last night."

I placed my hand over hers. "I hope she died peacefully." *Unlike Alice.*

Meiling smiled with a tear shimmering in the corner of each eye. She wiped them away with the tips of her fingers. "If we all could die so well, we would be fortunate. Day after day Grandmother slept for longer and longer periods of time. Finally she just did not wake up, she stopped breathing, and that was all."

"You know you have my deepest condolences."

Meiling inclined her head. "I do, and I thank you. Now I must get on with my plan, though prematurely. The funeral rites for Grandmother will take place the day after tomorrow. My not so honorable cousin insists that our betrothal ceremony must be performed tomorrow. I told him it is too soon, that he will displease the spirits of the ancestors by doing this, but he only laughed and said that my grandmother wished the betrothal and would approve."

"What will you do?"

"I will disappear. I am not going back to the camp of the Lis,

Fremont. Though I loved my grandmother with all my heart, I cannot be present at her funeral. I feel both sad and angry that this cousin's wishes should take precedence over mine simply because he is a man, but what can I do? If I go forth with the betrothal I will never get away!"

Meiling's eyes met mine. Hers were blazing dark fire, like black opals, and I expect mine were doing a paler version of the same.

"I am in total sympathy," I said. I wanted to add, "How could any woman not be?" for it was something I did not understand at all. The source of my bond with Meiling was that, from the first time I met her, something in her manner, something in her eyes had told me we might be of different races but we were alike under the skin. Most other women I knew would have believed that Meiling should subject herself to the cousin, which I found abhorrent.

Meiling broke eye contact, took a quick breath, and continued. "My preparations are incomplete, but I must move on nevertheless. Only two days ago I found an intermediary whom I can trust to sell the pearls. I had to be careful in my choice, which took precious time."

"What will you do for money in the meanwhile? How will you live, and where, Meiling?"

"I have a little money. I have brought it with me, just the money, nothing else. I will go by train down the Peninsula to Palo Alto and take rooms there until I hear from Stanford University, which as you know is also in Palo Alto. If I am not accepted, well"—she shrugged, an elegant gesture the way Meiling did it—"I will deal with that when it happens. Today I need to buy clothes, dresses and skirts and blouses such as you wear, Fremont. I hoped you might advise me in the shopping?"

"I would enjoy that."

"We must transform me into a fashionable woman who only happens to have a Chinese face. Such a transformation will be as good as any disguise—or so I hope. I have even thought of changing my name, but since my application to Stanford is in the name of Meiling Li, I cannot."

"This is so exciting! You would have no way of knowing, but in a way I changed my name too when I left Boston. Fremont is my middle name. Until I came to San Francisco I was always called by my first name, which is Caroline."

"Caroline?" Meiling raised her eyebrows. "I think you do not seem much like a Caroline. Fremont is better."

"For me, at any rate," I said, and then for no good reason we both burst out laughing.

When our laughter subsided I said, "If I may make a suggestion: perhaps it would be best for you to wear one of my outfits on the shopping trip. We will attract less notice together in the street. Your trousers fit me, so my skirts should fit you. Although it does seem a shame; as you are about to discover for yourself, your type of clothing is far more comfortable than mine."

"That is most kind of you. I accept." Meiling inclined her head; when she raised it, she had a troubled expression on her face. "But I am undeserving. I have a confession to make, Fremont. If Grandmother's death had not been—what is the word—imminent, I would have confessed to you several days ago. You recall telling me about the dead things that were left on your doorstep, and I said it was a form of curse?"

I nodded.

"The next night after the one on which we found the pearls, I came late and hid in the bushes outside this house, keeping watch. I thought, to return the favor you did me in helping to find the pearls, I might catch the person who was—how do you say—hara, har—"

"Harassing?"

"Yes, harassing you. Unfortunately, either I had not hidden myself well enough, or the evildoer has exceptionally sharp senses. He approached, bent down with a burden on his back. But he stopped in the street too far away for me to see his face. Fremont, it was as if he sniffed the air and knew there was danger to him, for he turned and ran. I ran in pursuit, but I was no match for this person, even with his burden. In the next block he vanished as if into thin air! I wanted to watch more nights, but that was when my grandmother began to sleep around the clock. We all knew she could die at any time, and I had to be there. So I failed you. Now we may never know who tried to put a curse on this house. I am sorry."

"That explains," I ruminated, "why there were no more after the dog."

"I beg your pardon?"

"There was a dead dog on the steps the morning after we found the pearls. That night was the one you just told me of. You need not be sorry, Meiling. You did do me a service after all, because after that he did not come again, which was a great relief. I suppose he must have thought we'd hired a guard, which made it too great a risk for him to continue his nefarious activities. Unless . . ." *Unless he did come back, with one of his cronies, and killed Alice.*

"Unless what?"

"Oh, nothing important. Come, now we must find you something to wear. And then we're going shopping!"

In the evening I returned to Haight Street in a pensive mood. I had spent the whole day with Meiling. It was a day I would never forget, full of unexpected contrasts that troubled me.

For example, in Western clothes Meiling looked very striking. I could not help noticing that she is much better built than I, though we both give an overall impression of being tall and thin. Meiling, however, has a fine pair of breasts whereas I am lamentably flat-chested. The fashions of the day played up her attributes, with an effect that both amazed and delighted her. While I shared her pleasure in the "transformation," underneath I felt sad. Why could the world not value her Chineseness? Why, in order to succeed in this culture, should Meiling have to make herself look like everybody else?

We ate an elegant luncheon in one of the better restaurants that had recently reopened. It was the first time Meiling had ever eaten in a restaurant that was not Chinese, using knife and fork rather than chopsticks. She giggled and so did I and we had a high old time, but again underneath I felt sad. The Meiling I had known for a year and some months was disappearing before my very eyes; this woman was someone else, Meiling-Yet-Not-Meiling.

She told me that she wanted to become a scientist. At Stanford she would study geology, which is the science of planet earth, and someday she hoped to teach at a university herself. She said other women at Stanford were doing similar things, as it was a progressive sort of institution. I was glad for her and a little envious, because my alma mater, Wellesley, still called itself a "seminary" in the prevailing manner of most women's colleges, and did not encourage its graduates to have careers. Envying my friend made me feel ashamed.

Then Meiling asked if I knew how she could get in touch with Michael Archer. When she said his name, memories flashed lightning-quick through my mind: Michael's long association with the Li family, his love of exotic places, the hint of mystery about him . . . I looked across the table at Meiling in her Western clothes, and I saw her, as it were, through Michael's eyes. She was beautiful, she was exotic, when the pearls were sold she would be rich, she was the same age as I, and she was asking about Michael. I did not want to know why. Unreasoning jealousy, sharp as a knife, ripped through me and I felt doubly ashamed. I told her that Michael was supposed to be at the Presidio in Monterey. She should be able to write to him there, but I could not be sure of anything where Michael was concerned because I'd heard nothing from him since he left San Francisco.

In the afternoon, Meiling and I shopped again, buying accessories to go with the clothes and a trunk to put everything in. Laden down, we piled into an open taxi and told the cabby to take us to the train station. In the taxi Meiling became a bundle of nerves, swiveling her head around and around until I told her she would twist her new hat off if she didn't stop. Thereafter, perversely, I caught her nerves and thought we were being followed. Nothing came of it. We reached the station and startled the porter by asking him to take the trunk into the ladies' lounge. There, amid much hilarity, Meiling and I packed her new belongings into the trunk.

Then we waited together until the train came, embraced, and said goodbye. Meiling declared that this had been the most wonderful day she'd ever spent. It *was* wonderful, but as I watched the train chug out of the station, I felt again the overwhelming sorrow that had been so often with me in the days immediately after the earthquake. I had tried to shake it off on the long way home, changing from streetcar to streetcar, and had only partially succeeded.

So you may be sure that I was not in the least pleased to see a tall, blond fellow dressed in an Army uniform sitting on the steps of the house at the corner of Haight and Belvedere.

"Private Albright," I said tonelessly.

He leapt to his feet. "Miss Fremont Jones! I had almost given up hope."

"I am surprised to see you here. I do not recall giving you my address."

With a faint flush of embarrassment, he hung his head. "I, uh, I followed you one day. I just had to know where you live. I hope you don't mind."

I most certainly did mind! I wondered if he'd followed me more than once, but I did not say so. Suddenly I no longer thought him such a harmless young man. I asked, "Do you have a message for me, is that it?"

"I thought, uh, maybe we could take in a show, or something. Dinner! It's almost dinnertime, I could buy you dinner and we could go somewhere . . . ?"

"I fear you will be missed at the Presidio."

"No, I won't, I'm off duty tonight, I mean today. All day and tonight too." He was as eager as a puppy, and I was having none of it.

"Private," I said, "you have a regrettable talent for coming up with these ideas at times when I cannot possibly accept. If you will excuse me, I've had a long day and I must get inside. My housemate will be waiting." I did not want him to know that I was alone here.

He regarded me oddly. "There's nobody at home. I rang the doorbell several times. When there was no answer I got worried, so I went around and looked in all the windows. There's no one in the house."

I gave the private my most withering look, which I had learned from Boston matrons, who themselves had studied at the School of the Medusa. "You are in error, and I am appalled to think that you would peek at windows like a common voyeur. My housemate has been ill, and in addition she is quite a shy person. No doubt you will have frightened her out of her wits, so that she is cowering in her room afraid to make a sound. And now, in addition to my difficult day, I will have to placate her."

"Hey," he said, backing away, "I apologize. I didn't mean any harm, I just wanted to see you. You're a really hard lady to get to know, do you know that?"

"Perhaps that is because I do not wish to be known. Good night, Private Albright." I swept up the steps and took out my key.

This young man either had more determination, or was more thickheaded, than any ten other men in the Western world. "May I come again? Just tell me when would be a better time. If I'm on duty I'll swap with somebody—"

I turned around in a swirl of skirts. "I do not think there will be a better time. Now goodbye!"

Night fell soon thereafter, and with the coming of darkness came a degree of apprehension such as I had never known before. I checked windows and doors twice over to be sure they were locked. I drew all the curtains and turned on every electric light in the house. I cursed myself for having removed the curtains in my office and was seriously considering rehanging them, when I got hold of myself.

I had decided, hadn't I, that it should appear as if all were normal in the house? Therefore I should not rehang the curtains. But I could no longer remember why I had made that decision. Whom was I hoping to fool? The neighbors? The police? Not the murderers—they and I already knew the truth, that Alice Lasley was dead. Fudge and double fudge! I left the window as it was.

My head felt about to split open. I had to do something to calm myself, so I took a long hot bath. I tried to relax in the deep tub, but couldn't keep my eyes from darting continuously to the bathroom door. I was afraid that, if I closed them even for an instant, someone would creep in and slit my throat. I could picture myself naked in the bathtub with streams of scarlet staining the water . . .

"Ye gods!" I yelped.

I don't know why, perhaps it was only my native stubbornness reasserting itself, but after that I felt better. I did close my eyes, I did relax, and when I was done I wrapped myself in my once-viridian robe and turned off the upstairs lights before going back downstairs.

I took pen and paper into the kitchen, where I could work away from the bay window's exposure. I thought I would work on the list I'd started to help me unravel the mystery of Alice and her death. Instead, as if the pen had a will of its own, I found myself writing to Michael Archer.

Dear Michael, I have just spent the most amusing day with Meiling—

I put the pen down. I had been thoroughly taught that a female does not make the first approach to a male, not under any circumstances. She does not call on him, he must call on her. She does not send round her card with a note of social invitation. At a party or a ball, she does not ask him to dance. And she does not write a letter to him unless he has written to her first.

On the other hand, had I not set out for San Francisco precisely because I did not intend to live my life a slave to convention? Do I not go without a corset because it is more comfortable; do I not habitually wear my hair down even though I am of an age to wear it up, simply because it takes less time and I do not particularly care how I look? Had I not already defied convention in many other, more significant ways? Yes, I had. So why should I care about writing to Michael first? Yet I did care.

"Fremont, you are being very foolish," I grumbled. "After all, he is only a friend, so the rules for males and females need not apply." I picked up the pen again. I would write to Michael, not a silly, superficial, chatty letter (I crumpled that sheet up) but what was most on my mind.

I produced a letter of some three pages that sounded entirely too confused, and somewhat desperate, when I read it over. I put it aside and chewed on the end of the pen, lost in thought. Vaguely I was aware of the stillness of the house around me, making its occasional creaks and groans. The tall-case clock down the hall marked the half hour with a muffled chime.

I attempted to clarify my thoughts. Why, really, was I writing to him? In a rush of decisiveness, I seized a fresh sheet of paper and scrawled:

Michael, please come back. I need you.

Then I looked at what I'd written and knew I could never send it. Never in a million years. So I tore up both letters and burned them in the stove, after which I went early to bed with the kitchen knife for a companion. I hid in sleep; I slept as if I had been drugged.

❦

It is really quite remarkable how a couple of nights of sound sleep can restore a person. I woke early, and upon opening my eyes I knew what I should do. Perhaps my sleeping brain worked better than my waking brain did of late; or perhaps Sherlock Holmes had paid a visit during the night and shot me up with a seven percent solution of cocaine. Whatever the cause, I was glad to discover that my brain cells had not completely turned to mush.

First, after a requisite amount of coffee, I addressed the problem of how the murderers had gained entry to the house. Feeling Holmesian, I examined every inch of both back and front doorframes and all the windowsills with my magnifying glass. There was no evidence that any opening to the outside had been forced.

As Nurse Bartlett would have said, *Hmmm*. This made me think of Alice's absent husband, who presumably would have had a set of keys. If he existed, about which I had my doubts. Keys! Oh, dear God, I must look for Alice's keys.

They were not in the hall drawer, where I always put them whenever I found them lying about, which was often; Alice was notoriously careless with her keys. I hastened up the stairs. A quick glance around her room showed me that they were nowhere in sight. I put up the window shade to let in the light so that I could see better, and while I was at it opened the window—might as well air out the room—then turned out all of Alice's purses and reticules and even a small carpet-bag, all without finding the keys I so frantically sought. I went through all the drawers, with similar results.

Hmmm, again. Of course Alice could have lost them, but I did not think so. If she'd lost them she would have told me. She would have wailed about it. To be thorough, I must search the rest of the house. I did that, with an apprehension that increased as I went from room to room without result. Just as I finished, the doorbell rang, announcing my first customer of the day.

Actually, it was more than one customer: a group of women from the tents in Golden Gate Park, all of them wanting me to type the letters they dictated, to relatives in far-flung places like Scotland and Alabama. Such letters constituted the bulk of my business at present, and though I do not charge much for this particular kind of work, I was glad to have it. As they say, every little bit helps.

Around noon the women departed in a flurry of smiles and thanks, after which I put up a sign announcing that I would be closed two hours for lunch. I walked to the market, where there was a public telephone, and called Anson. He answered, and I identified myself.

"I know your voice, Fremont," he said warmly. "I hope there is a pleasant reason for your call, although to speak with you is always pleasant, whatever the circumstances."

A pretty speech! I said, "You are too kind. I was hoping, if it would not be too much trouble, that you could help me with something at the end of the day."

"Certainly. When I'm done in the office I have a few house calls to make, but after that I could come to Haight Street. May I know what it is that you need help with?"

"It is a private matter, better not discussed over a public telephone. Do you own a screwdriver, Anson?"

"Of course, but what a non sequitur!"

"I would be obliged if you could bring it with you. Alice probably has one, but in the event she does not, it would be prudent for you to bring yours."

"You're very mysterious."

"Not really. Upon your arrival, all will be revealed."

Anson made the chuckle that always surprised me with its buttery warmth. "My dear, I shall hang upon tenterhooks until then."

We said our mutual goodbyes. I depressed the hook, then rang again and asked the operator to connect me with the telephone company's business office. When the connection was made, I canceled my order for a telephone on Haight Street. I didn't know how much longer I could remain at Alice's house, but surely it would not be long enough to justify the expense of having a telephone installed. With those two things accomplished, I asked the market's proprietor if he knew the location of a hardware store.

He obliged by giving me directions. I was soon the owner of two new locks of shiny brass, one for the front door and one for the back, plus their keys. A close examination of the locks led me to believe that their installation would not be terribly difficult. Likely I could do it myself, if I had not already asked Anson. I could have hired a locksmith, but I did not want anyone around the house whom I did not already know and trust.

With an hour still remaining of my lunch break, I thought I might replace my trusty weapon. In an upbeat frame of mind, I boarded a streetcar and rode it all the way downtown. A prodigious amount of building was going on, to the accompaniment of an equally prodigious amount of noise. I was very glad to see it; also to hear it, even though my acute aural sense is usually offended by loud sounds. At the end of the line I debarked.

The waterfront and docks had been preserved from the fire, by dint of heroic effort and water hauled and pumped from the Bay. The Ferry Building rose up, undamaged by the earthquake, with its clock still stopped at twelve minutes past five. Along here there were vendors, such as the woman from whom I had bought my walking stick last year. She had left her accustomed place outside the train station after the earthquake and I hoped to find her again. I went into this rough area unafraid, for our disaster had so upset daily affairs that a woman alone could go almost anywhere now, without remark. Everyone was far too busy to care, or even to notice.

Concealed weapons were no longer in vogue, it seemed. The hastily thrown-up stalls that I passed were trafficking in more mundane wares, such as clothing and household goods and, in one case, live chickens. I did not see the snaggle-toothed Chinese woman who'd sold me the walking stick. There was nothing for it but to return home.

As I rode the streetcar back, a radical idea began to form in my head. Forget walking sticks with secret blades; I would rather have a pistol. A small pistol, silver perhaps, sized for a woman's hand. One heard that such things existed, and surely I could learn to shoot it. I was quite good with a rifle—my father had taught me to shoot traps at an outdoorsmen's club he belonged to on Cape Cod. Now, how would I go about acquiring a pistol?

Michael would know, a small voice inside me piped up. I told it firmly to hush and, furthermore, not to utter those three words ever again. My stop was coming up; I slung my bag, heavy with door locks, over my shoulder and hopped out.

On an impulse that I was sure was a good one, I walked a block in the opposite direction from Alice's house. As I'd hoped, Mickey Morelock was still in the outdoor kitchen business. He seemed an eminently streetwise sort of person, the sort who would know about pistols.

Completion of the inspections in this part of town had not notice-ably diminished Mickey's customers, because many from the tent city bought their food from him. He greeted me enthusiastically as I stopped to one side, without joining the line. "If it isn't one of my favorite young ladies!" he said. "Where've you been keeping your-self?"

"I can cook at home now," I explained, "but I thought I might ask your advice on another matter. I'll wait until you are free."

I waited, shifting my weight from one foot to the other and having second thoughts. My stomach rumbled in response to a delicious chicken-and-dumpling smell, but my mind was too full of doubts about pistols to recognize hunger. I had almost decided to make an excuse and leave when Mickey ambled over, wiping his hands on the splattered apron that spanned his considerable girth.

"Well now," he said, grinning, "when it's advice you want you couldn't come to a better place than old Mickey. So how can I help you, darlin'?"

In the face of his good humor, my doubts evaporated. I lowered my voice confidentially. "I would like to buy a pistol, for protection, and I do not know how to go about it. I want something small, that I can handle easily."

He winked broadly. "Nothing to it. I'll be glad to take care of that for you. You just come on back here tomorrow morning, early, and we'll see what we've got."

I felt an enormous flood of relief, as if the pistol were mine already.

My intention was to tell Anson the truth about Alice. I planned what I would say while I changed into a rose-sprigged dress, more feminine than the tailored skirts and blouses that are my habitual daily garb. When I was dressed and he still had not arrived, I brushed my hair upside down for fullness and pinned it in a pouf on top of my head. I stood back and examined my appearance in the cheval glass, part of the bedroom suite brought from upstairs. I had lost weight, when already I had none to lose. My dress was loose at the waist, but not enough to be concerned about. I would gain it back eventually. I was also too pale. The doorbell rang and I pinched my cheeks to give them color before answering it.

Anson, carrying his black medical bag, took off his homburg and smiled. "Good evening, Fremont."

"It's good of you to come," I said, stepping back.

He brushed my cheek with cool lips as he passed through the door. While I closed it, he rummaged in his bag, which he had set down upon the Monstrosity. He came out with the screwdriver, which he held up, inquiring, "Where is the patient?"

I laughed. "We will begin in the kitchen. This way, Doctor, if you please."

I had laid out the locks and keys on the kitchen table. I gestured to them and launched into my explanation. But I astonished myself; the words that came out of my mouth were not those I'd planned, they were just short of prevarication: "We have had some trouble here. In point of fact Alice has disappeared, and I am concerned for my safety. Therefore, I decided to change the locks," I babbled, "and as you know, every workman in this town is beyond busy, I'd have to wait days for a locksmith and I dare not. That is why I asked for your help. Anson, if you would change the locks for me I would be eternally grateful."

Anson furrowed his brow. He said, "Let us sit down and talk about this further."

"There is no need to talk about it, only to get it done!"

He, who had always been so courteous and soft-spoken with me, said severely, "Fremont, I insist. Now sit."

I sat. As did he.

"What do you mean, Alice has disappeared?"

"Just that." I squirmed on my chair. That is the trouble with prevarication, once you have begun there's no end to it, and afterward one has the trouble of remembering what one has said. Anson looked at me as if I were on the dissecting table. I snatched a breath and went on. "The night we went to dinner, you recall, the night I wore my green dress—"

He nodded, but his intense scrutiny did not lessen.

"—after you accompanied me to the door, I let myself in and called out to Alice, as usual, but there was no reply. The house was dark. Well, that was not so unusual because it was before the electricity was turned on, but anyway, there should have been a lamp in the hall, or something. I just, well, the house seemed too quiet somehow. It felt wrong. I went up to Alice's room, but she wasn't there. She wasn't anywhere in the house. Nor had she left me a note."

"What did you do then?"

My mind felt like the Maxwell with its motor racing. "I waited until it got to be quite late and she still had not come home. Then I went out and took a cab to the police station, where I reported Alice missing. The police were no help. They said they aren't taking any missing persons reports at the moment."

"That doesn't sound right, Fremont."

Oh, dear God, help. "Exactly what I thought, Anson, but they said the city is in such disorder, with so many people homeless and so many others having decided to leave, that it is impossible to tell who is missing and who is not."

Anson bobbed up like a cork. "I'll go to them myself. Such treatment of your concerns cannot be tolerated!" For punctuation he threw down the screwdriver, whose point made a nick in the table before toppling over and rolling onto the floor.

"Please, Anson," said I, grabbing his hand and holding onto it for dear life, "do not! I . . . they . . . that is, earlier I had some dealings with them in which I made a report that they disbelieved. One of the officers had proof that I was in error, so I am not in good favor with the police. I'm very much afraid that if you go to them it will only cause trouble for me. You wouldn't want that, would you?"

He allowed me to tug him back down into his chair. Then he wiped his balding brow and mumbled. "I don't know. This just doesn't seem right. Of course I would never cause trouble for you, but. . . ."

At that moment, I wished heartily that I had never asked for his help! "I'm sorry to have involved you. Please go. I can take care of the locks some other way."

"But if your friend comes back—and surely she will come back—how will she get in, if the locks have been changed? This is not your property, Fremont. You have no right to alter it."

I do not particularly like to be told that I am in the wrong, even if I am. I said testily, "I will let her in, of course. Anson, Alice's keys to the house are missing along with her. What if she has fallen victim to foul play? Anyone might have those keys now. I am afraid to stay in this house alone, not knowing who might use them to get in here. Alice would not want me to live in fear, I assure you!"

A myriad of emotions played across Anson's open, honest face. He would never make a successful poker player. First, distrust: "You say you've had a run-in with the police—"

I nodded, feeling anxious.

Concern: "But you did go to them again, about Alice, and they declined to become involved."

I nodded again.

Worry: "Keys are missing. Of course you would be afraid. How well do you know Alice, Fremont?"

"Not well. She has proven hard to get to know, so that I haven't a clue how to proceed with looking for her on my own. I am trying, of course, and will continue to do so."

Anson's face cleared, and his jaw hardened, by which I surmised that he had come to some conclusion. *Good,* I thought, *he will help me change the locks and we can put all this behind us.* But that was not what happened.

He reached out and captured my hand, which he then held so tightly that I found it difficult not to wince. "Fremont," he said, "this is a questionable situation, but it has made me bold. Indeed, we are living in an unusual time, which may very well call for unusual measures. You know that I think you are an admirable woman. The skills you displayed when you were driving for the Red Cross would be put to good use in a medical office. You are not squeamish, and you have a true compassion for the sick and the injured."

I wondered where this was going. Did he intend to offer me a job?

"You would make an excellent helpmeet for one of my profession. In addition, I feel a true affection for you that in time can only grow. I do not know what you feel for me, and I realize that we have not known each other very long. Nevertheless, I could not bear for anything to happen to you here in this house while I proceed in the conventional fashion. As I said before, these are unusual times. The obvious solution is for you to come to my house, without delay."

I tried to take back my hand, but he held it fast. "Anson," I said firmly, "that would not be proper. Nor is it necessary. We have only to change the locks and I'll be quite safe."

He closed his eyes and shook his head back and forth. "No, no, no. You misunderstand me." When he opened his eyes, they showed a new emotion. Imploring: "Fremont, I am asking you to be my wife!"

A Possibly Premature Prothalamion

I was struck dumb.

Taking my silence as encouragement, Anson pressed on. "We are well matched, you and I. I already care for you, and I think you care for me. I am sure that in time I will grow to love you. Probably in no time at all!"

I found my tongue and uttered a prophecy: "More likely you will grow to hate me."

"I could never hate you!" He pulled me to my feet and into his arms. Anson was surprisingly strong, especially his hands. But then, I supposed doctors need strong hands for the setting of bones and so forth.

I placed my own hands against his chest and pushed away, but he did not allow it. He kissed me, earnestly if not quite skillfully.

When our lips parted I said, "I do believe you mean it."

His eyes bored into mine so intently that I began to wonder if he were trying to plot the anatomy of my brain through my pupillary openings. "Fremont," he said, "I am not in the habit of making proposals—of any nature—that I do not mean. You have a problem, and I have the solution. Marry me. Say that you will."

My throat went dry. "I, ah, I have to think about it."

"For how long?"

"I don't know." I pushed at his chest and this time he released me. I walked over to the back door, held back the curtain, and looked out. But I was not seeing anything; it was merely a delaying tactic. "I suppose until I'm satisfied that I've done all I can to find out . . ."

Anson strode over and put his hands on my shoulders, his chin against my hair. "In all likelihood your friend will be back soon, though it is odd that she did not say where she was going. Nevertheless, after what you've told me, you should not stay here. Isn't there someone else—"

"No, Anson." I turned around and skirted past him, back to the kitchen table. "I am going to stay here for the time being. If you prefer not to help me with the locks, I expect I can do it myself."

His face took on a reddish tint, as if he were about to become belligerent, but he changed his mind, the color faded, and he smiled instead. "Has anyone ever told you, Fremont Jones, that you are the most stubborn woman in all creation?"

I smiled too. "Yes, Doctor. Many times."

He changed the locks.

Mickey Morelock will have a gun for me this morning, I thought as soon as I opened my eyes the following day. He'd said to come early; I got out of bed with more alacrity than usual.

The novelty of being able to make my own coffee had not yet worn off, so I had no desire to drink Mickey's. Mine was better, in any case. I poked up the stove and set the percolator on it to brew while I dressed. Delicious coffee smells soon wafted down the hallway to tease my nose and to lead me, still fastening my hair, back to the kitchen.

I stood leaning against the sink, sipping from the brown mug in a kind of morning daze. I was thinking vaguely about Anson's proposal when I heard the clank of bottles on the back stoop. I looked over my shoulder out the window and saw the top of the milkman's head go by.

There was something related to the milkman that I had been forgetting to do. Caffeine had not yet sharpened my wits enough for me to recall it; but as is so irritatingly often the way of things, as soon as he was gone I knew what it was.

I set down my mug and opened the back door. As always, he had left two bottles of milk, doubtless Alice's standard order. Even when she had been here, it was more than the two of us drank. I brought them in and put them away. Tonight I must remember to leave a note for the milkman, reducing the order to one bottle—that was what I'd forgotten. I do not like to waste things, and since the earthquake, I can no longer take for granted the availability of even the simplest things. Food, for instance. There had been days when I would not have eaten were it not for the charity of others. Including Alice. I sighed; at least I had repaid her—in money, if not in sufficient care.

With my second cup of coffee I cogitated upon those two bottles of milk. Were they evidence of a husband formerly in the house? Perhaps, and of the missing maid also. More and more I was inclined to believe that I had misjudged Alice. She had certainly behaved strangely about her supposed husband, and there were no traces that I could find of a man about the place. Yet someone had got in, torn the study apart looking for something, killed Alice in a brutal way, etc. This husband made a likely candidate. I resolved to do everything in my power to find out more about him. I would begin as soon as I had kept my appointment with Mickey.

"How much do I owe you?" I asked, turning the pistol over in my hands. It was exactly as I had imagined, small and silver, and I was quite pleased. I knew better than to ask where he got it. I did not know the laws about sale and possession of firearms, and considering the unreasonable treatment I'd had from the police, I did not care to learn.

"Oh, nothing," Mickey replied, waving a hand like a ham hock. "I got it from a buddy who owes me, so it didn't cost me a nickel. Glad to do it for you."

"If I do not pay you for it now, then *I* will owe you," I said, not keen on the idea. Mickey seemed an agreeable person, but one can never be too sure.

"I wouldn't know what to charge you, and that's the truth. So you just run along, pretty lady, and think no more about it." He grinned, stuck his hands into pockets beneath a flowing apron, and ambled back to his customers. Viewing Mickey from behind, I observed that he had a vast sort of roll to his walk, as if at some point in his life he'd spent a long time at sea.

I stuck the pistol—which he'd told me was a single-shot Deringer, whatever that was—in my bag, where I'd already stashed a box of bullets also courtesy of Mickey. The pistol did not come with instructions, and I hadn't thought it wise to reveal my ignorance, so I would have to figure it out by myself. One thing was certain: I wouldn't ask Anson's help.

The morning passed quickly and profitably, with the advent of a new client, a writer who was living in Golden Gate Park. He had hastily (not to mention untidily) written a book entitled *The Great San Francisco Quake,* and was in a fever to get it in the hands of a publisher as quickly as possible. He gave me an advance payment and promised a bonus if I produced the typed manuscript in three days. I told him I would try, and that I would make more rapid progress if he left me to it, rather than looking over my shoulder while I typed.

At one o'clock I hand-lettered a sign: NEW HOURS: NINE A.M. TO ONE P.M. CLOSED AFTERNOONS UNTIL FURTHER NOTICE. This I posted on the door. If I were to get anywhere with the Alice Investigation, I would need some time to myself.

I took my lunch—a hard-boiled egg and an apple—upstairs to

Alice's room. I had an idea that a woman who writes poetry would also have kept a journal, and that I would find it if I looked diligently enough. I munched as once again I went through her drawers. In my previous search for the keys, I hadn't seen anything like a journal or a diary, but there was always the chance I'd simply overlooked it. In my formerly mush-brained state I hadn't gone about anything very well.

The excellent quality of Alice's underthings distracted me. *Trousseau,* I thought. More evidence that there really had been a husband? Lace and ribbons, the finest, sheerest silks and cottons, all so delicate to the touch. I put aside the apple core, wiped my fingers on my skirt, and took up an exquisite camisole. It was of ecru silk and had the tiniest pleats down the front I'd ever seen, alternating with bands of peach-pink satin ribbon. A spinster would not buy such a garment for herself, would she? I would not buy it for myself, probably not even if I were putting together my own trousseau. It must have been dreadfully expensive, and there were many others that had cost as much.

Fremont, you are wasting time! I folded the camisole—which was like folding a cloud, it was that wispy—and returned it to the drawer. As I went meticulously through the remaining drawers of the lingerie chest, I tried not to think about Anson's proposal, but the trousseauish nature of Alice's belongings had brought it to the forefront of my mind.

It was interesting, to say the least, that I had not immediately refused him. The mind has its reasons, I suppose. Such as: Very likely Anson was right in thinking that he and I would work well together. Or, if I wanted to keep up my typewriting service, I doubted he would object. He had said more than once that my desire to work was one of the things he admired about me. Certainly it was not easy to find a man who would allow me to continue working; on the other hand, I had not thought that I would ever marry. . . .

Enough of that! The lingerie chest had been aptly named, for there was nothing but lingerie in it. I turned around, scanning the room and tapping my foot. Where next? I did not currently keep a journal, but when I had in the past, the notebook had resided on the table by my bed. The round table next to Alice's bed was covered with a crocheted cloth in the pineapple pattern, and on it sat an oil lamp with a rose-colored glass globe, a miniature brass clock that had wound down, a clear crystal water carafe and matching glass, and a heart-shaped silver box. I took the lid off the box; it held a single small key of the sort that might open a little chest or a tiny drawer. I put the key in my pocket, and as I did so I had an inspiration.

I have heard that people hide things beneath their mattresses. That would be a good place to hide a journal, or anything flat. I flipped back the crocheted spread and lifted the mattress with one hand while feeling underneath it with the other. No notebook, but there was certainly something under there. I hefted the mattress until I got one shoulder beneath it, and then I looked.

Money! Between the mattress and the covering of the bedsprings was a layer of paper currency in large denominations: twenties, fifties, and hundred-dollar bills. I hunched farther under the mattress to get a better look. Actually, there was more than one layer. There must have been thousands of dollars in Alice's bed!

I was appalled. "I have plenty of money in the house," Alice had said—what an understatement! So much money belonged in a bank. My father is a banker, and I cannot help having picked up an opinion or two from him. Banks are safe; mattresses are not. But what could I do? It was not my money.

"Oh, botheration!" I swore, letting the mattress down. I smoothed the spread and sat on the bed. I felt as if I were sitting on a powder keg. How could Alice *sleep* on it?

This discovery had not helped my main investigation in the least. It was just one more thing to worry about when I had enough already. I should put it out of my mind, not allow all that money to distract me.

I took the little key out of my pocket and studied it, then scruti-nized the room. Some dressing tables have tiny drawers, but Alice's did not; its drawers were deep, with no keyholes. The key would no doubt prove to be a red herring, like everything else I came across in this bothersome business. I should continue to look for the journal—or anything else that might tell me more about Alice and her putative husband—in an orderly manner, room by room, upstairs and then down. By my reasoning, the study should come last, because anything in there of significance to Alice's murder would most likely have been removed along with her body.

At about four o'clock in the afternoon the doorbell rang. Too early for Anson; I wondered who it might be. I hurried down from the guest bedroom, which I had just finished turning inside out with no result.

"Oh dear," I said involuntarily at the sight of a policeman in uniform on the front steps.

"I'm Stephenson, ma'am," he said, politely touching the brim of his hat.

"Yes, I remember you." I laced my fingers together—they were suddenly ice cold. "You may as well tell me quickly what I've done wrong now, and get it over with."

He looked over first one shoulder and then the other, up the street and down, before asking: "May I come in?"

I would have liked to decline but didn't see how I could. I stepped back from the door without saying yes or no, and Stephenson entered, politely removing his hat. After a brief hesitation, he went into my office and sat in the client's chair beside the desk. I sat in my usual place, which gave me a bit of much-needed confidence.

As Stephenson did not seem inclined to begin the conversation, I asked, "Do you have a rank, a title to go with Stephenson?"

He gave an aw-shucks grin, raising one shoulder. At that moment he looked painfully young. "They just call me the Rookie, because that's what I am. I guess you wonder what I'm doing here."

"Yes, but I would still like to know how properly to address you. *I* can't very well call you the Rookie."

"Oh, yeah, well, you can call me just plain Officer Stephenson, or you can call me Wish. My real name's Aloysius. Awful, isn't it?"

In spite of his uniform and my recently found fear of the police, I felt a smile play with my lips. "Wish. I like it. I shall call you Wish, then, unless Sergeant Franks is around. You may call me by my first name, which is Fremont."

"I remember, Miss Fremont."

"Not *Miss,* just Fremont."

"Fremont." He grinned, then immediately sobered. "If the sergeant knew I was here, he'd skin me alive. Get me thrown off the force, I guess."

"So why are you here, Wish?"

He ran a skinny finger inside his tight collar and craned his neck a bit before answering. "I'm on my own time, I just got off duty. It's like this. I believed you, Miss, I mean Fremont. You know, the other night, about your housemate."

I let out a long, deep breath with great relief, as if, without knowing, I'd been holding it ever since then. "Thank you, Wish."

"It's just the sergeant, I mean Sergeant Franks—there's other sergeants and so on that are different—he can be kinda hard. He takes against people sometimes, that's just how he is. Never can see any reason for him to do that, myself, but then I'm just the Rookie. It's not my place to apologize for him, but anyway, I do. You just mustn't tell him I did."

"Your apology is accepted, and you needn't worry about me saying anything to the sergeant. I fully intend never to see him again."

Wish rocked his lean body forward, rubbing the heels of his palms against his kneecaps. "Any new developments? About Alice Lasley, I mean?"

He had a good memory, this young man. I would have bet a penny to a pound that Franks could not recall her name. "No. It's very frustrating. I'm staying on in the house for now, in the hope that I may be able to find something here. So far, I've found nothing the least bit enlightening."

"How about you? Anybody bothering you?"

"No, and in a way that's worth remarking." I wondered how much I dared tell him. My instinct was to trust Wish Stephenson; in particular, I was vastly tempted to tell him about the money under the mattress, as that was for me a burdensome secret indeed. But I dared not. He might mistake my intention, interpret it as a bribe, report it to his sergeant. Then I would be in an even worse pickle!

"I don't quite take your meaning," Stephenson said.

I made a mental note of that educated turn of phrase. "Before Alice was killed, she often complained of hearing someone in the house, usually when I was not home. I didn't believe her, much to my later dismay. Alice was a nervous type, the kind who makes a fuss over nothing."

"Like the Boy Who Cried Wolf."

"Exactly. She also said she often felt as if someone were watching her, and I sometimes felt the same, but I thought it was my imagination. Now, since her death, this house has been perfectly peaceful."

"Sounds to me like whoever did it got what he wanted. Including her, dead."

The awful bluntness of his words made me shiver. "I suppose so. I just want to know who did it, and why."

Wish rose to his feet—a motion that he accomplished in a coltish manner, as if he were not entirely in control of his long arms and legs. "I'm sorry, Miss Jones, but Sergeant Franks was right about one thing. Unless we find a body, or the bones even, we can't do anything. How long do you plan to stay in this house?"

"I haven't decided. I'm still trying to find out if there are any relatives to take it over. It's difficult. Alice does not appear to have left records of any kind. They *must* be here. I just haven't found them yet."

"Well"—he put on his hat, giving a little tug at the brim to set it in place—"if I can be of any help, call the station and ask for me by my real name, Aloysius Stephenson. They'll think you're my mother because she's the only one calls me Aloysius. She calls the station a lot. I think it's mostly that she just likes to use the telephone."

I smiled. "That must be difficult for you."

"Yeah, it is. They tease me something terrible."

I saw Wish Stephenson out and closed the door with a smile still on my face. Wish: I could not have said why, but the nickname suited him. His brief visit had gone a long way toward restoring my faith in the police. As no doubt he had intended it should. Had he been sent? Or had he come, as he said, on his own?

I wondered if I would ever be able to trust people again.

For two days I typed in the mornings and searched the house—fruit-lessly—in the afternoons. The evenings I spent with Anson. He conducted himself circumspectly for the most part, but had flashes of impatience that were understandable. "Soon," I told him, "I will let you know my decision soon."

At around eleven on the morning of the third day, I finished *The Great San Francisco Quake*. It came out to one hundred and ten pages, short for a book, and not particularly well written. No doubt it would be a great success anyway, if, as the author hoped, it was the first on our disaster. I stacked the pages in a neat pile on the corner of my desk, then plunked a paperweight on top of them for good measure. The writer would be pleased and so was I—I wanted that bonus.

He came in due course, paid me the bonus, and left all smiles with a promise of more work to come. *Now what?* I thought, but I knew what. Dragging my heels, I went down the hall to the one room I had not yet searched: the study. I did not like to go in there. Every time I did, I saw Alice's body again, with the broad band of scarlet at her throat, grotesquely wavering in the lamplight.

I could not do it. Suddenly I was swamped by an overwhelming need to get out of Alice's house. Where I might go, what I might do, were not the issue; I just had to go.

Because it was a typically cool and foggy early summer day, I went to my room for the aubergine cape, and while I was there had an inspiration: I should practice shooting my new pistol!

The place I had in mind to do it would make a good outing. I put the pistol and a handful of bullets tied up in a handkerchief into my bag, then changed into my most comfortable shoes, for I would be doing a lot of walking. I tucked a wool scarf into my bag for good measure.

Alternately walking and streetcar-riding, I made my way to the northwest corner of the city, an area called Seacliff. There are a few grand houses here, but mostly it is wild. I kept walking north, looking for the path that would take me along the cliff's edge. I had been here once before, with Michael. With Golden Gate Park now so full of people, this was the only place I could think of where I might practice with my pistol safely and undisturbed.

Aha! I found the path, which led through cypress trees bent by the wind and choked with dense undergrowth, all full of greeny dark. It was, not to put too fine a point upon it, spooky. Quite a delicious sort of spookiness.

The ocean crashed on unseen rocks not far away. Droplets of thick mist bathed my face, and the wind whipped my hair. I paused to tie the wool scarf around my head. A foghorn gave out a low, hollow moan. The nearness of the sea sent a thrill rippling through me, and I quickened my steps.

I came out of the trees and a fog-shrouded vista opened up before me, all in shades of gray and silvery white. Oh, it was magnificent! The sea-smell alone transported me. If there is a God, then surely He lives in the ocean, not in the sky; surely those great rolling, foaming waves are the horses He rides, and He sleeps in the vasty deep amidst dreaming whales.

Exulting, I walked along the cliff's edge toward Land's End. The wind tore at me; I did not care. I let go my plan to practice with the pistol, for I could not be bothered with anything so mundane. Again and again the crashing surf sent its spray high into the air, higher than my head. Mile Rock was out there, nothing on it but a lighthouse. I could not see it for the fog, but I well remembered the sunny day when Michael, sailing his boat the *Katya,* had taken me near it. That was the day I first saw Michael Archer as a man, strong and in the fullness of his prime, not merely an elegant, rather bookish older neighbor.

The path was a narrow track, and perilous; it is a wonder I did not fall to my death that afternoon. Certainly I did not watch my step, because my mind and my heart were both too full. I do not believe in angels any more than I believe in God, but perhaps an angel was watching over me. I do not know; all I know is that at Land's End that June day I made a decision that shaped my life: I decided not to marry Anson Tyler.

It was not a clear-cut decision, of the sort where one says, *I have decided and so that is that.* No, it was more that I finally let myself think honestly about Michael. Yes, he had gone away, but he would return, and when he did, he would come to me. He had not written . . . and that disturbed me much more than it should have. I had felt angry with him . . . but the person I was most angry with was myself. I was angry with Michael because it was easier to be angry than to admit my true feelings for him. I was angry with myself for having those feelings: *I was in love with Michael Archer!*

There, the truth was out. And I owed Anson a debt of gratitude I could neither mention nor repay, because thinking about his proposal of marriage had forced me, at last, to acknowledge my love for Michael.

I stopped on the path and turned my face to the moisture-laden wind. I snatched off my scarf and the clasp that held my hair, letting the wind stream through it. I was completely alone, not another soul in sight. "I love Michael!" I shouted, and the wind bore my words away.

The foghorn moaned, a reminder that love is not all joy, it comes mixed with pain. For me the pain was that I knew Michael did not love me. He had loved once, deeply, a woman called Katya, for whom his boat was named. She was dead; he blamed himself; he would never love again.

I resumed my steps. My long hair streamed into my eyes and wrapped itself around my neck; I could not see, nevertheless I walked on, lost in my thoughts. Michael did care about me, as a friend, or perhaps—and this was rather humiliating—as a daughter. For he was some twenty years older than I, and while this difference in age was not a barrier to me where love is concerned, it was to him. True, he did not treat me like a child. Indeed he had always, from the very beginning, when I was more than a little green at being a woman on my own, treated me as an equal. I amused him. Sometimes I even seemed to provoke his admiration. But he did not love me.

When I reentered the greeny dark among the cypress trees, it no longer seemed deliciously spooky but rather somber; its somberness matched my mood. I wished I could regain those few moments of exultation, but they were gone. After a while, I realized it was all right, *I* was all right. I felt somehow clean inside. By admitting that I loved Michael, no matter how he might feel about me, I had achieved a kind of inner balance.

It is good when one is able to be honest with oneself.

I returned to Haight Street to find an old woman picking her way carefully down the front steps from my door. I hastened to help her, because she looked as if she could fall and break an ankle as easily as blink an eye.

"May I help you?" I asked.

She looked at me with eyes as black and inquisitive as a bird's. "Oh, it's you, isn't it? I almost didn't recognize you with your hair all down around your face."

"I'm Fremont Jones," I said, mentally bracing myself; cruel fate had given me a taste of self-honesty only to confront me once more with the necessity of lying to others. I was getting sick of this. "I'm Alice Lasley's housemate. I don't believe we've met?"

"No, we haven't, but that doesn't mean I don't know who you are. I've seen you going in and out. I thought at first Alice got you in to help with her aunt, but then I saw your sign. You're just a boarder, that right?"

"I rent two downstairs rooms from Alice," I said, thinking, *Aunt? What aunt?*

She pulled in her chin and rocked back on her heels, regarding me in a way that said *nosy neighbor*. Nosy neighbors know things; she could be useful to me. She could also be a liability. I was on my guard.

"In trade, are you?" she asked.

"No, what I offer is a service. As the sign says, a typewriting service. What may I do for you, Mrs.—?"

"Weeks. Miss Lola Weeks. I'm a maiden lady, just like poor Gertie."

"Poor Gertie." I have observed that repeating a person's words back to them in a certain tone will often draw them out.

"Gertrude Lasley, that child's aunt. Humph! Though she's not such a child no more, the way she gets herself all gussied up—"

"I beg your pardon, Miss Weeks, but you still have not told me how I may assist you. I assume you want some assistance, since you were at the door."

"Was no answer," she sniffed.

"That is because I was out."

"You the only one in the house can answer the door, is that it?"

"Something like that."

"I thought as much. Haven't seen Alice for a while, and I wondered if she's took sick. Wondered who was taking care of poor Gertie if the child was sick. Thought I'd inquire."

Even as I opened my mouth to speak, I had not the slightest idea what I was going to say.

⊰ 12 ⊱

Mens Sana in Corpore Sano, or Some Such Thing

"How kind of you to inquire!" I said brightly. "Have you known them long, then?" I took her arm and turned her away from the house. "You must allow me to accompany you to your door—we can talk as we walk."

"I've known Gertie for dog's years. Alice since she came here, let me see now, that was two years ago. Gertie first took sick not long after Alice moved in. I guess it was Providence, the girl being there to help out at just the right time and all."

"Yes, most providential. I must admit I don't know either of them very well. I happened upon Alice right after the earthquake—Oh! That reminds me: how did you do in the quake? I hope everything is all right at your house?"

Lola Weeks stepped into the street without looking, with me hanging on her arm and on her every word, as well. Fortunately we did not get run over. She gushed, "It was really the most unpleasant experience I have ever had in my life! I simply couldn't deal with it. My dear, I just got right out and left all the cleaning up to my house-keeper. I went over to Berkeley, to my sister's children. They're all grown up now and I must say they were really very kind, treated me like royalty, they did."

"How nice for you."

"I just came back a few days ago. Wanted to wait until everything was back to normal. The housekeeper sent word."

"You were very wise." We had reached the steps of a house across the street and one down from Alice's. She put her foot on the step and I let go her arm, ready to flee.

"I do pretty well," she said complacently.

"I've enjoyed our little chat," said I, walking backward. "It was so nice to have met you."

"Are you sure you won't come in for a cup of tea?"

"Not now, thank you." I stepped off the curb, waved, and turned away. "Perhaps another time."

"Oh, wait! You forgot to tell me how they are, Alice and Gertie!"

From the middle of the street I called over my shoulder: "They are both as well as can be expected!"

"Well!" said I, closing the front door with relief. My head was positively spinning.

I had assumed that the Haight was a neighborhood in which people kept their distance out of respect for one another's privacy, as often happens in cities. I based the assumption on the fact that none of the neighbors had come to see Alice; and while at first that had seemed odd to me, I'd gotten used to it. Now here was Lola Weeks.

I hadn't quite lied to her, but she would be back. Which meant my days—if not hours—in the house were numbered. I couldn't keep putting her off *ad infinitum*.

I puttered around, changing shoes for slippers, brushing my hair, checking what food there was for dinner, and so on, and all the while I was thinking, thinking, thinking.

If Alice had a husband, that nosy neighbor would have known. She would have said. Especially if something had gone wrong in the marriage—she would have spouted gossip of that nature, I was sure.

There was no husband. This large house belonged to the aunt, Gertrude Lasley.

Gertrude *Lasley,* Alice *Lasley* . . . When a woman marries she always takes her husband's name, *always.* I must say it has never seemed quite fair to me, but there it is. If one's surname were Smith or Brown—or even I daresay Jones—then one might marry and still have the same name. But Lasley? Not likely.

I stood in the middle of the formal parlor with the sherry decanter in one hand and two glasses, by their stems, in the other, and my mind was working like clockwork. It was all coming together. Yes. Yes, it was.

Mystery #1 solved: There never was a husband. Alice made him up out of some pathetic emotional need.

Mystery #2 solved: The house belonged to the aunt, which was how a librarian had afforded to live in it.

Mystery #3 solved: The aunt had liked milk, which was why the standard order was for two bottles.

Mystery #4 solved: The money hidden in Alice's bed properly belonged to the aunt. Well, maybe not; but anyway, my mind rushed on to—

Mystery #5: Where was the aunt? The aunt had been sick, the aunt was now . . . DEAD! And buried?

I almost dropped the decanter. And at that inopportune moment the doorbell rang. It was Anson on his nightly visit, I had expected him. I set the sherry and the glasses temporarily on the Monstrosity and opened the door.

"Good evening, Anson."

He kissed my cheek and presented me with a small bouquet of daisies. "Fremont. You are looking lovely tonight."

I didn't; I was rather a mess, since I had not changed clothes after my windblown walk. And I felt that I was accepting the flowers under false pretenses because of what I had to say to him. It wouldn't be easy, because I really did like Anson Tyler.

"I thought we might have a glass of sherry together," I said. "Do you mind the kitchen? The parlor is so stuffy, and my office is, well, an office."

"I enjoy being in the kitchen with you. The cozy atmosphere is as pleasant as your company."

Ouch! I thought. No, it wouldn't be easy.

Anson went on, "Is this the sherry here? Ah, yes, and the glasses. I'll bring them, shall I?"

I thanked him, and tried to compose my speech while I arranged the daisies in a water glass, not wanting to take the time to look for a vase. I plunked the flowers in the middle of the kitchen table and sat down.

Anson had poured the sherry. He picked up his glass. "I propose a toast: to us!"

"To friendship," I said carefully, touching glasses. I drank; he didn't. He raised his eyebrows and a wary look came into his eyes.

"I cannot marry you," I said, getting right to the point, "but I hope that we will continue to be friends."

He had gone very white, with a pinched look to his nostrils. "Friendship is not what I had in mind, Fremont."

"I know. You made me a gallant offer, but in all honesty I cannot accept it. On the other hand, I will be glad to be your friend, for life. People need friends too, Anson. I know I do. Will you still be a friend to me?"

He put down his glass untouched and turned his head away. A great silence reigned. I sipped at my sherry. All of a sudden I wanted to gulp the whole bottle, get disgracefully drunk, scream like a banshee, tear my hair so that he would look at me in horror and run from the house. Later he would realize how lucky he was, what a near escape he'd had.

But of course I just sat there, suffering his silent disapproval. My mother had been good at that, silent disapproval; eventually she would sigh, look at me, and say something like *Caroline, how could you?* And I would feel about two inches high.

Anson sighed. He looked at me. He said, "Fremont, why? Will you at least give me a reason?"

I felt about two inches high. My voice squeaked a bit, but I got it under control. He was a kind man, generous and considerate to me. I owed him this. "As man and wife we would not suit. I have something of a wild streak in me, Anson. Please do not misunderstand, it is not sexual—"

He looked horrified that I had uttered such a forbidden word.

"—but rather I am more unconventional than you realize. As a wife, I would be expected to settle down. *You* would expect that, and though I might try, I do not in all honesty think I would succeed. Believe me, you would be happier married to someone else."

"But, Fremont, I love you! I know I have not said it before, I only fully realized it over these past three days when it has been such agony waiting for you to say yes. I do, I *love* you!"

I hung my head. I never meant to hurt him. "I didn't know," I murmured into my lap. "I thought we were only discussing an arrangement between two people who care about each other, who might at best grow into love someday."

He went down on his knees beside me and looked up into my face. "It has already happened to me. I don't care if you're—what was that you said?—unconventional. We will . . . we will learn to accommodate each other. You must reconsider. Please, Fremont, marry me!"

Now I felt as low as a worm. I shook my head. "I had not wanted to tell you this. I am in love with someone else."

"So. You're going to marry *him,* then." Anson got up off his knees and slumped dejectedly into his chair.

I shook my head again. "He doesn't know how I feel, and I doubt I will ever tell him. I'm not going to marry anyone, Anson."

Another silence. I drank the rest of my sherry. Anson stared at the wall. When at last I could stand it no longer, I said, "I suppose, after what you've told me, we cannot even be friends now."

He glared at me, which I thought was quite a healthy sign. Then, in the manner of a mild man who has at last been pushed too far, he exploded. "How can you ask that of me? What do you think I'm made of? Doctors have feelings, you know, we just have to keep shoving them down all the time. I thought you were so understanding, so compassionate, so brave. . . . Ah, the hell with it!" He picked up his sherry and tossed it down in one astonishing go. "I'm leaving. Goodbye, Fremont Jones. I hope I never see you again!"

I sat sniveling for longer than I like to admit. Why does life have to be so complicated? Why do people have to go around falling in love with the wrong people when it can never possibly work out? How can we have such good intentions and still end up hurting one another?

After a while I got up and threw out the daisies. I hated to do it, but I couldn't stand their bright little faces looking at me, reminding me what an awful person I am. Then I did what I always do when I need to change my mood: I took a bath. What is it they say: a clean body makes a clean mind? No, it's *a healthy mind in a healthy body,* or something like that. Oh, well. At least the bath did its job, which was fortunate, because I had much work yet to do. It was entirely possible that I would not sleep at all.

Wearing the old once-viridian robe for both comfort and courage, I clenched my teeth and entered the study. In my pocket I had the small key I'd found in Alice's room. Somewhere in this room I would find something significant, I had to! There was nowhere else to look. I was no longer looking only for clues as to who had killed Alice, but also for clues about the aunt's fate. I had the most ghastly suspicion, nigh onto a conviction . . .

But no, I would not allow myself to entertain these thoughts, I would keep an open mind. Who knew what I might yet find?

The study had been put together by someone who had never intended to spend much time in it. The thick, handsome rug (which was no longer here) had given the room some dignity; without it, the hodgepodge nature of the furnishings stuck out like a sore thumb. The types of wood did not match, nor did the styles of the various pieces, nor were the colors of the upholstered furniture in harmony with one another. Indeed, it looked a good deal like a display room in a used-furniture store.

There were two large bookcases of dark wood, constructed in a utilitarian style, with glass-fronted shelves filled with books. There was a small desk of pale fruitwood in more or less a Queen Anne style, rather pretty, rather useless if one were serious about desks. Pulled up to the desk, a walnut chair with a padded seat and back (faded green), and straight legs that were a bad match for the desk's curving lines. Three more chairs that had the look of side chairs from long-gone dining sets were placed randomly against the walls. In front of the window sat a drum table that might have been a squat companion to the Monstrosity in the hall—it was ringed about with hideously elaborate carving and sat on three splayed pedestal legs ending in clawed feet. To either side of the drum table were two shabby overstuffed chairs, one deep pink brocade, the other mouse-gray plush, with crocheted antimacassars pinned on to cover the worn patches. One of those sword-leafed palms, the kind that never really flourishes nor ever gives up and dies, took up an entire corner. A few undistinguished paintings in dull frames hung on the walls where someone had decided something was needed.

I began by looking behind the paintings; I also examined their backs. It would have been nice to find a hidden safe, but of course I didn't, nor anything stuck to the backs of the paintings. Next I opened each drawer of the desk. None were locked. None contained anything at all—in other words, someone had cleaned out the desk. Once I would have thought Alice's murderers had done it, but now I was not so sure.

On top of the drum table was a collection of knickknacks, among them a wooden chest shaped like a small casket. *Aha!* I thought, pouncing. But the little key did not fit its lock. It was unlocked anyhow, and contained the sort of things one picks up idly, such as a badly tarnished silver button in the shape of an acorn, a lovely blue bird feather, and other items not worth attention.

This was really most odd. Alice had been a passable poet. Where were her poems? Not in her bedroom, and this was the only other place. With a sigh I began to go through the bookshelves, looking for thin volumes either untitled or with titles written by hand. I scanned along with such impatience that my vision blurred and I gave myself the beginnings of a headache. I didn't really want Alice's poems, I wanted a journal. I would have settled for a cache of family papers, most particularly a will. A family Bible with a genealogy in the front would have been welcome, too. *Where were these things?*

I closed a glass panel with such force that the pane rattled. Some Sherlock Holmes I made! I was getting absolutely *nowhere,* and time was running out. I needed to think about this, if I could get my mind to work. I stomped over to the mouse-colored chair and collapsed into it, half sitting and half lying in the most deplorable posture.

If I'd been sitting up properly I never would have noticed the keyhole. Keyhole*s,* plural. They were cunningly concealed among all the ugly carving around the drum table. Scarcely daring to believe my eyes, I reached out one finger and inserted its tip into what I thought was a keyhole. It also felt like one. I took the tiny key from my pocket and tried it, holding my breath. It fitted; the key turned, clicked, and unlocked a drawer shaped like a pie wedge.

There were six such drawers around the table and they were deep. The one key unlocked them all. Only one drawer had anything in it; I might have wished for more, but with the way things had been going I was more than satisfied. I had found Gertrude Lasley's bankbooks.

She'd had five accounts in five different banks: Crocker's, Wells Fargo, the Bank of California, the First National Bank of San Francisco, and one I'd never heard of, Bay Western. The Wells Fargo account showed the most activity, with both deposits and withdrawals made on a regular basis. The others showed only deposits paid in at regular intervals several months apart. The Bay Western account was the smallest, containing only a little over five thousand dollars when it was closed out by one withdrawal of the entire amount on May 15, 1906. Good timing on someone's part, and I thought I knew whose. I also thought I knew where a good portion of that five thousand dollars was at this very minute. If I were to go up and count it, I would know how much Alice had spent. I could even guess what she'd spent it on: clothes. Who knew how much of the regular withdrawals from the Wells Fargo account, doubtless the household account, had gone the same way?

I went out into the dark hall and to my rooms, using the faint street light that fell through the uncurtained office window to guide me. *Tick-tock, tick-tock,* went the grandfather clock. At the moment its sound was not companionable but emphasized my aloneness.

Where did I put it? I cursed the addle-brained state in which I'd spent my first days in this house. Finally I found it rolled up in one of my old petticoats, along with the large blue jewel: the lace-trimmed nightcap that had been forgotten in the corner of a drawer upstairs.

Gertrude Lasley's nightcap, I was certain. I held it in my hands and sat on my bed with my eyes closed, as if waiting for this bit of un-washed cloth to tell me its secrets.

I felt awful to suspect that sweet little Alice had slowly poisoned her aunt Gertrude, but such a suspicion was unavoidable. Sweet little Alice had also been manipulative and cunning. She was one of those people who can appear to sit and do nothing, while actually pulling invisible strings that make others dance around her. I should know, I'd been a principal dancer.

I had quickly learned that the sisterly feelings I'd had at first for Alice could not last, but I'd never thought her capable of actual mal-ice. She was so good at acting the victim, while in reality she was a villainess! There were poisons in the garden shed. I did not know much about poisons, but I had heard that rat poison contains arsenic, and arsenic given in sufficient amounts on a regular basis will produce a long decline and finally death.

I wondered when Lola Weeks had last seen Gertrude Lasley. It didn't really matter; what mattered was that Lola thought she was still alive, which meant that Alice, for some reason, had not tried to pass off her aunt's death as natural. I supposed the earthquake had intervened. . . . Or, because of the date the bank account was closed, perhaps . . .

I jerked and my eyes flew open. I'd heard sounds at the front door. I am blessed (or cursed) with exceptionally keen hearing, yet I had to strain to make it out again. There it was, a metallic sort of scrabbling. Someone was trying the lock.

There was no time to think, only to act. I fumbled under the pillow on my bed and got the pistol. It wasn't loaded, but it was still a deterrent. I toed off my slippers so that I might move silently in bare feet. Keeping close to the wall (although anyone who might look through the bay window would easily see me), I crept into the front hall. The sounds had ceased, but my vigilance did not. Whoever it was would now go to the back door, and so did I.

Standing in the kitchen, I braced my feet wide apart and held the pistol with both hands, arms stiff, as I have seen done in stage plays. My breath came rapid and shallow. I could see a vague outline of a human head through the sheer curtain at the back door's window. I heard him try, and try again, to open the lock. I knew that I was afraid, but I did not feel afraid, I felt excruciatingly alert.

Not knowing that I was going to do it, I heard myself scream: "Go away! I have a gun and I will use it!"

❧ 13 ❧

A Most Frustrating Kind of Hide-and-Seek

"I repeat," I yelled, moving closer, "get away from this house or I will fire my gun right through the door!"

The silhouetted head simply faded away without a sound. I stood rigid as a catatonic for long enough to make my elbows ache, then slowly I lowered the pistol. I put it in the pocket of my robe, opened the back door, and peered out. Anyone could have remained hidden in the shadowy yard. All my bravado was spent; nevertheless, I made myself go down the steps in my bare feet with my right hand on the pistol in my pocket. Crinkling through the scrubby grass, I made a circuit of the house. I poked into the bushes. The street side was better lit, the street itself deserted. The erstwhile intruder had gone.

On reentering the house I began to shake all over. I felt freezing cold—not just because of my bare feet but on account of some sort of delayed reaction. I could not even think of getting warm until I'd checked through all the rooms; stealthy as this person was, he could have slipped in through the back door while I was walking around outside.

He had not. I was quite alone, with no confidence that I would remain that way for long. I poked up the fire in the stove and made a fresh pot of coffee, though it was the middle of the night. Gradually, warmed by the stove and the drink, I stopped shaking.

I could not stay in this house for even one more day. I didn't dare. I hope I am not given to paranoia, but it did seem that I was in danger from all sides. The nosy neighbor, Lola Weeks, was more than likely to appear on the doorstep again, asking after Alice and Gertrude Lasley, neither of whom I could produce. She might very well get suspicious and report me to the police—a thought not to be borne.

I considered the young police officer, Wish Stephenson. I was inclined to trust him, but my natural inclination is to trust people, and where has that got me? "Into this mess," I muttered. Even if Stephenson were trustworthy and took my side, he was only the Rookie. The detestable Sergeant Franks would run over the two of us like a steamroller. So much for that idea.

I was certain now that Alice's murderers had taken those keys I could not find, and that one of them had used the keys just now in an attempt to get back into the house. Therefore, whatever they had been looking for they had not found; they must have come here for a reason other than, or in addition to, murdering Alice. My mind whirled unproductively: What did they want, why had they killed her, and was there a connection to what Alice had done to her aunt?

"Fudge!" I said, banging my coffee mug down for emphasis. The grandfather clock struck 2 A.M. Dawn these days came early, around five. I felt excruciatingly frustrated at the thought of leaving this house with so much unanswered. On the other hand, it seemed eminently wise to escape at the first opportunity.

I must work quickly. I turned out all the lights in the house as if I had gone to bed. Then I returned to the study. I had broken off my examination of the bookshelves too soon; those poems and possibly a journal should be there somewhere. Alice was too vain by nature to have discarded them.

I had all but given up the search when it occurred to me that sometimes people hide documents and letters and such among the pages of books. I happened to be standing in front of a shelf that had, at my eye level, a tripartite volume of the romantic poetry of Byron, Keats, and Shelley. I pushed up the glass panel and took it in hand. Riffling through the pages was not especially helpful, in fact it was distinctly unhelpful in that I had an urge to sit down in the middle of the floor and start reading (I am particularly suscepti- ble to *La Belle Dame Sans Merci*). Resisting that urge, I held the volume upside down by its front and back covers—a terrible way to treat a book!—and shook it. Aha! Several single sheets of paper rained out.

I picked one up at random and read:

> *Awaken me, my ruddy love,*
> *As dawn awakes the morning,*
> *And 'pon my lips your kisses drop*
> *Like new day's dew aborning.*

"Aborning?" It went on in that vein. Sounded like Alice, all right. This poem was handwritten and I thought I recognized the penman- ship as well as the style. "Ruddy love"—if I were still puzzling over her husband, I'd have pounced upon that description as a likely indi- cator that he was a redheaded man. Perhaps he was, perhaps he did exist and was her partner in the crime of poisoning the aunt, and perhaps Alice really had been looking for him when I'd found her. The hell of it was that now I'd probably never know.

I continued to shake out books, and when I'd been through them all I'd found forty-three poems, including the twenty I'd typed for her the previous year. I got tears in my eyes; silly, maybe, but what had happened to her, as well as what she likely had done, seemed a terrible waste of humanity.

Still, I had not found a journal or any of the family records I'd hoped for, and time had run out. I left the bankbooks where I'd found them, locked all the pie-shaped drawers, and put their key in the box that resembled a little coffin. An appropriate resting place for it. Then I gathered up Alice's poems. I had decided to keep them.

What I would do with them I had no idea; publish them, some-day, in a volume titled something like *Love Poems of a Slain Mad Murderess*? I giggled insanely at the thought—this night of much ten-sion and no sleep had me deranged. Nobody would want to publish, much less read, anything so lurid; some people say our society is depraved, but surely we are not *that* depraved yet!

As I dressed in the half-light of coming dawn, I realized I was lightheaded and jangly-nerved. Nevertheless my mind clicked along smartly. Before leaving the house I drowned the fire in the stove, then wrote a note to the milkman:

We are going away. Please cancel our order until further notice.

I signed it *A.L.* I put it under an empty milk bottle by the back door as I left that way, scurrying around the far corner of the house and down Haight Street on the lookout for a cab.

Damn and double damn! ("Fudge" had quite outlived its usefulness, considering the gravity of my situation.) The guard on duty at the Presidio gate was none other than Private James Albright. I'd had the cab driver drop me half a block away, thinking that somehow I might sneak in without attracting attention, but now I realized that would not be possible. I strode purposefully forward, ignoring the way Al-bright's eyebrows rose and his jaw hardened at the sight of me.

"Good morning, Private," I said. "I have come to retrieve the Maxwell from the garage. There is an emergency in which the auto and I are both needed. I trust you have no problem with that?"

"No problem, Miss Jones," he said stiffly, saluting.

My cheeks burned as I passed through. It was a long hike from the gate to the garages, and I was huffing like a steam engine by the time I got there. If the auto refused to start up, I would have a hissy-fit of major proportions.

"Come on, Max, I need you, start for me," I crooned, cranking. It was really ridiculous how fond I had grown of this automobile—I had actually missed it, and it seemed to have named itself inside my head while we'd been apart.

Perhaps Max was as glad to see me as vice versa, for "he" started and we chugged off. Private Albright stood in the road as we approached, but I did not slow down, rather waved with false gaiety, and at the last moment he stepped aside. Actually I was rather glad he was on duty—at least he could not follow me this time.

The sky was grayish and overcast as Max and I returned to Haight Street. The sun had not yet risen, the streets of San Francisco were quiet except for the auto's steady chugging. I planned to be out of Alice's house by full daylight. I did not park on the street but drove around back and bumped into the yard, out of the neighbors' sight.

In my haste, the clumsiness that had accompanied my forgetful period some weeks ago returned—with worse results. I had not really hurt myself back then; now, I did. With my arms full of clothes, I tripped going down the steps and turned my left ankle. It hurt like the dickens, but I ignored it. Limping, I nevertheless finished loading my possessions in record time. Last of all, I took down my FREMONT JONES TYPEWRITING SERVICES sign and pasted in its place another that I'd hand-lettered on cardboard: CLOSED FOR RELOCATION. SORRY FOR THE INCONVENIENCE, FREMONT JONES. Then I limped out the back, locked the door for the final time, and made my getaway.

Unfortunately, it was not an entirely clean getaway: as I crossed Ashbury Street, Mickey Morelock flagged me down. I did not want to stop but felt I should, on account of his having been so kind as to get me the pistol.

"What's all this, pretty lady?" he asked, putting a foot on Max's dashboard. "Don't tell me you're leaving us!"

"Not exactly. It is only that my living arrangements did not turn out to be quite what I'd hoped, so I am moving on."

He cocked his large head. "Got something better, didja?"

"Well, no. I expect I shall be living in Golden Gate Park for a while—assuming there's a tent available." Suddenly the enormity of my situation burst in on me—no home, *again,* and no office, which meant no income—and I felt quite deflated. "I honestly am not quite certain what I will do."

"Tell you what. It's early yet, but I got the coffee made. Whyn't you park that auto over here where we can keep an eye on it—say, what's that you got there?" He leaned over, peering across me at the passenger seat.

"It's a typewriter. I have a business, a typewriting service, if I can only find a place to set up again."

"Oho! So you're smart as well as pretty. I shoulda known, shoulda known." He winked and smiled, and I smiled in return. He continued, "Like I was saying, whyn't you park where we can keep an eye on your stuff and tell ole Mick all about it? Who knows, maybe I can help."

Probably the last thing in the world I needed at the moment was more coffee, but Mickey's warm-hearted Irish manner, so reminiscent of Mrs. O'Leary, was irresistible. There was no one else around other than Mickey and me, so I felt safe. "All right," I agreed.

I parked the auto and got out, forgetting about my ankle. A blinding pain shot up my leg, all the way through my body and up into my head. I staggered and would have fallen without Mickey's brawny arm suddenly coming around me.

"Hey, you okay?" he asked. I allowed myself to rest for a moment against his comfortable bulk.

"I'm quite all right," I lied, pulling back. He frowned but did not question me further. I gritted my teeth and without much of a limp made it to a stool near the huge sheet of metal that was Mickey's cooking surface.

"Here ya go." Mickey handed me a steaming mug of coffee, then turned away, bending over so that his ample backside was almost in my face. He looked so comical that I, feeling suddenly quite giddy, could barely restrain myself from laughing. Rummaging around, he mumbled, "Now let's just see what we've got here. . . . Yeah. That'll do, that'll do the trick." He straightened up with a covered pan in hand. "Last night's leftovers—corned beef hash. How about I fry us up some? It'll only take a minute."

"Thank you, that would be lovely."

My ankle hurt so much that I didn't see how I could eat, but I did. Not only that, I enjoyed it. Mickey was really an excellent cook. I engaged him in conversation about the restaurant he'd lost in the earthquake, his plans for its rebuilding, and so on.

After a while Mickey said, "Now looky here, you got me to talking all about myself, when this was supposed to be about how I could help you out."

I felt so warm and cozy, replete with good food, that I really did not want to think about my problems, much less talk about them. I demurred: "You're very kind, but I expect I can work things out."

"What kinda things?"

I laughed. "Oh, the usual. Where to live, where to have an office so that I can earn my livelihood. Little things like that."

Mickey nodded sagely. "Things like that, I can help. I know lotsa people, got plenty o' contacts. Do anything in the world for ole Mick, they would, or so they tells me."

I believed him, but I didn't say anything. I was fresh out of hope.

"So what's it to be, pretty lady? You want I should find you a coupla rooms, a nice apartment maybe?" He wrinkled his brow, and a calculating look came into his eyes. "Typewriting service, you said. That means you'd want to be near the business district, on the beaten track like they say."

"Ideally, yes. But, Mickey, I must tell you the truth: I haven't much money." I knew that rents had gone sky high overnight.

He waved my remark away with a big hand. "On Fillmore, that's where you wanna be, that's where the best business is going on these days. Think you could come up with a deposit on a coupla days' notice?"

"As I said, if it's not too large."

He winked. "Don't worry your pretty head about that. You just give me about a week and I'll see what I can do."

I was virtually certain that he would never find anything I could afford, but I said, "I would be most grateful." Then I got to my feet, gingerly, because a few customers were straggling in.

Mickey called out over his shoulder, "Be with ya in a minute!" Then he placed a hand on my arm. "Where can I reach you?"

"I expect I'll be in the park. Considering its crowded state, it would be easiest for me to contact you when a week has gone by. Now you must let me pay you for that excellent breakfast."

"Nope, that was on me. My pleasure."

"I can't—"

"Yeah, you can. But one thing before you go, pretty lady. I don't even know your name."

Amazingly enough, that was true. I'd never told him, yet I felt as if I'd known Mickey Morelock for years. "Fremont Jones," I said.

"Fremont, huh?" He gave my arm a squeeze before removing his hand. He winked again and leaned toward me confidentially. "Any relation?"

I grinned—this man knew the history of his state. "Yes. Fremont was my mother's maiden name. John Charles Frémont was her cousin."

"Well, fancy that! See ya later then, Fremont Jones."

My ankle had ballooned up to thrice its normal size. It looked positively grotesque. I had removed my shoe and doubted I could get it on again.

"Well," said the nurse at the aid station in Golden Gate Park, "I've found a tent for you, but we have to do something about that ankle. For sure you have to stay off it."

I wished Bartlett were here. This nurse was named Annie Fuchs, and I had never met her before. She was young, certainly not older than I, but I had to assume she knew her business. I said testily, "I can't very well stay off it. I have to unload my things."

"Don't worry about that," said Annie, sitting opposite me and taking my foot into her lap. "We have plenty of volunteers around here to do it for you. Let's hope your ankle isn't broken. Can you move your toes?"

I moved them, nearly passing out from the pain.

"Um-hm. How did you say this happened?"

"I tripped coming down the steps with my arms full. I just turned my ankle, that's all. I can't imagine why it hurts so much."

"You stay here and keep that leg elevated." She propped my foot on the chair she vacated, then slipped a rolled blanket underneath it. "It's probably only a sprain, but I think the doctor should take a look."

"No, please!" I yelped. "I really would rather not have a doctor."

The nurse looked at me strangely. "Why not?"

Why not, indeed? Because the doctor might turn out to be Anson Tyler, and he was about the last person I wanted to see in my semi-helpless state. But I couldn't tell her that, so I shrugged. "I just don't much like doctors."

She smiled. "A lot of people feel that way, but there is nothing to be afraid of. Anyway—even if you can walk on it, which I doubt—I can't take the responsibility of letting you go to your tent until a doctor has examined that ankle. Be back in a minute."

Luck was with me: the doctor who came was not Anson but another whom I'd driven and knew slightly, an older man called Dr. Stuart. He manipulated my foot, pronounced the ankle unbroken, and told me not to put my weight on it for twenty-four hours, after which he would examine me again. He gave me a supply of pills for pain—by that time I was so glad to have them that I did not even ask what drug they contained—and summoned two brawny young men to carry me to my assigned tent. I suffered the indignity in silence; bantering words came to mind but I could not utter them on account of biting my lip so hard against the pain.

Nurse Annie Fuchs had perhaps been taking lessons in generalship from Bartlett, for she stood in my tent barking orders: put this here, that there, bring more pillows, set her down carefully, and so on. While I had been with the doctor, she had found someone to unload the Maxwell. The canvas cot that I was placed upon by the brawnies seemed as comfortable as any bed.

I sighed, "Thank you."

"Get her a pitcher of water," Annie barked.

"Ay, ay, sir," said one brawny, who soon returned with it.

"Thank you so much," I said again, with tears in my eyes for their kindness, "all of you."

The young men left, and so did the older volunteer, who had been carrying my things into the tent, but the nurse stayed. She supervised my swallowing of two pills, fluffed pillows behind my head and beneath my injured foot, covered me with a blanket, and said to me: "Rest."

I did; but not until I had made sure that my bag was where I could reach it and my pistol was inside. My last thought as I fell asleep was: *I must learn how to shoot that thing!*

I dreamed I was playing a game of hide-and-seek, but this game was not fun. I was child-sized in a world built for giants; instead of finding a secure hiding place I kept getting lost in this huge castle full of long corridors with many tall doors and long windows whose white curtains billowed out in a most threatening manner. I did not want to play anymore, I did not want to be "it." The scene shifted, in the abrupt manner of dreams, but I was no better off. Now I was outdoors in a maze of dark hedges higher than my head, and I could not get out no matter which way I went. Outside the maze there were people laughing and talking, making a happy sort of racket, but I could not find my way to them. I ran and ran, until finally I realized that I was dreaming and managed to wake myself up.

For a panicky moment I did not know where I was, but my ankle soon reminded me. Sunshine glowed through the canvas walls of my tent, turning them quite golden. Golden, for Golden Gate Park. The happy racket I'd heard in the dream came from all the people outside, thousands of them. "There is safety in numbers," I murmured, and went back to sleep.

When I next woke, it was to the feel of a cool hand on my brow and a voice that said, "Hmmm." I opened my eyes to the prune face of Nurse Bartlett, and smiled up at her.

"I am glad to see you," I said.

"Wish I could say the same to you, but under the circumstances, I can't. What happened, Fremont?"

I struggled up on my elbows; the effect of the pain pills had worn off, and I winced. "The short version is that I decided I could no longer stay at Alice's house, and in the process of moving out I fell and turned my ankle."

"Turned? More like halfway wrenched your foot off from the looks of it. You must have been running to fall that hard."

"I suppose I was." I leaned back against the pillows. Sitting up was too much of an effort.

Bartlett clucked, shaking her head, and poured a glass of water, which she handed me with two more pills. "Take these. I'd like to hear the long version but it will have to be another time. There's someone outside who wants to see you."

"I don't really—" I started to say, but too late. Bartlett had already pulled back the tent flap and Anson, ducking his head, came in. He looked formidably grave.

"I have already seen a doctor," I said.

He sniffed; I remembered that pinched look around the nostrils too well. "When I saw your name on the list of patients, I felt I would be derelict in my duty if I failed to look in on you."

"I understood that you never wanted to see me again."

A faint flush chased along his cheekbones. "Words said in anger are seldom meant once the anger fades. You should know that, Fremont. Now I will examine your ankle."

"I really wish that you would not be nice to me," I said through clenched teeth. Actually, his present idea of "nice" was quite painful, as he manipulated my foot. Anything else I might have said vanished clean out of my head.

"I am not being nice, I am being what I am, a doctor. Fremont, at what time did this accident occur?"

"About five o'clock this morning," I said, gasping. Then he released my foot; the relief was tremendous. "Why?"

"I'm concerned about the amount of swelling. If I had been on duty when you came in, I would have insisted that this ankle be packed in ice. Perhaps it isn't too late, although it's almost noon. How did it happen?"

"I tripped and fell, that's all," I grumbled. I did not like the idea of having my foot iced; I had been enjoying the cozy warmth of my tent.

"Was there anyone else involved?"

"You mean did anybody push me? Of course not!"

"You cannot have forgotten that I know your situation. Were you, perhaps, running from someone?"

"No, Anson, I was only clumsy. I did this all by myself. And before you ask, Alice did not return, and I simply felt it was time for me to leave her house."

He left my foot and came closer to my head. The old kindness beamed from his eyes. "Other than the ankle, you are in no distress of any kind?"

"No," I said shortly. I did not want to become involved with him again, and if that meant I must be somewhat rude, I would.

He put his fingers on my wrist.

"I don't need my pulse taken."

"Sssh."

I sighed. The pills were making me groggy again.

"Your heart is beating strongly and evenly."

"I could have told you that."

"I am only doing my business."

"You are not my doctor. Dr. Stuart is."

"We share patients here. The treatment is free, so who is the doctor of whom does not matter."

"It does to me. Anson, you and I will be far better off to stay out of each other's way. I would not have come here if I'd had any other place to go."

"Actually, I'm glad you're here, Fremont. I presume you have some medication for pain? Ah, yes, I see." He picked up the small brown bottle of pills. "This will do. When did you last take your medication?"

"Bartlett gave it to me right before you came in, and it's working. I believe my eyes are beginning to cross."

He chuckled. "You haven't lost your sense of humor. That's good. All right, I'll leave you now, but I'm sending a nurse with ice to pack around your foot. We'll see if we can't get that swelling down."

I stood the ice until nightfall, by which time I had decided it was less a cure than a vengeful torture of Anson's devising. I hopped to the tent flap and distributed melting ice chips outside under cover of darkness. Fear of fire loomed large in this encampment; we were each allowed one oil lamp, which lit the tent's interior well but did not penetrate beyond. Many people had gone to sleep with the setting sun, and their tents were dark; but many more glowed like Chinese lanterns of peculiar size and shape. The tents were only about six feet apart. Mine was on an outside row so that the forest that occupies so much of Golden

Gate Park loomed on one side. Ordinarily, because of my liking for privacy, I would have been glad of this location; as it was, I would have preferred to be somewhere in the middle.

Standing on my right foot and clutching the canvas for balance, I gazed into the dark wood. By listening hard, I was able to separate the dull hum of conversation in the tents from other night sounds: the soft whir of summer insects, a far-off cry of sea gulls, the sighing of the wind in the trees, and once, a liquid spill of notes from a songbird who did not want to tuck its head under its wing and go to sleep. I leaned down rather precariously to pick up the basin that had held the ice and went back inside.

Much to my dismay, there was no way to secure the tent flap. I supposed it did not matter, as canvas would offer little resistance to a determined intruder, but I would have felt more at ease had I been able to lace or button myself in. The safety-in-numbers theory did not seem to work for me at night. I told myself there was nothing to fear, the intruders—the murderers—would not have followed me here. They were not interested in me, they would only be glad that I had vacated Alice's house. But it did no good; I was still afraid.

I decided to take no more pain pills. That damn ice torture had kept me awake all afternoon in spite of the pills, and now I longed for sleep. I hopped back to the canvas cot and arranged the pillows so that I was more or less sitting up, with my left leg propped higher than the right. The sprained ankle looked disgusting; in fact, I didn't have what you could properly call an ankle anymore. I smiled grimly as I compared the injured one to the other. I have heard that men are attracted to ankles; in this condition I might perhaps attract half a man.

Both feet were bare and, with the night chill in the tent, uncomfortably cold. I covered them with the blanket and wondered what I could do to keep myself awake. My book of Nathaniel Hawthorne's tales lay on the floor by the cot; I'd tried to read during the afternoon but had not been able to concentrate. I took it up again. Then I bent down once more and rummaged in my bag for the pistol.

The feel of the metal in my hand gave me false confidence—I supposed false confidence was better than none. I turned the weapon in my hand, admiring the way the silver surface gleamed in the lamplight. Perhaps I should load a bullet into it, perhaps I could fire if need be without having practiced. No, particularly in my rather fuzzy state of mind, I should settle for the false confidence, plus the likelihood (no matter how remote) that the sight of the pistol would discourage an intruder. After all, it had worked last night and I'd only yelled through the door.

But, Fremont, how many times can you bluff? I have often observed that the small voice we all have inside has a most perverse way of telling us things we do not want to hear. Fortunately, when I so choose, I am quite good at ignoring it.

With the pistol in my lap, I began to read . . . nodded . . .

I snapped my head up and my eyes flew open in the same instant. There was a scratching sound at the flap of my tent, and a low voice I could scarcely hear over the terrified thumping of my heart. I seized the pistol, forgot my ankle, and was up from the cot in a flash with my weapon held stiff-armed in front of me. I opened my mouth to say, "Go away," but no sound came out.

Someone drew back the tent flap; I saw a black triangle of night. A dark suit of clothes, a dark head, bent down.

"Don't come any closer or I'll shoot!" My voice miraculously reappeared, so harsh and threatening that I did not recognize it as mine.

⫷ 14 ⫸

What Fools These Mortals Be!

"Fremont, no!" The intruder was through the flap. Hands went up in front of his face, palms out.

I was panting, sweat pouring down my neck from pain I felt but distantly, as if it were someone else's pain; my elbows were locked, my fingers clamped upon the gun like a vise. There was something familiar about this man, but in my terror I shouted again, "Stay back!"

"Good God, Fremont, what's happened to you? Don't you know me?"

I shook my head. I blinked in disbelief. I lowered my arms. "Michael? *Michael?*"

"I see you were expecting someone else," he said dryly, folding his arms across his chest. He stayed where he was, on the other side of the tent.

"I, ah, no. You should have told me you were going to shave off your beard. You look different." Actually he had a very nice chin, with a depression like a thumbprint in the middle of it. He had kept his dark sideburns.

"I tried to tell you about the beard, among other things. I wrote you a letter, which was eventually returned to me stamped *Addressee Unknown*. That letter's round trip from Monterey and back took three whole weeks. Can you imagine how I felt? Fremont, I have been concerned about you. And now I'm even more concerned. What are you doing with that—" He crossed the floor and attempted to take the pistol from me, but I held onto it like a leech. I believe I was in some sort of shock.

"It is a single-shot Deringer, with one *r,* not an imitation," I said haughtily, raising my chin.

He withdrew his hand. He was looking at me curiously, his changeable eyes very blue at present. "I see. So you know all about it."

"Of course." I took a step sideways; my ankle was killing me but I'd be damned before I'd let him know it. "Have a seat, Michael. I must admit I've wondered if I would ever see you again. I am sure you found my note."

Michael sat on the folding chair, and I lowered myself to the side of the cot. I would have liked to put my leg up but did not want him to see my grotesque ankle. Suddenly I was all too aware of my appearance—I must look disreputable, I had not attended to myself or looked in a mirror all day.

"What note?" he asked.

"The note I left on the bed in your room at the Presidio." Which said that I'd gone to Alice's, so how—

"There was no note on my bed. I've been looking all over San Francisco for you for two days. If I hadn't by chance recognized my Maxwell tonight at the edge of the park, by that aid station, I would not have found you yet. This was the first place I came looking for you yesterday, and you were not here then."

"That is true. I was not here yesterday." I put the pistol down next to me on the cot. My ankle was throbbing so much I could hardly think. Was it possible I hadn't written that note but had only meant to? I wasn't quite myself then, but—

"Fremont, never mind." Michael's voice went soft. He leaned over and took my hand, brought it to his lips, kissed my knuckles.

I looked at the hand he'd kissed as if it belonged to someone else. I felt decidedly odd. My head was spinning.

"Let us start over," he said. "I'm just glad I found you. I don't care why you left or where you've been or any of that. Someday I might like to know, but not now. I'd like to tell you what was in that letter, if I may, and something even better that has come up since then."

"Pray, do." I took back my hand and interlaced my fingers in my lap. He was smiling at me, and while I had been rather fond of his beard, I liked his clean-shaven face even better. I tried to smile back, but in truth I was feeling so very unwell that I could not be sure I succeeded.

"I wrote to you of my discoveries, such as: the Monterey Peninsula, which has other little towns on it in addition to Monterey, is even more beautiful than San Francisco."

"No." I shook my head and immediately wished I hadn't. "That is not possible. Nothing is better than here."

"I did not say better, I said more beautiful, in terms of the natural surroundings. If you go up into the hills and look down on Monterey Bay, you will see the sweetest curve of white sand, the bluest water, not to mention an abundance of fish in the water. Monterey is now primarily a fishing port, Fremont, but the town has a distinguished past. Your famous ancestor, and his wife, who I hear was quite a character in her own right—"

"Jessie?" I perked up a bit. "The family did not approve of her. They would never talk about her and I've always been curious."

"The colonel and Jessie Frémont lived in Monterey when California was voted into the Union. There are people still living there now who remember them. I wanted you to come down, Fremont, that is why I wrote."

"All this is in the letter I did not get?" The tent was going around and around. I stiffened my backbone, clenched my hands tightly, and forced my eyes open as wide as they would go.

"Yes, but I suppose it's just as well because in the meantime I visited Carmel-by-the-Sea, an artists' colony on the other side of a great hill with a magnificent forest. That's an even better place for you, because there are writers in Carmel—novelists, poets, journalists. Where there are writers, you may be sure a typewriting service will flourish."

"I live here," I pointed out. This conversation was not making a lot of sense to me.

"We will come back to San Francisco in time. This would be a temporary thing, while the earthquake repairs are going on. The Monterey Peninsula is a kind of haven, Fremont, and I've wanted—one might even say needed—to find a haven, for longer than I like to think about." Michael reached into my lap and took both my hands, the hands I had been gripping as if somehow they were keeping me upright. He said earnestly, "Come with me—"

I am loath to admit it, but I fainted dead away.

I do not know how long I was unconscious, but for certain it was too long, for when I came around there was another man in my tent. It was Anson Tyler, and he was arguing with Michael in low tones but a heated manner. I could not quite make out what they were saying.

I leaned up on one elbow, and a nurse pushed me back down. There was a veritable crowd in my tent. "What happened?" I whispered to the nurse. Her name tag said *Rose,* but whether that was her first or last name was anyone's guess.

"You must have overexerted yourself, and as a result you fainted. Dr. Tyler is furious with your visitor for allowing this to happen. Are you feeling better? Would you like a drink of water?"

"Yes, please." The water tasted good. "This is my fault, not my visitor's. For one thing, I did not have any supper. I couldn't go get it, and no one came by, so I thought I'd just wait until breakfast. Then, ah, when my friend came I didn't want him to see my ugly ankle, you know how it is . . ." I said in a chummy fashion, though I was not entirely sure why I suddenly felt a desperate need to have this Rose on my side.

"Well, no wonder!" she said. "I think I could rustle up a sandwich for you. Would you like that?"

I was rather torn; the thought of food made my stomach rumble, but I did not particularly want to be left alone with Michael and Anson and their disagreement. My stomach won. "Yes, I would like that, if it isn't too much trouble."

"Not a bit." Rose left, and both men came over to my bedside, keeping a wary distance between them.

"I wish you had told me you are not well," said Michael grimly. "I wish you had told me a few other things, too."

"What other—"

"Fremont," Anson interrupted, "it's very important for you to have peace and quiet and plenty of rest at this time. I have filled Mr. Archer in on the particulars and he has agreed to leave."

"But—"

Michael turned to Anson. "You have no objection if I kiss her goodbye?"

What in the world was going on?

Anson took a step back. Michael bent down and kissed me on the lips, the first time he had ever done so, and he did it tenderly, but I could hardly enjoy it under the circumstances.

I grasped his lapel and whispered, "Michael, please—"

He placed his finger on my lips. There was an odd expression, almost of sadness, on his face. He murmured, "It's all right, Fremont. I understand." Then, so that only I could see, he drew something silver—my Deringer—part way out of his pocket and murmured again, "I'm taking this with me because you are in no condition to have it."

"I beg your pardon!" I said loudly, suddenly irate.

Michael paid no attention. He turned his back on me, and a second later he was gone.

"What did you say to him?" I demanded of Anson, fiercely.

Anson picked up the little brown bottle and peered inside. "When did you last take these?"

"I don't remember, and you haven't answered my question."

"If you had taken them on schedule, you'd be getting the proper rest and would not have had this recent problem."

"If *you* had not prescribed that foot-torture-by-ice, I would have had quite enough rest this afternoon! As it was, I was extremely uncomfortable, and for nothing! Just look at my ankle! The swelling hasn't gone down one single bit, and it hurts like hell, and, and—" My fury spent itself and left me speechless.

Anson chuckled in his mellifluous manner. He tucked the blanket around my feet and brought it up to my waist, where he tucked it in again. I glared at him. He said, "You do have a temper. Now, if the storm is over, I suggest you take your medication and get a good night's rest. Dr. Stuart will see you in the morning."

I took the pills obediently. I no longer cared if Jack the Ripper himself were to materialize on this side of the world, in my very tent. At the mention of Dr. Stuart, though, I wondered: "Anson, what are you doing here at this hour of the night? And by the way, what time *is* it?"

He consulted the watch that he kept in his vest pocket. "It's a few minutes before ten. I was here to deliver a baby, which I did, not long before you fainted. I was at the aid station, washing up, when your friend came running like a bat out of hell and yelling that you needed attention. I must say, he is a rather impetuous fellow."

At that moment, Nurse Rose came through the tent flap with my sandwich, and I decided I would rather eat than have anything more to do with Anson. I had never felt so depleted, physically and emotionally, in my entire life. Not to mention confused.

The pills did their job: I slept.

I was awake the next morning long before any nurse came around, and in spite of the sandwich I'd consumed at a late hour, I was starving. I lay on the cot, listening, as the encampment came to life around me, and tried to remember what had happened the night before. Normally my memory is quite reliable; I can reconstruct a conversation word for word long after it has taken place. Yet the inner workings of my mind now gave me only vague flickering pictures, like a moving picture show of remarkably poor quality. Perhaps if I kept trying the words might come through.

Michael had come, and he no longer had a beard. I smiled, seeing that clearly enough. *Most likely,* I thought, *he grew the beard in connection with his spy activities, for with it he looked older and slightly sinister.* In a clean-shaven state Michael was devastatingly handsome. Yet no matter how hard I tried, I could not recall a single word of what he'd said to me. I did recall how I'd felt: glad to see him, and also quite ill.

"Oh, no!" I exclaimed. I thought, *How humiliating, I fainted!* I, Fremont Jones, who have always believed that females cause themselves to faint for frivolous reasons. Certainly in the future I should not be so quick to judge.

I realized that my face was burning, and raised a hand to it. My skin felt hot, which I put down to embarrassing thoughts, and went on trying to reconstruct events. Anson had been in my tent when I woke out of the faint, and he and Michael had not got along. He'd made Michael leave. Michael had kissed my lips. . . .

I thought about that for a long time, wondering why the memory of the kiss did not please me more. If only I could remember what he'd *said!* There had been more times than I could count when Michael had kissed my forehead—or my cheek, but usually the forehead, in a fatherly manner—but I had greatly desired a kiss on the lips instead.

Finally I recalled asking Anson exactly what he'd said to Michael. He had not given me a straight answer, which was really very irritating. I decided it did not matter, since all I had to do was ask Michael when he came again.

"Oh, damnation!" I had just called up a vision of Michael taking my pistol, its silver winking at me from his pocket. He had no right to do that, none at all! Just wait until I saw him again, I would give him a piece of my mind and no mistake.

The trouble was that Michael did not come back. Dr. Stuart did, and pronounced me healing nicely although for two days I ran a slight temperature. Anson came and checked my ankle as if he did not trust his colleague, which I pointed out was rather rude of him; but he only smiled and acted kind, which made me more uncomfortable than the ankle.

By midweek I was itching to get out and go somewhere. I hobbled to the aid station and found Nurse Bartlett on duty. I asked her how long I was to be an invalid.

She felt my forehead and placed her thin fingers along my cheek. "Your fever's gone," she said.

"Yes," I agreed. I extended my foot for her inspection. "The swelling has also gone down. As you see, I was able to work a stocking over it this morning."

"Hmmm. Well, I never thought you'd be content to sit around in your tent for very long. Tell you what, Fremont, I'll bind your ankle to give it support. You can watch and learn how to do it yourself."

"A splendid idea."

"But mind you," she said as she removed the stocking I'd worked so hard to get on, "you must take it slowly. The longer you put weight on this injured joint, the more it will swell, and you could be right back where you started."

"I understand." I watched her work, admiring the deftness with which she wrapped a narrow strip of white cloth under my instep and around and around the ankle itself. "It feels stronger already."

"Um-hm. Today you can walk around here a bit, get an idea how much activity you can take. You must not push it, Fremont. Strength of will, which you have in abundance, cannot force an injury to heal faster. Though I admit the lack of it seems to be a deterrent to healing. Now stand up and see if I made the binding too tight."

I stood, shifting my weight and testing. "It really is much better. I will take all your cautions to heart, Mrs. Bartlett. Thank you."

"You are entirely welcome."

On my way out of the treatment tent I paused. "Mrs. Bartlett, do you remember Michael Archer?"

"To be sure, I do. What about him?"

"I don't suppose you've seen him around here lately, have you?"

"No, I can't say that I have. I thought you told me he'd gone someplace out of the city."

"He did, but he came back. He visited me and I was expecting him to come again. I was thinking—" I bit my lip, as it had begun to quiver.

"Come on, Fremont, out with it. This is old Bartlett here, you can talk to me."

"Well, I was thinking that perhaps Michael had been here and Dr. Tyler had turned him away. They had a kind of disagreement in my tent, though I'm not sure what about."

"Oh ho ho! The plot thickens."

I blushed. "I do not believe it had anything to do with what your tone implies."

Bartlett came up and put her hand on my shoulder. She had a mischievous expression peeking out from among all those wrinkles.

"For such an intelligent young woman, you are remarkably blind in some areas, Fremont."

I frowned at her, unable to think of a rejoinder.

"At any rate, I haven't seen Michael Archer, but if I do you may be sure I won't let Dr. Tyler run him off. Now get along with you."

"Thanks again."

I moved at first cautiously, and then more confidently, out among the people who were always milling about the place. I felt rather as if I were at a summer camp for adults; in spite of our dire situation, there was a kind of holiday atmosphere. I supposed it came of having no jobs to go to at present.

I decided that I might as well make sure that Max was where I had left him. He was, and there was a note tied to his steering wheel.

How interesting! I recognized Michael Archer's handwriting as I untied it and pried open the envelope.

Dear Fremont, If I know you, and I believe I do, as soon as you are well enough you will want to be out and about, and that will bring you to the auto. I want you to keep the Maxwell, my dear. Consider it a gift in recognition of the coming event. With every wish for your happiness, Michael.

My heart leapt. "Max," I said, "you are mine!" I climbed in and sat there, touching the wheel and the controls and smoothing the leather of the seats with an affection now tinged by pride of owner-ship. I did not have the ignition key with me, or I would immediately have gone for a spin.

I decided to go back to my tent and get it, and along the way my delight subsided enough that I began to think about the exact wording of Michael's note. I stopped where I was, oblivious to the jostling I got from someone in a hurry to get past me, and read the note again. What "coming event"? And while I was certainly glad that Michael wished for my happiness, it did seem an odd way to end. "He has probably gone away again," I muttered; "the note has that ring to it."

I went out for a spin anyway, putting aside a twinge of unhappiness. As I have so often observed, Michael's ways are mysterious and to try to fathom them is usually a waste of time.

Another day passed. I got stronger and more curious. Michael still did not come, nor had I seen Anson for two days. I drove by Mickey's Kitchen, intending to inquire if he had found me a place—not that I had any real hope in that direction—but he was not there. The surly woman was there instead, so I drove on by.

I needed distraction. I begged a folding card table from a nurse and dragged it behind me to my tent, where I set it up outside with my typewriter upon it and my FREMONT JONES TYPEWRITING SERVICES sign propped in front. Within an hour I was typing letters as people dictated them to me. I did not take any pay for my services. In the camp at Golden Gate Park we gave to one another freely, that was the way of it, and I wished it could be possible always to live thus.

On the fifth day after my accident I was very restless indeed. I wanted to see Michael, if he was still in town. I wanted my pistol back. Anson was quite getting on my nerves with his solicitousness, which was of a degree that seemed more than professional. Though I had plenty of typing business—in fact, if I had been charging I would have done very well—it did not hold my attention. My thoughts began to stray in a discomfiting direction, toward the mysteries I'd left unsolved in the house on Haight Street.

I had an idea what Alice had done with her aunt; and if, as I suspected, it was Alice herself who had cleaned out all the records one might expect to find in any house, I thought I knew what she had done with them, too. One thing often leads to another; therefore, if I could find the aunt's body and the records, I might have a clue or two as to who had killed Alice. Who knew, I might even find Alice's body, and then, perhaps, I could set about clearing my reputation with the police.

I am by nature much concerned with the concept of justice, and to my way of thinking, there had been a lot of injustices perpetrated recently that in one way or another involved me. My reputation with the police was the least of them, though Sergeant Franks's attitude still rankled. There was the business of the Sorensons and all the contraband, now disappeared—I had given up on that, except for a nagging feeling that I should get rid of the blue jewel in a beneficent manner, if I could ever figure out how. Then there was Alice, about whom I still felt guilt no matter how hard I tried not to, no matter if she had poisoned her aunt. And finally there was the aunt herself, Gertrude Lasley, whom I had never known but whose nightcap I still had in my possession, burning a hole in my suitcase as it were. Yes, I should certainly like to see some justice done!

By the dinner hour I had convinced myself that I must return to Alice's house under cover of night. I was quite excited, and in a positive frame of mind; in other words, I was more myself than I had been in some time. As I worked out the details of my plan, the location of my tent so near the trees seemed, for the first time, fortuitous. In the twilight I moved Max to a side street that I could reach by walking (or rather, sneaking) through the wood. It would have been best if I could have walked to Haight Street, which after all was not far, but my still healing ankle could not take it.

Waiting was difficult. Time after time I peered out from my tent flap only to find lights still burning in nearby tents. I kept checking my pocket watch, the one Bartlett had given me eons ago, chafing at the delay as minutes and then hours went by. Finally, with all but two tents dark, I judged it was time to dress.

First I bound my ankle twice over, flexing my leg to be sure the binding was neither too loose nor too tight. Then, with loving care, I removed the black silk outfit Meiling had given me from the tissue paper in which I'd stored it. The trousers glided over my nether limbs like a silken second skin; likewise, the tunic slithered sleekly down my body. I would not bother to hide these exotic garments under my aubergine cape tonight; if I performed as well as I intended, I would not be seen. I tucked Alice's keys, with Max's key attached, into the waistband of my trousers. I blew out the lamp, and in darkness, by feel, wrapped the black scarf around my face so that only my eyes showed. There! I had once more transformed myself into a dangerous Ninja. Suppressing a giggle, I stole out into the black night.

I parked on Belvedere, a block away from Alice's house, and flitted from the auto like a silent shadow. There was no fog tonight but also no moon. For a moment I wished we were still without electricity so that there would be no streetlights, but only for a moment, because I would not have gone back to the discomforts of those post-earthquake weeks for anything.

I approached Alice's house from the rear, as it faced onto Haight. I wished I could run but could not on account of my ankle; what I lacked in speed I had to make up in stealth. Slowly, stealthily, I crept across the yard until I reached the garden shed. Equally stealthily, I opened its door. The shed was old, not used much anymore, and the door hinges creaked—not a loud creak, but it might as well have been the crack of a rifle for the effect it had on my heart.

I waited, breathing shallowly through the silk scarf, blood pounding in my ears. The creaking door had not attracted any attention. I slipped into the shed. What I wanted here was to ascertain that the various poisons I had previously seen were still in place on the shelves.

Owing to the darkness of the interior, I could see nothing. It was black as pitch in here. I took a step forward and my shinbone collided with something hard—I almost cried out, for though I hadn't hit my ankle it was the same leg. My ankle made its objections known in a literally nauseating manner. I should have known better than to come on this expedition without a lantern. I sighed, which sounded rather eerie in the small enclosed space, and felt behind me for the door. I could do nothing in this darkness, I might as well proceed to the house.

Carefully, carefully I pushed open the door and felt quite satisfied with myself when I edged through sideways without a single creak. Sometimes it is advantageous to be slim.

My self-satisfaction did not last long. No sooner was I all the way out of the shed than an arm came from out of nowhere around my neck. I could not even cry out, though I tried. Someone was strangling me!

❧ 15 ❧

A Fire in the Heart

He was very strong. One of Alice's murderers had me, I was sure of it, and I was done for. I squirmed and kicked and flailed my arms about and all the while my windpipe was being crushed. *Better crushed than slit,* I thought, kicking harder. The next thing I knew, he had flung me to the ground, pinning me down with a knee in my stomach. The dastardly creature brought his face inches from mine as he ripped off my scarf.

I said, "Michael!" while he said, "Fremont!" and then we both said in unison, "What the *hell* do you think you're doing?"

I laughed (rather more hysterically than I might have wished), until Michael said, "Hush! We don't want anyone to hear us," and put his hand over my mouth. Whereupon I bit him, not very hard.

"You are a devilish creature," he hissed, pulling me to my feet.

"So are you," I said.

He drew me over to the steps where we were in shadow, and gave me a quick up-and-down glance. "Where did you get those clothes? I thought you were a Ninja, even though we have never had the Ninja in San Francisco as far as I know."

"I suppose you have encountered Ninjas in your Japanese escapades?"

"Not firsthand," he said evasively. "Looking more closely, I see your costume only superficially resembles that of a Ninja. Your gar-

ments are not Japanese but Chinese. They are Meiling's, is that it? You
and she have been up to something?"

"You have it right in one, Watson. Congratulations. Now, why
don't you tell me what you're doing here?"

"I am watching this house. What are *you* doing here? Damnation!
I've just remembered your injury." He touched my leg lightly. "How
is your ankle? Did I hurt you, Fremont, was I too rough?"

Involuntarily I rubbed my throat, which was a little sore. "I shall
live, though I confess the opposite thought did enter my mind for a
few seconds."

Michael wrapped both his arms around me and pressed my head to
his chest, murmuring near my ear, "I'm so very sorry. I would not
hurt you for all the world, Fremont Jones."

It was quite worth a little scare to be able to stand within his arms
and hear his heart beating beneath my cheek. His mouth brushed my
ear. But just as I felt a desire to snuggle, indeed to purr like a cat, he
dropped his arms and moved away, saying, "I beg your pardon. Momentarily, I forgot. Please forgive me. Now, I will take you home.
Are you still in the park?"

"Michael!" I said loudly. Previously we had talked in a near
whisper.

Predictably he shushed me.

"I am not going back to the park," I said sotto voce, "I'm going
to do what I came for, and as long as you're here you may as well help.
I suggest we go inside and I'll explain. And may I remind you, you
owe me an explanation or two." Or three, or four, but who was
counting?

"I won't pretend that I have never broken into a building, but in
this case I would rather not."

"You don't have to. I have the keys."

We went up the back steps. Michael said, "Sometimes, Holmes,
you amaze me."

"Elementary, my dear Watson." I unlocked the door.

The house had already acquired a musty, lifeless smell, though I had been gone from it less than a week. I had drawn all the shades before leaving, so I did not have to do that, but I preferred anyway not to turn on the electric lights.

"Wait here," I said. "The kitchen is as good a place as any to talk, but I want to fetch an oil lamp."

"Any sort of light will attract attention. We can talk in the dark. I rather like talking to you in the dark."

I forbore to inquire what he meant by that. "If I am correct, it probably will not matter if we turn on every light in the house, but still I would rather not. Anyway I cannot do what I came here to do without some kind of illumination, so as I said: wait here."

"I'm coming with you."

Really! I strode out into the hall, observing that there was a strange feeling in returning to a place where one has lived when it is empty of habitation, even if one had not particularly enjoyed one's time there. I went on through to the rooms that had been mine, because the lamp that I kept on the desk was relatively light and easy to carry.

Michael was a cool character, I gave him that. He said not a word, made not a single sound at the mess in the rooms I'd occupied: pictures pulled off the walls, desk drawers thrown on the floor, and so on. As for me, my stomach fell down to the vicinity of my feet, which was ridiculous considering that I had expected no less. The handmade relocation sign I'd stuck in the window had been pulled down and torn to pieces—and somehow that bothered me most of all. However, the lamp was not broken. I lit it with a slightly shaking hand, forgetting that I was making a spectacle of myself in the curtainless bay window.

Michael was more alert. He put his arm around my waist and walked me backward into the hall. I turned, holding the lamp high. The poor Monstrosity had its mirror cracked and its drawers pulled out and their hapless contents scattered around . . . which was nothing compared to the parlor. That fussy furniture was not my style, nevertheless I could not help feeling sorry for the chairs and the camelback sofa with their stuffing ripped out. The panel door in the tall-case clock stood open; the wretched beasts had yanked its chains out, and its pendulum was nowhere to be seen.

I mused, "I wonder what they thought they might find in the clock?"

"None of this is a surprise to you, is it, Holmes?"

"I'm afraid not."

Michael started up the stairs, but I called him back. "There is no need to go up there. We will only find more of the same."

"The woman who lives here—I understand she is a friend of yours—she may be there, she may be hurt. If not worse."

"Michael, the worst has already happened. Come into the kitchen and I will tell you everything."

We sat at the kitchen table and I told him all I knew about the occupants of this unfortunate house. Actually it did not take much time in the telling, for there were more questions than facts. Michael rubbed thoughtfully at the sides of his chin, in the way that he used to rub the silver streaks in his beard.

"It seems you have a talent for making connections with odd people," he said. "I wonder how you do it."

"Probably that is what attracted me to you."

He grinned. "What now? How do you wish to proceed?"

"I'll tell you, but first I would like to know why you were watching this house, and how you knew that Alice was my friend—if one could call her that."

"I had a letter from Meiling, forwarded to me from Monterey. I received it today. She told me about the dead things left on the doorstep here. That continued to bother her, and she was concerned about you. I knew, of course, that you were no longer living here but thought it would be wise to do a little surveillance. I was too late, obviously. I'm glad you got out before this happened."

"So am I." I thought for a moment. "You know, Michael, I think it's quite possible that whoever did this deliberately waited until I was gone."

"Do you have any idea at all who is responsible?"

"I really do not."

"Would you care to take your best guess?"

"Holmes never guesses," I said with mock scorn; then I planted my elbow on the table and chin in hand. "What I believe is that Alice put her aunt's body in the basement. When I was looking for Alice herself I searched the basement, which is really more like a big crawl-space. I didn't find anything, but I did smell something rotten. In thinking over these things recently, I wondered why I hadn't seen any sort of storage space beneath the house."

"You mean like a wine cellar, something of that sort?"

"I had more in mind a root cellar, but to each his own. I entered the basement from an outside door, but if there is a separate storage room, there should be an entry to it from the inside."

"Shall we look?"

"By all means."

"After you, Holmes," said Michael with a flourish.

I rather spoiled the Sherlockian effect by limping; my ankle had begun to hurt like blazes. I limped across the kitchen, through the butler's pantry into the storage pantry beyond. I had not spent much time—really, not *any* time—in this pantry, because when Alice was alive we could not cook, and when cooking was permitted again, I had bought my own food day by day. Over my shoulder, I asked Michael to bring the lamp.

As I had suspected, there was a trapdoor cut into the floor of the storage pantry. This trapdoor had been skillfully installed, fitting its space so tightly as to be almost invisible unless one were looking for it. I took the lamp while Michael lifted the door back on its hinges. A faintly rotten odor spread from the hole like a miasma. We looked at each other. "I will go down," Michael said.

"Not without me!" With lamp in hand I followed him, far more easily than I could have done had I been wearing skirts.

The room at the base of the steps was a kind of root cellar, claustrophobically small, and undoubtedly the source of the rotten odor I had smelled in the basement a couple of weeks earlier, though it was fainter now. I said, "I don't understand. How is this possible?"

Michael knelt to one side of a heap of human bones that lay at the bottom of the narrow flight of steps. Indeed, I had just stepped over them. He bent down, poking and sniffing like a bloodhound. "Lye," he said. "Alice Lasley was a clever woman. She used lye to dissolve her aunt's flesh. Otherwise the stench of the decaying body would have been so overwhelming that neither she nor you nor anyone else could have lived in the house for months. Not many people know that lye is corrosive enough to eat away human flesh."

"She was a librarian, she would have looked it up, you may be certain." I crouched beside Michael, curiosity having overcome my initial repugnance. "I think we may assume, from the distribution of the bones in a huddled shape, that Alice simply pushed her aunt down the steps and left her as she lay. Ugh!" I shuddered. "I can almost see her standing at the top of those steps and raining lye down upon the poor woman's body."

"Yes, undoubtedly that is what happened. Look, Fremont: there is still a bit of hair attached to the skull. Not enough to be used for identification, but because arsenic concentrates in the hair and fingernails it will be proof of poisoning." Michael stood. "Let us go back up and decide how to proceed."

"Just a moment, please. I am looking for—yes, I believe this is it. Michael, will you carry it upstairs?"

I had found a pasteboard box containing a lot of papers, which Michael placed on the kitchen table and began immediately to sort through. "In the study there are some bankbooks we should add to this material," I said, and went to get them. As I'd hoped, the intrud-

ers—thinking they were already done with this room—had not included it in their recent raid.

"Here they are," I said upon my return. I sat down rather heavily.
My ankle was throbbing; I did not need to look to know it was
swollen. I would have liked to put my foot up, but chose not to. By
way of distracting myself from the pain, I untied the black scarf from
around my neck, where it had been hanging like a cowl all this time. I
also undid the knot I'd made of my hair and shook it out, and I
stretched, as one does in the morning.

Michael glanced over at me. "If I may say so, Fremont, you look
rather fetching in Meiling's clothes."

I grinned. "Thank you. I wish I could dress this way all the time."

"Think of the scandal!" said Michael with a wink.

"It would be delicious!" Our moment of levity passed. "I suppose
this may sound cold-blooded, but I'm glad we found Alice's aunt."

"Let us hope no one will question the fact that the bones are
Gertrude Lasley's. Assuming that tests show the presence of arsenic in
the hair, Alice would be indicted—if she were alive. I confess I haven't
a clue how to find Alice's body."

"Nor have I, and I have nearly broken my brain on the subject. Is
there a journal, or a diary, in that box?"

"Yes." Michael passed a cloth-bound notebook over to me; it was
not Alice's but Gertrude Lasley's. I had wanted to find something like
this for so long, yet for now I was too tired to read it.

"Watson," I said, "would you think it awful of me if I asked you
to take that box back to your room at the Presidio? That is, if you are
going to be in San Francisco for a while longer. Your note sounded a
bit as if you might be leaving—Oh, how could I have been so stupid! I
haven't thanked you for giving me Max. Thank you, very much indeed."

He looked up and smiled. "Max?"

I smiled too. "Yes, Max. He and I have become friends of a sort, and while I know it isn't proper for me to accept such a valuable gift—"

"Say no more. Of course you must accept it. You and the Maxwell are well known around town, you are quite the pair, as I heard often while I was trying to locate you." He looked away; in the dim lamplight it was hard to tell, but I believed that his face flushed slightly. "Besides, in the circumstances, a substantial gift is not necessarily inappropriate. It is not as if I cannot afford it, and you deserve the best, Fremont."

"I'm grateful, but a little confused. What circumstances are you talking about?"

"Why, your marriage, of course."

"Marriage?" My eyes opened wide. *"Marriage?"*

"Yes. Your, ah, fiancé—Dr. Tyler, is it?—told me. The night you fainted. That was a horrible time; I don't like to think about it even now." Michael busied himself once more in the papers.

I grabbed his hand. "Stop that! Look at me. Just exactly what did Anson Tyler tell you?"

"You must understand, I put the man under some pressure or else he would not have said anything. If you are trying to keep it a secret at present, I'll stay mum."

I gritted my teeth. "It's not a secret, it's not—oh, just get on with it, tell me what he said."

"All right. When Dr. Tyler was examining you in your unconscious state, I thought his manner too familiar, and I made objection. He told me in no uncertain terms not to interfere, which of course I did not take kindly and said so. But then he took me aside and explained how well the two of you had come to know one another, how well you worked together—Fremont, spare me relating all the details." Michael ran his hand over his head, as he does when he feels frustrated. "Suffice it to say, when he told me he had asked you to marry him, I got the picture, and of course I agreed to bow out."

I dropped Michael's hand, leapt up, and planted both fists on my hips. I would have liked to stride back and forth if I could have done so without limping. "Let me be sure I have this straight. Anson told you that he had asked me to marry him, and so you just . . . just more or less handed me over with your blessing? As if the two of you had made some sort of deal concerning me, is that it?"

"How could I interfere? The man seems suitable. He's a doctor, so he earns a decent livelihood; then there is the fact that he is closer to your own age. I admit I've had some bad moments since, particularly when I realized that you and I are not likely to be able to have many more nights like this, playing at Watson and Holmes, though tonight we are hardly *playing*. . . ." Michael's voice petered out.

My brain was boiling so fiercely that for a while it did not connect with my mouth. When it did, my voice came out soft but lethal. I leaned down into Michael's face and said: "You . . . are . . . not . . . my . . . father!"

"Fremont, I assure you, my feelings for you are not in the least fatherly."

Some part of me registered that statement as significant, but my anger carried me on. "I am not a piece of chattel to be handed from one *man* to another."

Michael drew his head back. "I never thought you were."

"Oh, yes, you did. Anson told you he had asked me to marry him, and that was that, as far as you were concerned. What he did not tell you was that *I refused him*."

Michael's eyebrows rose; his face brightened. "You refused?"

"I refused, and you needn't look so relieved, Michael Archer. You are not off the hook, not by a long chalk. I thought we were such great friends, I thought—God help me—that sometimes you even regarded me as an equal, and yet you could treat me this way. I am appalled."

"I do regard you as an equal, Fremont. In fact, sometimes it seems

to me that you are my better half. That is, if I had a half. If you know
what I mean."

I had never before heard Michael sound confused or seen him
flustered. It gave me some satisfaction. I stood to my full height again.
"You and Anson discussed me, you decided things between the two of
you about my very life—not while my back was turned, or while I
was in another room—that would have been bad enough—but while I
was lying unconscious! Man to man, right, Michael? Man to man!"

"We did it in a gentlemanly fashion, if that's what you're trying to
say."

"Your gentlemanly fashions make me sick," I spat. "Did it never
once occur to you that it was *my* life, that you should have talked to
me? Don't bother to answer that. I already know the answer. Now I
am going home, if you can call a tent *home.*" I half stalked, half limped
to the door. "And don't expect me to give Max back to you, even if I
did obtain him under false circumstances. I love that auto, and I'm
keeping him!"

"Fremont, wait." Michael rushed up and put his hand on my arm.
I shook it off, glaring at him. He said, "You are right. Everything you
said is right. I apologize."

"I expect someday I may forgive you, but for now I have had quite
enough of men. All men, including you. Will you take that box to the
Presidio?"

"I will. Surely we must continue to work together on this? I
gather from what you said earlier that we cannot report what we've
found tonight until it can be done in such a way that you will not be
implicated."

"You gather correctly," I said stiffly. "And I believe I will take
Gertrude Lasley's diary, if you would be good enough to hand it to
me."

He did, asking, "Did you drive here tonight?"

I nodded, desperate to escape.

"Would you like an escort, or do you prefer to be on your own, Fremont?"

"I most definitely prefer to be on my own," I said, thinking, *For the rest of my life!*

I slept for a few hours, though not very well. I could not get comfortable, what with various new aches and pains from Michael's throwing me to the ground, in addition to an exacerbated ankle injury. My mind would not be still, either. Awake or asleep, my thoughts and dreams kept going around and around and getting nowhere. The unyielding surface of the canvas cot was not a bit of help. I wondered crossly how soldiers could be expected to win wars when they had to sleep on these things.

Eventually I got up, not much later than my usual rising hour. *Oh, fine,* I thought as I looked into the mirror: I had a great purple bruise around my neck where Michael had almost strangled me. I inspected my abdomen and found another bruise there (from his knee), and more on my elbows. I could not very well go into the communal shower with other women looking like this. What a bother! I should have to wear a blouse with a high collar, and I do not particularly like high collars—although they are fashionable, they are also uncomfortable, as is so often the case. Fashion is really quite perverse.

My ankle was as swollen as it had been two days previously. Bartlett had warned me not to overdo; obviously I had overdone. It hurt a good deal. I bound it up, muttering, "Since you are attached to me, ankle, you had best get used to a little discomfort and stop puffing yourself up at the slightest provocation."

The anger I'd felt at Michael had grown during the night and generalized to my whole situation. That anger drove me like an engine. Only action would bring relief. I went *stomp, limp, stomp, limp, stomp, limp* through the encampment, got into the Maxwell, and chugged over to Mickey's Kitchen. One cannot live on anger alone, I needed food to fuel me. I parked, and joined a straggly line over which Mickey himself presided.

"Fremont Jones, you're a sight for sore eyes," he said, pouring a mug of coffee without my having to ask.

"I'll have a plate of hashed potatoes too, if you please," I said, "and a rasher of bacon."

"That's the way! I like to see a gal with an appetite." He dished up and said in a lower tone as he handed me a plate, "I got some good news for ya. Coupla furnished rooms available in a big house on Fillmore that they've just divided up into apartments. Be ready day after tomorra!"

I went around and stood next to Mickey as he continued to serve. "I wish I thought I could afford the rent. How much will it be?"

Mickey closed one eye in an exaggerated wink. "I fixed it, said it was for a friend." And then he named a figure that I could barely afford.

I decided barely was close enough. "Thank you. I will take it. Shall I give you a deposit, or will you direct me to the landlord?"

"I vouched for you so's you could skip the deposit. All you gotta do is go on over there, day after tomorra like I said, and he'll come around for the first month's rent. Name's Smythe, with a *y*. Hold on a minute, I got the address wrote on a piece a paper. Yeah, here it is."

I managed to take the greasy slip of paper even though my hands were full, and thanked Mickey again. *Things are looking up,* I thought as I returned to Max. I ate my breakfast sitting in the auto, and then drove on to Anson Tyler's house on Valencia Street.

The transaction with Mickey, and his good food, had damped my anger but not put it out. As I drove toward the Mission District it flared up again, then settled down to burn with a steady flame that I was getting used to. It gave me energy, and purpose, and I decided that I could do worse than to go around an angry person. Of course, I should take care not to be entirely offensive.

I knew that Anson saw patients in the morning hours, so I did not knock but went on in. A bell over his door rang, reminding me (sadly) of the one I'd had on my own office door. I went into the waiting room and sat down. It was empty. I had scarcely arranged my skirts when Anson, wearing a crisp white coat, came from across the hall. He looked quite the professional.

"Fremont! I did not expect to see you here."

"I did not come as a patient, Anson. I need to speak with you on a private matter. It will not take long."

"Come into my office." He led the way into a plainly furnished room that was spotlessly clean. Whatever else one might think of Anson Tyler, as a doctor he could not be faulted. He took a seat behind his desk and folded his hands upon it, beaming at me. "Now, how may I help you? Your wish, as they say, is my command."

I started to sit, thought better of it, and remained standing. "It has come to my attention that you led my friend Michael Archer to believe you and I are to be married."

"Oh, that." He looked a little shamefaced. "If you will allow me to explain—"

"I am not interested in explanations. I don't care why you did it, I care that you *did* do it. You perpetrated a lie, Anson, a lie about me."

"It's not really a lie, Fremont. I was upset with you, you know, that night on Haight Street, and I admit I was hurt by your refusal. But when you came to your senses and left that house, which you should have done in the first place, I thought we would have another chance. I still love you, you see. I had rushed you before, so I thought I would give you time—"

"Really, I cannot listen to this! You must get it into your head once and for all: I am the wrong mate for you. Time will never change that. I am so angry with you for misleading Michael that I can scarcely speak in a civil tone. I have set Michael straight. If you have *misled* anyone else, I expect you to set them straight without delay."

Very quietly Anson said, "He's the one, isn't he?"

I felt color rise in my face. "I take your meaning, and it is none of your concern. Because of what you did, and the way he reacted, I am done with both of you! So get that through your head once and for all. I've found another place to live and will be leaving Golden Gate Park in two days. Stay out of my way, Anson. Stay out of my life!"

I swept out of there, borne on an anger so strong that I did not even think of limping. I left Anson with his mouth hanging open like a beached fish.

When I had calmed down somewhat, banked the fires of my anger as it were, I consulted Mickey's greasy note and drove over to Fillmore. I located my new home and parked at the curb, admiring it from the outside. Of course it might be a pigsty within, but from the exterior that seemed unlikely. The house was big, square, and modern, three stories, with a handsome mansard roof. It had been painted on the outside since the fire, in a pale gray that gleamed. The roof was black. The location was perfect. I hoped my apartment would face the street, so that I could hang my FREMONT JONES TYPEWRITING SERVICES sign in a window. I could hardly wait to move in. *Thank you, Mickey Morelock, thank you, thank you!*

As I returned to Golden Gate Park, I reflected that such good fortune had made me feel less angry but no less purposeful. There was a kind of hardness, an adamance inside me that had never been there before. I felt as if the fires of San Francisco and the fire in my heart had burned away my soft places and tempered me, like steel.

❧ 16 ❧

Wonders (and Horrors?) Will Never Cease

It is easy to lose track of the days when anything like a regular schedule has vanished from one's life. I stopped on my way back to the park and bought a *Chronicle,* both for the news and to be sure that it was (as I thought) Thursday. It was, which meant I would be moving to Fillmore on Saturday. I was highly satisfied.

I spent the afternoon in my tent with my foot up for the ankle's sake, since my talking to it had not done a bit of good. First I read the paper, which was full of extremes: at one end of the spectrum lay the building boom, and on the other a good deal about crime and graft and so on. I suppose it is ever thus, people being what they are.

Then I read Gertrude Lasley's diary. She must have been a sweet old lady; certainly she had done her best to keep her spirits up even as her condition deteriorated. One could read her steady decline through the quality of her handwriting alone: in the early pages she wrote a fine hand, but by the end it had become a shaky scrawl that was difficult to decipher. Throughout, she chronicled an illness characterized by painful gastric disturbances, with frightening episodes of paralysis toward the last.

Gertrude's attitude toward Alice progressed from an initial enthusiasm to a long period of making charitable excuses for her niece's behavior, and finally—when she was too weak to do anything—to complaint. She complained not of being poisoned, which she never suspected, but of neglect. Alice had dismissed the maid for stealing (so that was what had happened to her! but I doubted it was she who stole) and was slow to hire another; Alice left Gertrude alone for long periods of time; Alice allowed the bed linens to go soiled, and did not often enough provide clean gowns and caps; finally, and most pathetically, Alice would not call a doctor. Gertrude knew she was dying. The last entry said, "I have no more strength to write."

I closed the diary and wept for Gertrude Lasley. I no longer felt guilty about Alice being murdered. To go swiftly with one's throat cut had to be an easier way to die, and after what she had done to her aunt, Alice had not deserved to live.

On Friday morning Michael came to my tent. I was refreshed after a relatively good night's sleep, clearheaded, and sure of myself, though I knew that what I had to say would be a surprise to him.

"I thought," he said, "that we should discuss how to proceed in this Lasley business."

I handed Gertrude's diary to Michael. "I believe there are enough details about the progression of the unfortunate old lady's illness here to make a case for poisoning. Also, there is no mention of Alice having acquired a husband; indeed, the diary sheds no light on the question of who might have killed Alice. As for our having a discussion, that will not be necessary. I turn the entire matter over to you, Michael. I have decided that my sleuthing days are over."

He raised one eyebrow, looking at me critically. "You have the right, of course, to make such a decision. Nevertheless, because you have been so closely involved—"

"I've thought of that. When it is necessary to do so, I will cooperate with the police. If I have to defend myself, I shall retain a lawyer, even if I have to ask my father for help with the expense. I am hoping that won't be necessary. I know you have contacts on the police force—you seem to have them all over the place. If your own contacts fail, you might want to make the acquaintance of a young rookie officer by the name of Stephenson. I do not know that he can be trusted, that is a judgment you must make for yourself. The reality is, Michael, that you are quite good at this sort of thing whereas I am out of my depth."

"I disagree," he said softly. "You have made an excellent Holmes to my Watson, and I had hoped we might go on."

I raised my chin. This was harder for me than I had envisioned. "You are only being charitable. My life is in a shambles, Michael. Beginning tomorrow, I have an opportunity to put it back together, and that is what I intend to do."

"May I inquire as to the particulars?"

"I will be advertising my new office, so the police will have no difficulty in finding me if they need to. As for the rest, you may as well know that I am still angry about the way you and Anson treated me. As a result, I do not wish to have anything to do with either of you. I have told Anson, and now I am telling you."

Michael released a breath through his teeth in a soft hiss; he rubbed at his head, rumpling and then smoothing his hair. He said, "Damn!"

I said, "I will leave Max in the garage at the Presidio on Sunday. Of course I can't accept the auto as a gift, it would not be proper. In the heat of the moment, I misspoke when I said I intended to keep it. I believe that concludes our business, Michael, and so I will ask you to leave now."

"How did we go so wrong?"

The expression in his eyes caused me pain, but I steeled myself against it and said nothing.

"I had hoped," said Michael, "once this Lasley matter was cleared up, and since you are not after all engaged to Tyler, that you would think seriously about Carmel."

For a moment I wavered; I did not recall his saying anything about this Carmel—whoever or whatever a Carmel might be—and so, of course, I was curious. But I got myself in hand and shook my head. "I want only to be left alone so that I can conduct my life in an orderly and profitable manner. That is all. Goodbye, Michael."

"If you insist," he said slowly, "goodbye, Fremont." He turned to leave, then turned back. "I almost forgot. About your pistol—"

"Keep it," I said quickly. "In my new life I will not need it."

Michael's blue eyes were clouded with gray, his expression troubled. He said not another word, but ducked and backed out through the tent flap.

Yes, my soft places had burned away. I watched him go and felt nothing: not sadness, not anger, not vindication. Nothing.

I had work to do. For once, I would pack carefully so that all would be ready on the morrow for my final move. In my hasty departure from Haight Street most of my clothes had become wrinkled, and the wrinkles had not hung out. I decided to sort the clothes that merely needed pressing from those that needed laundering, and was doing so when Nurse Bartlett poked her nose into my tent.

"Fremont, there's someone here to see you."

I looked over my shoulder as I continued sorting. "I am not particularly in the mood for company, Mrs. Bartlett. Could you put them off?"

Bartlett shook her wrinkles and withdrew her head, and through the tent flap popped a plump pink person who said, "Wotcha up to, Fremont?"

"Mrs. O'Leary!" I cried, flinging myself into her bosomy embrace.

"There, there," she said, patting me, "it's lovely to see you, dearie, but watch out for my new hat."

I took both her hands and moved back at arms' length. "Mrs. O., you look very grand."

"You're a sight for sore eyes yerself, Fremont, and no mistake." She nodded, and her new hat, which boasted a quantity of pink ostrich feathers, bobbled atop her faded red hair.

"A new hat, and if I am not mistaken, that is a new dress also. A traveling costume, is it not?"

"That it is. Oh, Fremont, I've got so much to tell ya, I hardly know where to begin."

"Do sit down." I gave her the one chair and pushed aside a pile of clothes so that I could sit on the cot. "I am all ears."

"Looky here," she said, thrusting her left hand in my face.

"Oh my. Could this be a *wedding* ring?" The ring was an extravagance, a circle of diamonds. Her traveling costume was pink shantung, beautifully cut to fit her large body.

"It surely could, Fremont, it surely could. Why, it's like a fairy tale! See, I was sittin' in a tent in this very camp, all snivelin' and sorrowful, and outside the fire was raging and all, when up comes this handsome gentleman and says to me, 'Maureen, is that you?' And I says, 'Who's askin'?' But already I thought I reconnized him. Fremont, it was Jack Ryan, who I knew before himself and me was married. Hadn't seen Jack in all these years. He was visitin' San Francisco when the quake hit, stayin' in one of them hotels wot burned, and he got evacuated to Golden Gate Park same as me. Well, one thing led to another, you know how it is, or maybe you don't—"

My former landlady broke off, actually blushing.

I smiled. "I think I can imagine. Do go on."

"Long about the time the fires stopped, Jack says to me, 'Maureen, what say we do what we shoulda done a long time ago?' and I says, 'Wot's that, Jack?' and he says, 'Let's get married and blow this town.' That's the way he talks, Fremont: 'blow this town.' Jack's a big tycoon, got some kinda business down the south part of the state. So I thought, why not? But I did have me a quiet conversation with himself of blessed memory before I said yes."

"I'm sure himself would wish you every happiness, Mrs. O. I mean Mrs. Ryan. As do I." I leaned over and kissed her cheek.

She positively glowed. "I declare, I didn't know an old woman could be so happy! Fremont, we been on a honeymoon. Went on a train all the way to Chicago and back. Then I told my Jack there was some people in San Francisco I wanted to look up before we settle down for good. We're gonna live in Los Angeles, Jack's already got a house there."

"You don't know how glad I am to see you. I'd given up looking for you. Now I understand why I couldn't find you: Those days when the fire was burning, I was so busy driving for the Red Cross that I couldn't think about much else. When things calmed down enough for me to start looking, you and your Mr. Ryan must already have been married and gone. The two of you didn't waste any time, did you?"

"Nope." She beamed. "An experience like that big quake makes a body realize there's not all that much time to waste! I'm glad I found you, too. So wotcha been up to, Fremont? Seen anything of our friend Mr. Archer?"

I hadn't the heart to tell her the truth about my activities, so I made up a gay story of adventures driving for the Red Cross, left out everything about Haight Street, and concluded by saying that I was preparing to move to very suitable quarters on Fillmore.

"Write down the address for me, dearie, so's we can keep in touch." I did, and handed it to her. She tucked it in a handbag that matched her costume, then put her head to the side (plumed hat dipping) and gave me one of her old piercing glances. "Ya didn't say anything about Mr. Michael Archer."

My guard was down, and I believe a bit of something may have momentarily shadowed my eyes, but I forced a light tone: "Oh, he went away as usual, and he came back, as usual. He is staying at the Presidio, if you want to see him. I'm sure he would like that."

"I'll tell Jack, and we'll go on over there when I get done visitin' here. Ya know, Fremont, I had some idea as how you and Mr. Archer might get together, romantically speaking."

I laughed. "Romance does not agree with me, Mrs. O. Forgive me, I shall have a hard time getting used to you being Mrs. Ryan."

"Well, we can fix that easy enough." She patted my knee. "From now on, you just call me Maureen. Well, I'd best be goin' but, like I said, I'll stay in touch. Jack's got a grand place in Los Angeles, he says, plenty of rooms. Maybe you can come down and see us sometime."

"I would like that," I agreed, giving her a farewell hug. *Wonders will never cease,* I thought as I watched my former landlady sail like a pink ship through the sea of tents.

Saturday morning, as I was putting the finishing touches to my packing, I came across a rolled-up old petticoat that I should have put in the pile of clothes to be laundered. When I picked it up, something fell out onto the hard-packed dirt floor of the tent.

"Botheration," I muttered, bending down, "I forgot all about this." It was the large blue jewel, the only remaining evidence of the contraband from Sacramento Street—and a reminder that, in my decision to give up sleuthing, I had abandoned the Sorensons to the status of unsolved mystery.

I heard the scratching that passes for a knock when one's door is canvas, and quickly stashed the jewel in my pocket.

"Miss Jones, may I come in?" a man's voice inquired. I didn't recognize it.

"Yes, come in," I replied, raising my voice slightly.

The Greek god in Army uniform—otherwise known as Private James Albright—ducked in. He politely took off his cap and stood at attention. "Your friend Michael Archer told me where to find you."

"Oh?" I crossed my arms and regarded him skeptically. Once again he had come at an inopportune moment (he seemed to have a gift for doing so), but I decided that this time I would not mention it.

"I, uh, I owe you an apology, and he made me promise to deliver it to you in person."

"I cannot wait to hear it."

Albright ignored my sarcasm, or perhaps it went over his head. "You see, I told you a lie when I said I had followed you, and that was how I knew you were living in the house on the corner of Haight and Belvedere. What I really did was, I got concerned when I kept knocking on the door of Mr. Archer's room and you never answered, so I filched a skeleton key and unlocked the door. I found the note you had left him on the bed, saying where you'd gone, and I took it. I'm sorry, I shouldn't have done that. I know I caused Mr. Archer a lot of trouble when he came back and didn't know where you were. I didn't work up the nerve to tell him what I'd done until yesterday. He was pretty mad, but he's a gentleman. He forgave me, and made me promise to tell you."

"Well, that's a relief, I must say! I had begun to wonder if something had gone wrong with my mind when Michael said there was no note on his bed. You are forgiven, Private Albright. As they say, it is all water under the bridge now. Thank you for taking the trouble to come."

He smiled, his equanimity restored, and advanced a couple of paces. "I had, uh, a kind of hankering for you, if you know what I mean, but I'm over it now. Maybe we could be friends, and I could go back to calling you Fremont, and you could call me Jim?"

I smiled too, a little. I had been quite hard on this young man; likely it was time for a truce. So I said, "Friendship is always a good thing, if you're sure you can stick to that, Jim."

"Yeah, I'm sure, Fremont. Looks like you're moving again. You must be pretty sick of moving."

"You are correct on both counts. However, I expect this will be the last time. I have finally found a place that is highly suitable."

"I'll bet you could use some help. I've got time. Let me help you move."

"Why not? It will go all the faster, and I should be glad of that. Thank you, Jim. Shall we get to work?"

Jim Albright was a strong and able worker. With his help I had accomplished the move by Saturday noon. Jim didn't linger, he was not a pest, but went cheerfully on his way.

Mr. Smythe-with-a-*y*, who said he was not the landlord per se but the property manager, had been on hand to direct me to the proper apartment. As soon as Jim Albright departed, Smythe returned for the rent; from his sudden materializations and dematerializations, I surmised that he lived in the building. He was a small man with eyes like black pebbles and a downtrodden air. I should make my cheque out to Fillmore Enterprises, he said.

My stomach lurched a little at the amount, which came to nearly half of all that I had left in the world, but the apartment was worth it. It was on the second floor and, as I had most desired, faced the street. Even before I unpacked my belongings I hung up the wooden sign that had last decorated the bay window of Alice's house.

Then I went outside and looked up. I should have to get yet another sign made, for from the sidewalk FREMONT JONES TYPEWRITING SERVICES was barely legible. Owing to this second-floor location, larger lettering was required. Perhaps I could obtain permission to have the sign painted on the window glass, such as I'd had on Sacramento Street. More expense, but it could not be helped.

I went back to my apartment, cogitating upon my financial status. Taking this place was a gamble, but one I had every reason to believe would pay off. Fillmore had become the city's business district. Being here put me right in the thick of things, and I anticipated the clients flocking to my door. Yes, it was worth it.

The rest of the day I spent putting away my belongings and rearranging furniture. There was no desk, so a table meant for dining had to serve. I set up my typewriter lovingly, sat down, and typed a letter to Father and Augusta. The table was the wrong height for typing, but I could put up with that for a time. It felt so good to be doing again what I did for a living that I typed another letter, this one to Meiling.

The only drawback to my new quarters was that, in the hasty division of this large house into apartments, no bathrooms had been added. It was necessary to share a bathroom at the end of the hall, which meant that I would not feel free to indulge in the long hot baths that were my favorite luxury. There was also something of a kitchen problem: my apartment did not have one. Rather, it had a long shelf against one wall of the bedroom, set off by a folding screen. A gas ring, of the type I'd had in my tiny kitchen at Mrs. O'Leary's, sat upon that shelf. But since I am not much for cooking, this arrangement was fine with me.

During my evening ablutions, I reflected that being in a real bathroom, however briefly, was an improvement over the communal situation at Golden Gate Park. I wondered about the other residents of the house. I'd heard them moving about but had not yet caught sight of any of them. I resolved to go around and introduce myself the next day.

I went to bed early. Oh, what a treat it was to sleep on a real mattress in a real bed! I fell blissfully, instantly asleep.

Some sixth sense awoke me. For perhaps the only time in my life, I was alert even before I opened my eyes, my keen hearing focused on footsteps so light they were all but inaudible. Running footsteps. *In my apartment!*

⫷ 17 ⫸

Nefarious, Precarious

For precious moments I lay frozen in fear. Then I rolled off the bed; I had begun to wriggle under it, crawling on my stomach, when a hand grabbed my injured ankle and yanked me out. The pain was excruciating, but I bit my lip and swallowed a yelp. No matter what happened, I was determined to be brave.

I twisted around to confront my attacker, who immediately clamped a hand over my mouth and hissed, "Be quiet or I will kill you!"

You will probably kill me anyway, I thought, and then opened my eyes wide in disbelief. For one insane moment I thought this was Meiling playing some sort of joke: the face so close to mine was masked, Ninja-style, with only the eyes glittering in the room's near darkness. Whoever it was jerked me to my feet, keeping a hand over my mouth. From the other room, I heard the shades being lowered— so this person had an accomplice. With the light from the street blocked off, there was a moment of total darkness; then the electric lights came on.

Of course, this was not Meiling. But it *was* a Ninja, or rather two Ninjas, in black costumes subtly different from mine and Meiling's. The Ninja who had me said more loudly, "Quiet or I kill!" and removed his hand from my mouth. I began to laugh hysterically, I could not help it.

My laughter confused them. They glanced at each other. The second Ninja advanced on me and said menacingly: "Why you laugh? What so funny?"

"N-nothing," I gulped, trying to get myself under control. "You would not understand." More laughter gurgled from my throat.

Ninja Number Two slapped me hard with the back of his hand. I staggered, my cheek burned, and the laughter died. The two of them nodded at each other. Number One untied a rope from around his waist and, with it, tied my hands behind my back. Then he prodded me to walk in front of him into the other room, where he pushed me down into a straight chair. His buddy came forward with another length of rope and tied my feet to the chair legs. In doing so, he noted the bruised condition of my poor ankle and made some remark in a foreign tongue, pointing at my foot. Number One said something in reply, and they both bobbed their heads and giggled in quite a nasty way.

The language they spoke did not have quite the cadence of Chinese; it was also less guttural. Though I had never heard Japanese spoken, I assumed that they were Japanese, and were in fact real Ninjas. A most sobering thought. Meiling, who was not afraid of much, feared the Ninja. Still, I did not like them giggling over my infirmity and decided to assert myself.

"I thought there were no Ninjas in San Francisco," I said.

Number Two raised his hand threateningly. "No talk!"

Oh well, I tried. I sat there, shivering in an old flannel nightgown without a stitch underneath, unbound hair streaming down my back, and watched in silence as the two of them ravaged my new apartment. I could not imagine what they were doing here. Why Ninjas, why me? They used wicked-looking knives to tear into the upholstery of the love seat and the one overstuffed chair, then did the same to the mattress. When one opened the wardrobe, pulled out my aubergine cape, and raised his knife, I could keep still no longer.

"If you would only tell me what you are looking for, all this destruction would not be necessary!"

I might as well have saved my breath. He paid me no mind, just held up the cape and slashed it to ribbons. He was joined by the other, and together they shredded every item of clothing I owned. Including my underwear, which they pulled lastly from the drawers.

One of them grunted—I could no longer tell which Ninja was which, for they appeared identical—and held the blue jewel up to the light. It winked and glowed, and both of them exclaimed over it in Japanese.

I hoped the jewel would satisfy them, but it did not. Rather the reverse: finding the jewel seemed to inflame them, and the pace of their destruction quickened. It was all the more horrible somehow because they were so quiet about it. People in the neighboring apartments would not hear a thing.

They slashed all the curtains. They took up the bedroom rug. They took down pictures and the mirror, punched them with their fists, and broke the glass. Vicious, pointless vandalism! They came back into the living room and moved me, chair and all, so that they could take up that rug. Of course, there was nothing underneath it except the floor. One of them spied the box that held my files, dumped it out, and they both set to, shredding papers with their knives. I shed tears, powerless to prevent them. I clamped my trembling lips together to keep back a sob. Finally, there was nothing else for them to shred, nowhere else for them to look. What would they do now?

A Ninja came over to me and, for no reason whatever, boxed my ears. I heard popping and felt sharp pain. Tears rose again in my eyes, but these I blinked away. Shock and horror were fading. I was getting angry instead.

The Ninja who'd hit me bent down so that his masked face was right in mine. He spoke slowly and distinctly. "Now you tell us: where are the swords?"

"I don't know what you are talking about. What swords?" As soon as the words were out of my mouth, I did know: *the contraband!* And Private Albright, with his all-American good looks and convincing show of friendship, was mixed up in it somehow. He had to be—no one else knew exactly where I was.

The other Ninja joined his pal. Now they were both having at me. "Sacred swords of ancestors. Samurai swords. Stolen. Not part of bargain. What you do with them?"

"There was only the one," I said, thinking of the exotic curved blade with the squiggly writing on it, "and it disappeared. The blue jewel, I suppose it is a sapphire, is all that's left, and you are welcome to it. I never intended to keep the thing, it's just that I have been rather busy lately—"

The one who seemed to do all the hitting hit me again. "No lie!" he yelled furiously.

Keep that up and someone will hear you, I thought, getting madder by the minute. Through clenched teeth I said, "I am not lying."

The two masked heads turned toward each other, nodded, and the Ninjas moved away from me. They held a quiet conversation in their own language, while I wondered if they'd ever left ugly gifts on the steps at Haight Street, ever ransacked the house, murdered Alice. Then one of them walked over to the table and stood looking down at my typewriter.

"Don't touch that!" I cried, knowing even as I did that I should have kept silent.

He cast me a glittering look. The other Ninja seized my hair with one hand and clamped his other hand over my mouth. The one at the table said, "This machine means much to you."

I nodded, a motion that pulled my hair painfully. My captor removed his hand and said, "Samurai swords mean much to us. We know you lie, know you work with Sollenson. Sollenson gone, dead. You alive. So now you tell us what you do with swords of ancestors."

Sollenson? My mind raced. "Oh, you mean the Sorensons. I think

I know now what swords you are referring to. I did not actually see them, only the hilts, which, to judge from their size, must have been the hilts of a very large pair of swords. But I did not touch them, I swear. I did not work with the Sorensons, either; I only rented an office in their building. You must believe me—"

My voice died in my throat as I watched the Ninja, with brute strength, rip the slender metal ribs from the inside of my typewriter. He bent them as if they were the softest gold—to me, they *were* more precious than gold—and threw them by handfuls onto the floor. He tore off the round, silver-rimmed alphabet keys and dropped them on the pile. The noise of it was terrible: metallic death. He came over to me. His buddy jerked my head back by the hair. *"Now* you tell," he said.

I was devastated, my anger consumed in black despair. Tears fell unchecked—so much for being brave. "I cannot tell you anything because I don't know," I said through my tears. "I only saw those things once, on the day of the earthquake. I went back to the building after it was burned, and all I found was the sapphire, which you have. All the other things were gone. I have no idea who took them, and that's the truth."

"You foolish lady," said the Ninja, turning away. The other let go my hair, and I thought for a moment they were going to release me. But the one who was the hitter and hair-puller gagged me instead. The one who had turned away now turned back, with something gleaming in his hand.

It was a hypodermic needle. I struggled against my bonds, I squealed, but I was helpless. He plunged the needle into my neck. Almost immediately my vision clouded, and I thought: *I am dying.*

I opened my eyes in the blackness of a tomb. I couldn't breathe, I was suffocating. *I have been buried alive!* I thought in panic. Immediately I knew that panic was no good, I should try to assess my situation objectively.

I was lying face down. Not in grave dirt, but rather there was a cool, dampish surface beneath my cheek. A hard surface. I moved my head: The surface was splintery, therefore wood. I rolled completely over onto my back, which proved to me that I was not in a coffin. My hands were bound behind me so I settled on my side. I told myself: *Easy, Fremont, easy.*

Less panicky now, I could feel bands of fabric on my face. One over my eyes, one over and partially in my mouth. A blindfold and a gag. Because of the former, I could not see; because of the latter, gasping for air through my mouth was like slow suffocation. But I had not been buried alive, and for the moment that was quite sufficient.

It is a good thing, I thought, trying to breathe normally, *that I do not suffer from nasal congestion.*

My head hurt. *Where am I, and how did I get here?*

After a few moments I remembered the Ninjas. They had destroyed my typewriter! They had destroyed everything I owned! I remembered being gagged, remembered the needle plunged into my neck, and then falling into darkness. I had thought I was dying, and so had come back into consciousness expecting the grave.

Perhaps I *was* dead, and this was some sort of very disappointing afterlife. A dark hell for people such as myself who have never had much use for religion.

Nonsense! My head still hurt, but it was rapidly clearing. The Ninjas had not meant to kill me, only to drug me so that I could be moved more easily; they had blindfolded me—why? I could not think why anyone would blindfold an unconscious woman, so I fell to wondering where I was.

My hearing is the most acute of my senses, but for the moment it was telling me nothing. My sense of smell was more informative: I smelled fish. No, not fish precisely, but fishiness in general. And something else that took me longer to identify: motor oil. I sniffed, detecting a hint of salt in the air. I listened again, harder. What I heard was no particular sound but rather the hush that is common to large, empty spaces.

So: I was in an empty warehouse or boathouse on the docks. San Francisco's docks, I hoped; I would be in a fine kettle of fish, to use an apt Neptunian phrase, if they'd spirited me away to some unknown port.

My feet were free—also bare and cold but no matter. Probably I could flee regardless of my hands being tied, if I could only see where I was going. Aha! That was no doubt why they had blindfolded me. Clever Ninjas. Well, I should just have to be cleverer still. They might destroy my typewriter and everything else, but I'd be damned if I'd let them destroy Fremont Jones!

There was a little—very little—give in the rope that bound my wrists. I began to work it back and forth, back and forth. Patience has never been a strong point of mine, but I knew it was called for now. Yanking at the rope would do no good, whereas steady, persistent pulling might stretch it enough that I could slip one hand through.

I have no idea how long I'd been working at it when I heard voices. I pricked up my ears and thought I recognized the foreign tongue of the Ninjas, though I could not make out individual words. In the space between sentences, I heard their quiet tread: they were walking in my direction.

Panicking, I yanked my wrists apart. Apparently I had chosen the right moment to do that, because I felt the rope give. But not enough—I still couldn't get my hand through. I kept on working away. The Ninjas had stopped moving. I would have given almost anything to know how far off they were, whether or not they could see me from where they stood. I thought not. I had an impression that this warehouse, or whatever, was fairly dark, or else I should have been able to see some light at the edges of the blindfold. I raised my head, peering in the way one does to cheat at blindman's bluff or pin-the-tail-on-the-donkey. I could not see anything at all, for whatever that was worth.

Heavy footsteps joined the Ninjas, who had begun to talk to each other again. They were near enough now for me to make out their words, but of course that did me no good, since I did not understand Japanese.

A man's voice boomed out: "Talk English, will ya? I can't make heads nor tails of that Jap gibberish!"

I knew that voice! Surely it was Mickey Morelock! I almost cried out, determined to make as much noise as I could in spite of the gag—but I stopped myself. I might be mistaken. Then, as I listened, I knew I was not mistaken . . . yet, in a way, I had been. The voice was Mickey's, all right, and he had played me for a fool.

A Ninja said, "We have brought the woman, Fremont Jones."

For a moment I didn't realize he meant me, because in his Japanese accent he said Fle-mont. I worked at my bonds.

The Ninja continued, "She no help. She know nothing, she have nothing. You must deal with her, we do not want more blood on our hands. Ninja do not come all the way from Japan to kill without reason."

Mickey said, "If you Japs wasn't so stupid, ya wouldn't have got the wrong woman in the first place. Besides, nobody told you to kill that—what's-her-name, Alice."

"We not want to kill her, but she no be silent when told. I slit throat to stop screaming. Too much blood, very messy, very much trouble to clean up. Hiding body more trouble."

A different Japanese voice broke in, more facile with English: "Mr. Morelock, you have not kept good faith with us. First you take our ancient samurai swords, not part of deal. Then you tell us there will be no payment because shipment has disappeared. You tell us Sollensons make it disappear with help of Jones woman. We no longer believe you."

My wrists were slippery. I knew the slipperiness was from my own blood, that I had abraded the skin off, but I did not care about that. Apparently blood is a good lubricator, for suddenly one of my hands slipped through the rope and I was free. I lay still as a stone, hardly daring to breathe, hanging on every word of that incredible conversation.

"Now, you just wait a damn minute," said Mickey, in an ugly tone I would not have believed could come from the mouth of a man I'd thought so jolly. "It's not me who double-crossed you, it was the Sorensons, and they cheated me too, dammit! I killed them for it, so you're not the only ones had to kill somebody in all this mess. Like I said, it musta been the Sorensons who wanted those swords that are so important to you. And I swear to God, it was Fremont Jones who got the stuff out of the Sorensons' place on Sacramento before the fire. I was there, I saw her, and I went in and got even with the Sorensons after. I woulda got rid of Jones for ya too, only something went wrong with that pistol I gave her that shoulda misfired and done the trick. Come on, where is she? I'll make her talk!" He took a couple of heavy steps.

My pistol? He gave me a defective pistol? Carefully I removed my blindfold and leaned up on my elbows. I would not have been surprised to find Mickey staring me in the face, but he wasn't. He was half the warehouse (for my assumption had been correct) away from me, and one of the Ninjas—they were unmasked now—had taken him by the arm. The three stood in a circle of light shed by a lantern placed on the floor. All the rest was shadows.

The Ninja who had Mickey by the arm continued speaking. "The Jones woman does not know anything, or she would have told us by now. We spend too much time on her, for nothing. Leave dead things on steps but she gets guard, so we have to wait. Kill other woman by mistake, so we have to wait. Jones goes to live in park with many people, we have to wait. Too much waiting! Tonight, you say, is the night. You tell us where to go. We make big fear in Flemont Jones, tear up everything, find nothing."

Nothing, I thought, *except for a valuable sapphire which apparently he didn't intend to mention to Mickey.* With a silent apology to Jim Albright for misjudging him, I removed the gag and began to inch backward.

The Ninja continued. "We destroy machine which means much to her, and still she says she knows nothing of our samurai swords. She has told us the truth, we are sure of this. So now we think you are the one not telling truth. We do not like this, Mr. Morelock."

The other Ninja echoed, "We do not like this."

They were circling Mickey now. "You will tell us where to find the sacred swords of the samurai!"

Mickey pushed at one of the Ninjas, then lunged past him. Mickey was larger than the two of them together, but the Ninjas had speed and skill. In a lightning-fast move, graceful as a dance, a Ninja kicked out at Mickey, spun in the air and kicked again, and Mickey Morelock went down so heavily the floor shook.

The other Ninja stood over the huge man and said, "You will tell us now or you will be very, very sorry. Ninja are skilled in ways of torture which we will be happy to demonstrate."

As much as I might have liked to see that, I decided it was time for me to leave. The problem was that they were between me and where, from the sound of their footsteps, I judged the door must be. Up to now they had paid no attention to me, but if I tried to move past them, they surely would.

I had never before been in one of these waterside buildings, but it seemed to me that I'd seen ships anchored between them and goods being moved in by way of a gangplank along one side. So there must also be a side entry. I chose the side to my right (praying that it *was* the *right* side) and crawled toward it. Mickey was blathering on. *Keep it up!* I thought, for as long as they were occupied with one another I was safe.

I reached the wall as Mickey gave out a yelp of pain. The Ninjas had made good on their threat: they were torturing him! I wondered how long he would hold out. At this point, I would have liked to know myself where the samurai swords were, but I searched instead for a way out. My eyes were by then quite accustomed to the darkness. In the lull that followed Mickey's cry, I heard water sloshing outside the building.

The side door was huge, a slab of wall. I had no idea how to open it, or even if I would have the strength to do so, but I had to try. I glanced over at the pool of light. Mickey still lay on the floor; at the moment the Ninjas were exchanging remarks in Japanese while they stood over him.

I pressed my back against the door and slid upward until I was standing, then grabbed the metal bar that I hoped was a latch. I pulled with all my might, but the door did not budge. Frantically I pushed on it, and still it did not budge, and then I understood that it must move to the side rather than in or out. I shoved once without result. Shoved again, every muscle straining, until with a great, rolling rumble the door moved.

"Hey!" yelled Mickey. "Stop, you!"

I had opened a space a few inches wide. The air that rushed in was full of sea smell, and of fog. Thick, white fog. Waves lapped below me, unseen. I squeezed through the opening as I heard behind me the light, running steps of the Ninjas. My bare foot encountered only empty air; nevertheless, I stepped out . . . and fell through the fog like a stone.

The icy-cold waters of the Bay closed over my head.

Out of a Nightmare

I feared the shock would stop my heart. I fought against the volumi-
nous folds of my nightgown, which at first billowed up around my
head and then, as the garment became waterlogged, threatened to drag
me down. Remembering my swimming lessons, I fluttered my feet
and felt myself slowly rise to the surface.

My head broke through; gratefully, I gasped air while remembering to tread water. My wrists smarted like blazes from the salt. The fog
was as thick as I had ever seen. While I was glad of the cover the fog
provided, it was disorienting in the extreme. I was afraid to strike out,
swimming. What if I went the wrong way and ended up in the middle
of the Bay?

That problem was resolved when one of my moving arms struck
something solid. Aha! I treaded over in that direction and explored the
solid object, deducing it to be one of the pilings that support the
warehouse. It was covered with nasty-feeling excrescences—barnacles,
I presumed. I presumed further that I needed only to move from
piling to piling to reach dry land.

It was not quite that simple. I did move in the wrong direction at
first and had quite a panicky time until I realized that I could not find
the next piling because there were no more, I must have passed the
Bay end of the building. Therefore I turned around and went back,
repeating the process in reverse. The whole time I was in fear that the

Ninjas or Mickey would come in pursuit of me, but they did not. I did not even hear them, and wondered what they were up to. I heard nothing but the lapping waves and, at intervals, faint and far off, the mournful foghorn over by the Golden Gate.

At last I reached a corner where two hard, slightly slimy surfaces met at right angles. I felt along the one in front of me, moving to the side, until my fingers encountered a ladder. I seized on it and hauled myself up on the dock, where I lay panting and shivering.

I did not feel particularly exhilarated by my escape. I was all too aware that I could be caught again, and for the moment I could not think how to get help. The fog enshrouded the landscape like a thick curtain. Finally I sat up and wrung water from my hair and night-gown.

This was quite the worst mess I had ever found myself in. Here was I, alone and wet and all but naked, not to mention freezing. I tried to picture the surroundings I could not see, without much success. Was there any kind of all-night establishment around here? I didn't know. I listened, and still heard nothing but the waves lapping against the docks. There was not much use in lingering. If for no reason other than to get warm, I should be on the move.

I had heard it said, and can now attest to the fact, that when one is fighting for survival one does not feel pain. Bum ankle and all, I walked the entire way from the waterfront to Fillmore Street. It took a very long time, and I thought more than once that I was lost. The city's geography helped, for whenever I found myself disoriented, I kept moving uphill. In the ordinary way of things, I doubt the ankle would have held up, but my two feet carried me to the large house on Fillmore where Max was parked out front.

The fog was not so thick here. I hung back, watching the house, thinking perhaps Mickey or the Ninjas or someone in their employ—

Mr. Smythe, for instance, who had taken half of all the money I had in the world—might lurk in the area. When I was ready to risk it, I ran across the street and up the steps, into the house, and up to my apartment on the second floor. I hardened my heart against the sight that awaited me.

My poor typewriter! I did not cry again. Instead I turned away, flinging the wet tails of my hair back over my shoulder. The Ninjas had dumped the contents of my leather bag onto the living-room floor, but they had not taken anything. The bag was slashed, but not clear through, so it was usable. I gathered up a coin purse and a few scattered dollar bills, plus other odds and ends, and stuffed everything back into the bag. Max's key I held in my hand . . . then I looked down at myself. My gown was still soaking wet, plastered to my body. Suddenly I felt the cold, and my teeth chattered until I thought I was in danger of biting my tongue in two.

At least, I thought, *I can put slippers on my feet.* I did not recall them cutting up my slippers. I went into the bedroom. One pair of slippers and four pairs of shoes were all that remained of my clothing. There was nothing, *nothing,* with which I might cover myself. I put on the slippers and deposited three of the four pairs of shoes in my bag, not having room for the fourth. Then I left Fillmore Street, and my decimated hopes and dreams, behind.

Dawn was breaking as I drove Max in the direction of the Presidio. I had to tell Michael not to fire that pistol! What if he already had? What if he, like Alice, was already dead—because of me? No, surely not, never! "Faster, Max," I said under my breath, "faster!"

I sailed through the Presidio gates without stopping, on the assumption that whoever stood guard would recognize the auto, if not me in my disreputable state. Fortunately, at this early hour there were no soldiers about the grounds. I did not go to the garages but stopped as close to Michael's building as possible and sprinted across the grass. Just as I reached the door, my ankle buckled and I fell; but I picked myself up and went on.

A minute later I rapped softly on Michael's door, praying he was there and would hear me. I did not want to rouse the whole building. Spies must be light sleepers, for he heard.

He opened the door in his pajamas, his hair standing up at the crown of his head. "Fremont! Dear God in heaven, what's happened to you?"

Simultaneously I said, "Michael, thank God you're all right!"

He pulled me inside and closed the door. "Of course I'm all right, which is more than can be said for you. You're soaking wet!"

"I have been swimming in the Bay. Michael, you must not fire that pistol you took from me."

"I suppose you have come here at this early hour, and in such a condition, to tell me that?" His mouth curved with a hint of a smile.

"Yes! And also"—I crossed my arms over my breasts as a paroxysm of shivering set in—"to use the telephone, if you will be so good as to take me to the nearest one."

"Not until you get some dry clothes on. Here"—he threw a sweater and a heavy woolen robe onto the bed—"put these on. I do not think my trousers would fit you. I'll turn my back."

Modesty was my last concern. I stripped the wet gown off and pulled the sweater over my damp skin. It, and the robe, felt deliciously warm and soft—a great improvement. While I was putting these things on, Michael said, "I know the barrel of your Deringer was jammed—I found that out when I cleaned it. I would have told you, but you said you had no further use for the pistol. I have to wonder, though, if you have rethought your decision as regards sleuthing. Why else would you be swimming in the Bay in the middle of the night?"

"It was entirely involuntary, I assure you. But most informative. Kindly lead me to the telephone, and then you shall know all."

"Fremont Jones," said Michael, shaking his head as he led me down the hall, "you never cease to amaze me."

"Elementary," I said lightly. At the moment I was amazing myself, with the oddest combination of exhilaration and exhaustion. I felt positively giddy.

I rang Central and asked to be connected with the police. When someone answered, I assumed a high, rather querulous tone: "I'd like to speak to Aloysius Stephenson. This is his mother calling." I doubted the rookie officer would be there at that hour, and further, I supposed I was making a mistake to trust him.

But my string of bad luck had at last run out. Wish Stephenson was there, and subsequently he proved to be entirely trustworthy.

I finished the conversation and hung up the telephone. Then I turned to Michael, opened my mouth to explain . . . and collapsed. For the second time in my life, I fainted.

Once again, I was living in a tent in Golden Gate Park. My ankle was quite all right now, but I could not say the same for my mental state. I was, not to put too fine a point on it, depressed. I knew that I should have to return to Boston, but the District Attorney would not let me leave until I had served as a witness at the trial of Mickey Morelock.

As it turned out, Mickey had long been suspected of shady dealings, particularly of the import-export variety, using contacts he'd made during his years in the merchant marine. The odious Sergeant Franks was a corrupt policeman in league with him. The Sorensons had provided storage space, for a price, but they'd got greedy, tried to haul away the stuff themselves after the quake, and been killed for it by either Mickey or the policeman—each accused the other. Officer Stephenson's work in bringing Morelock and Franks to justice (with some quiet help from Michael) had brought him a promotion. He was a detective sergeant now, no longer just the Rookie.

The Ninjas had disappeared, gone back to Japan probably, with or without their samurai swords. I would never know. Nor, unless by purest chance, would Alice Lasley's body ever be found. Gertrude Lasley's bones had been laid to rest in a service arranged by her neighbor, Lola Weeks. I had not attended, as I could not bear the thought of the woman's questions. Gertrude had had no kinfolk other than Alice, so the house on Haight—with all contents, including the money hidden in the mattress—had passed into the limbo of public domain.

On a rare sunny afternoon in early July, Nurse Bartlett and I sat at a card table outside my tent. We were cutting and rolling clean, soft, old diapers to make bandages—a soothing occupation. I was in need of something soothing; I had been feeling quite despondent, in spite of everyone's being so kind to me, providing me with clothes and so on.

"I keep thinking about Alice," I said.

"What about her?" Bartlett asked, raising her eyebrows.

"I had a dream about her the other night. A nightmare, really. In it I saw Alice tie up her aunt's body in a blanket and drag it—bump, bump, bump—down the stairs. You know, Mrs. B, in reality I have often wondered how she accomplished that. Alice was a tiny person. But come to think of it, she was strong."

"Um-hm. That type's usually stronger than they let on."

I mused for a moment. "I know she had strong hands. Well, anyway, the dream went on. Alice dumped poor Gertrude's body into the root cellar, and then the dream became really horrible. She was sprinkling lye down on the body, which we know she did do, when she went quite insane. As if what she'd done had gotten to be too much, driven her over the edge, so to speak. She slammed the trapdoor down and went tearing out of the house.

"This next part is really the worst, because in the dream I became one with Alice. She—or I—no longer knew who she was, or where she was. She, or we, wandered through the streets, with fire and smoke all around, like walking through hell. You know how it can be in bad dreams, when you walk and walk without getting anywhere—the most awful feeling. Mrs. B, do you suppose that's what did happen to Alice, before I found her outside the train station that day?"

"Maybe. On the other hand, people like her don't seem to have conscience enough to drive them batty."

"I think Alice had some conscience. She did act guilty, on more than one occasion. I believe the guilt was, in part, what made her paranoid."

Bartlett shook her wattles. "There's no telling what was going on in that girl's head. What the medical profession understands about the workings of people's minds would just about fit in a thimble, if you ask me."

We worked on in companionable silence. At length Mrs. Bartlett said, "What're your plans now, Fremont?"

I sighed. "I have to go back to Boston when Mickey's trial is over. I really should write to Father, but I keep putting it off. I have almost no money left, and without my typewriter I cannot earn a living. Michael Archer has offered me a loan, but of course it would not be proper to accept."

"Have you ever thought of nursing? There's ways to earn a little salary and get your training at the same time, and right now we need more nurses. I could help get you started."

I smiled wanly. "I do not think I would make a very good nurse, but thanks all the same."

Again a silence fell. I stopped in the midst of my bandage-rolling, thinking of Michael. Wondering if I were soon to make the greatest mistake of my life—and God knew, I had made some big ones already.

"Mrs. Bartlett, have you ever heard of Carmel-by-the-Sea?"

"Carmel-by-the-Sea . . . sounds familiar. I know: that photographer, that Mr. Genthe who was taking all the pictures after the quake, that's where he went. I read it in the newspaper. Carmel's down south of here, I think. Why do you ask?"

"Because Michael wanted me to go there with him."

"Hmmm." She peered at me, eyes twinkling among their many folds. "So that's how it is. No wonder things didn't work out between you and young Dr. Tyler."

"Hah!" I tried to laugh but it fell flat. "I was very angry with both of them for a while, but now I have no feelings of any kind at all, for anyone. Too much has happened. I have neither the energy nor the will to start over; I am quite hopeless. Carmel does sound interesting, but I cannot go anywhere except back to Boston. I'll tell Michael so the next time I see him. Whenever that may be—he seems to have given up on me, and I can't say I blame him. I haven't seen Michael in at least a week."

"Hmmm," said Bartlett.

I returned to my folding, muttering, "I must write to Father."

Two days later I heard a voice calling from outside my tent: "Fremont? May I come in?"

Though it was midday, I was lying on my cot with an arm flung across my eyes. The book I could not concentrate enough to read slid off my stomach as I sat up. The voice sounded like Michael's. "Come in," I said.

Michael ducked through the tent flap, smiling broadly. "I have a surprise for you."

He stepped aside, and the most extraordinary hat appeared in the tent flap, a large-brimmed creation all covered in blue flowers and green feathers and swathed in bluish-green veiling. The owner of the hat emerged, raised her face, and my spirits lifted for the first time in many, many days.

"Oh, Meiling," I said, hastening to embrace her, "I am so very glad to see you!"

"And I you, Fremont," she said.

"You are quite the elegant lady," said I, stepping back to survey her dress, which matched the veiling on the hat. The ensemble was not one we had bought on our shopping trip; it looked far more expensive.

Michael cleared his throat. "Um, I will leave you two to visit while I go out and scare up some refreshment for us."

"As long as you do not scare it too badly," I said.

He winked at me, grinning. "I see you have rediscovered your sense of humor at last," he quipped, departing.

Meiling and I sat next to each other on the cot while she told me her news. She had received her acceptance from Stanford. The university was still closed for earthquake repairs but would reopen in September, at which time she would matriculate.

"My other good news is that my intermediary has sold the pearls, and they brought an even better price than I had hoped."

"That accounts for the excellence of your outfit. It is new, I presume."

"Yes. I adore Western clothing, and I think it looks quite well on me, don't you?"

I laughed. She even sounded different, and while I somewhat missed the old Meiling, she was so obviously happy that I could not much lament the change. "Yes, you look wonderful."

"Fremont, I hope you do not mind. I asked Mr. Archer to meet the train and bring me here to see you. I feel safe traveling through the city in his company."

"That, I completely understand. How could you think I would mind? I am delighted to see you."

"He told me something of what happened. Real Ninjas! You are a heroine, Fremont."

I shook my head. "I do not feel much like a heroine, but thank you for saying so."

Meiling opened her very fashionable reticule. "I have brought you something. It is a cheque from the bank for your share of the pearls."

I started to shake my head again, but stopped mid-shake as a stern expression came into Meiling's eyes.

"You will please not argue. You will dishonor me, Fremont Jones, if you do not accept this small offering of gratitude. I have a new life now, which would not have been possible without your help, and so I have a debt to you that I am in honor bound to discharge. Truly, my soul cannot rest until you take it."

"If you put it that way . . ." I said slowly, taking the cheque. I unfolded it and saw the amount. My eyes grew wide. "Meiling, surely this is too much!"

"It is merely what I received for the pearls I offered but you would not take at the time. I always planned to give you the money, when I had it, instead. You accept it, yes?"

"Yes," I nodded, somewhat stunned. I put my arm around my friend and my head on her shoulder, saying again, "Yes. *Thank you!*"

Michael returned at that moment, carrying a tray with a pitcher of iced tea and three glasses. Space being somewhat cramped, he set it on the dirt floor and took the chair. His eyes twinkled. "A reunion of good friends is cause for celebration. Tea, Fremont? Meiling?"

We had a joyous celebration indeed. I suggested that we continue with an early supper at a restaurant, but Meiling declined. "I am uncomfortable in San Francisco, and anyway, it is nearly time for my train back to Palo Alto."

We said our farewells, and I promised to visit her soon. My heart was singing: I would not have to return to Boston after all! Meiling's generosity had made all the difference.

Meiling preceded Michael from the tent. As he ducked, I plucked at his sleeve. "Michael, would you come back here after taking Meiling to the train? I should like you to tell me more about Carmel-by-the-Sea."

He arched his black eyebrows, smiled, and said, "That would give me the greatest pleasure."

I stood outside my tent, waving Michael and Meiling out of sight. After many bleak days and nights I could feel again, and what I felt was love.